THE LADY
WITH
THE WOLF

Dennis Forster

In loving memory of my mam and dad,
Isabel and John.

THE LADY
WITH
THE WOLF

First published in Great Britain as a softback original in 2022

Copyright © Sarah Gedney and Jonathan Forster

The moral right of this author has been asserted.

Editing, design, typesetting and publishing by UK Book Publishing

www.ukbookpublishing.com

ISBN: 978-1-915338-29-7

Cover photos:
Backside The Royal Wedding © Piano Piano! – CC BY 2.0
Back Lane between Simpson and Spencer Terraces © Andrew Curtis – CC BY-SA 2.0

Chapter 1

M s Isa Weddle had a secret. MI5 paid her to keep a watchful eye on the safe house, number thirty-nine Chillingham Grove. She watched it through her lounge window while watching television.

When it was empty, as it was now, she claimed expenses for her cousin, Malcolm, to keep its gardens tidy. A safe house had to look like all the other houses in the street. And all the other houses in Chillingham Grove had manicured gardens. It was that sort of street.

She'd been watching for years. During that time, all sorts of people had come and gone. She'd never had any bother.

For the last year her London contact had been a chap called Desmond. From an independent source she knew he called her The Witch. Tit-for-tat, she called him Mr Wonderful. She'd never met him, but a gut instinct told her he was the type you'd meet at the Henley Regatta wearing a striped blazer.

When she'd rung him to report a tramp peering through number thirty-nine's front windows, he'd said: 'Just testing, Ms Weddle,' (he never used her first name) 'just testing ... making sure you are working for your money. The chap you spied a-loitering was a plant; nothing vegetable, if you know what I mean, but one of my chaps testing to see if you were on the ball. So glad you were. We must give

1

the taxpayer value for money, mustn't we?'

The job was a sinecure until one day the phone rang. She always remembered it had rung while she'd been watching a TV documentary about the forthcoming royal wedding. The year was 1981. In a few months' time Prince Charles and Lady Diana would be husband and wife.

At first she heard heavy breathing and was about to put the phone down, when an RP voice said: 'Good evening, Ms Weddle. Have I given you a fright? Ha! Ha! Eton and Harrow speaking.'

'You mean, Heaton and Jarrow,' said Isa, giving the response agreed between herself and London, as proof of identity. 'You don't sound like Desmond.'

'I'm not. Many years ago you and I worked together in Lebanon? Don't you recognise my dulcet tones?'

'No, I do not.'

'I am disappointed to hear that. Another dream dashed on the rocks of reality. And I thought I was unforgettable. I am your new control. You have a new boss, Ms Weddle. I am now looking after number thirty-nine. Those with the power to hire and fire have sent dear Desmond, with an overnight bag, to Quito. A good man, Desmond. A damn good bridge player. He'll love South America. He's moaning like the toothache, calling everyone he knows, including the prime minister ... isn't she wonderful? That he should be travelling First class; that he's not a pleb and won't be able to read official documents in "Economy" because plebs wearing sombreros will be a penumbra on his reading. Dear, dear Desmond; if only he wasn't such a snob. I have heard rumours on the old boy's network ... but you wouldn't know anything about that, would you? That you and he were oil and water.'

'Who are you?'

'You should have a better memory for voices, shouldn't you? I do so enjoy teasing people like you. You are giving me pleasure, Ms Weddle. Does that not make you feel all warm inside? That you are making a toff happy?'

'You have hit my hot spot. If I were twenty I'd be having an orgasm.'

'Dear me; I really have gotten under your skin, haven't I? You know, I don't think I will tell you my name.'

'In that case, why have you rang?'

'As your control I am responsible for looking after you. We don't want anything to happen to you, do we?'

'Are you threatening me? In case it's slipped your mind we are on the same side. Asshole.'

'I can see I've pressed the famous Ms Weddle straight talking button. Excellent. Game, set and match to me. I will be in touch.'

****

Who the hell was he? He'd known the punning passwords she and Desmond used to verify their identity. He knew too much to be a freelancer working outside the MI5 loop. When she'd worked for MI6 in the Lebanon, there'd been lots of men like him, bottom pinchers and teasers. She'd not recognised his voice. Why should she? The Lebanon years belonged to a different era. Why the anonymity? Why the insinuated threat?

As she lived alone, she posed these questions to her dog, Chippy. A big dog. A cross between a Husky and a German Alsatian. The dog was a good listener; albeit he did prefer a dog biscuit to listening to one of the boss's soliloquies.

****

A few days later a postman rang her doorbell.

'Are you sure it's for me? I'm not expecting a parcel. You are not the usual postman.'

'Special delivery. You are Ms Isa Weddle?'

'I am.'

'And you live at number thirty?'

'I do.'

'Then it's for you. You'll have to sign for it–' handing over a form on a clipboard. 'Print your name in block capitals, please. Sign where I've put a little cross. Usual signature. I don't know what's in the parcel but it must be valuable. I was told to be certain I gave it to no one but a "Ms I. Weddle". Have you any ID? I have to fill in the bottom part of the form, you see, to say I've seen some ID. Without showing me some ID, you can't have it.'

'Dear me, will my driver's licence be good enough? I always keep it in my purse. I have done so ever since I was stopped for speeding.'

'Doing thirty-five in a thirty zone, were you?'

'I was doing a hundred and twenty on the M1. My car is a Mercedes, not a Model T Ford; give me a second and I'll go and find my purse. Chippy, say hello to the nice man. He doesn't bite.'

'But I'm a postman.'

'But in a van and not with a sack over your shoulder.'

'Does that make a difference?'

'All the difference in the world. My dog is highly intelligent. He likes you.'

'How'd you know that?'

'He hasn't bitten you.'

'Eh?'

'Chippy, give the nice postman a smile.'

Chippy's growl made the postman place the parcel he was delivering over his crotch.

'Do you watch "Match of the Day"?' said Isa, smiling.

'Eh?'

'That's what footballers do when they stand in front of an opposition free kick. I'll get my licence.'

****

The package contained a Glock 9, a box of ammunition and a typewritten note.

She read: 'Dear Ms Weddle,

As a reward for the year I have looked after number thirty-nine, I have been promoted. I have always wanted to be a gaucho; something not many people know. My new posting is Quito. Not quite "gaucho country" but a step in the right geographical direction. Hold your breath. My replacement is Tony Adder, who I believe you worked with many years ago in Lebanon. Now you know why I am sending you the Glock.

Yours, Desmond

AKA: Mr Wonderful.

PS. You may be surprised that I know my nickname. Folk will gossip!

'Chippy,' she told her dog, who as usual was at her side, 'I need to talk and you need to listen. If I didn't have you to talk to, I think I might go mad. Chippy, what are Mr Wonderful and 'TA' (behind his back she'd always called Tony Adder by his initials) up to? What's their game? I don't trust them. As far as the British Secret Service is concerned, I'm a disposable nappy. Nappies, Chippy, are like poo bags. When you have used them, you bin them. You see, Chippy darling, I don't fit in. I'm not top drawer. My dad was a bricklayer and I'm female. The British Secret Service found my gifts for languages and mathematics useful. When they needed a female to infiltrate a harem, I was the doll what fitted the bill. My ability in those subjects, Chippy, won me a scholarship to Cambridge. That is where I met

'TA' and his ilk. When I met him, it was like meeting a human being from another planet. He is not a nice man. In a gharry in Cairo, I had to slap his face to stop him groping me. In Beirut I put salt in his coffee to stop him pinching my bum. I knew the game he was playing. He wasn't interested in me. His behaviour towards me and other women was a red herring. He wanted gossip to spread that he was a womaniser. But everyone in the embassy in Beirut knew the love of his life was Tobias. Tobias Lacy. They were always together. They drank too much. They smoked too much. Their claim to have played Russian roulette with staff from the Russian embassy was bullshit. Their pedigrees enabled them to get away, quite literally, with murder.

'They were in Beirut, Chippy, when my beloved Yuri, the love of my life, was blown to smithereens by a terrorist bomb. I was having a beer with my love when the bomb went off. My friend, Doctor Lucy, told me the shrapnel which hit me came as close as four millimetres to my left ventricle. Do you remember the cigar smoke you smelt a few months ago? It made your nose twitch. On the anniversary of Yuri's murder, I smoke a cigar. It helps me remember him. Yuri liked a cigar. You won't believe this, Chippy, but some folk in the street think I'm the daughter of a bishop. Others think I'm a lesbian. I don't mind; just so long as they don't think I'm a spy. That would never do. I do my best to appear respectable. I never fail to pick up your poo. No one would believe the amount of money I spend on poo bags.

'What are they up to, Chippy? From now on, 'TA' will be my London contact. Mr Wonderful is by all accounts off on a new career. If that is true, Chippy, why is he interfering? He is breaking all the rules. But then, Chippy, my darling, when did posh boys ever follow rules?'

Chapter 2

Isa had two close friends in Chillingham Grove. Beatrice and Mari. The trio took it in turns to host chatty, get-together coffee mornings.

Beatrice's husband was an accountant but always off work with depression. Mari's husband was sea-going and away from home for months at a time. In their different ways, Beatrice and Mari were single women, just like Isa.

They looked up to Isa. They were full of admiration for a single woman who drove a Mercedes with a hood that folded into its boot. They were awed by a single woman who kept a dog that looked like a wolf. They were impressed by the expensive clothes she wore; the tailor-made outfits they could not afford.

They knew, many years ago, she'd won a scholarship to Cambridge; that she had worked as a civil servant in British embassies throughout the Middle East. They knew that the love of her life had been killed in a terrorist attack in Beirut. They knew she had taken early retirement from the civil service because it had been offered and she'd thought 'Why not?'.

They knew she had a gift for languages and mathematics. An alcove in her sitting room was full of books on prime numbers. She had books in Russian, Arabic and Farsi and the collected works of P.G. Wodehouse in Mandarin. They knew as much about their friend Ms Isa Weddle as Ms Isa Weddle wanted them to know. They knew nothing of her clandestine life; that she had killed for her country; that, at a private ceremony, the Queen had awarded her the George Cross.

To the suburbanites, Beatrice and Mari, Ms Isa Weddle was a symbol. She represented style and freedom from male oppression. She made Chillingham Grove seem glamorous. She had taught them conversational Russian; how to say, 'Good morning', 'Goodbye' and 'Which way to the loo?' in Mandarin and Farsi.

Isa was hosting the trio's usual coffee morning get-together when the idea of Chillingham Grove having a street party to celebrate the forthcoming royal wedding was first mentioned.

'The royal wedding?' said Mari. 'I think it's exciting.'

'I'm not a great fan of royalty,' said Beatrice, 'but the wedding does make one want to fly the flag. A shop in town is selling Union Jack knickers.'

'Are they?' said Isa. 'Bol'she kofe?'

'Yes, please,' said Beatrice, handing Isa her coffee cup. 'The Russians murdered their royal family, you know.'

'We chopped off Charles the First's head,' said Mari.

'Murder, mayhem and anarchy,' said Beatrice, 'as far as I'm concerned they all belong to the masculine world. Men love watching war films, don't they? I know Ken does. I sometimes think that watching tanks in World War Two films is better for his depression than the tablet he takes.'

'To celebrate the royal wedding,' said Mari, 'some people I know are talking about organising a street party. If the Grove had one, it would help people get to know each other. Mrs Thatcher says there is no such thing as society. I disagree. On New Year's Eve this year no one came out to first-foot; that's another dying tradition; such a shame. A street party would shake the street up.'

'Oh dear,' said Isa, 'do you think the street needs shaking up?'

'Streets, Isa, are like curtains,' said Mari.

'Are they?'

'Yes, they are. They hang at windows for years gathering dust. Every so often they need a good shaking.'

'Street parties are très working class?' said Beatrice. 'I mean, Chillingham Grove is not a row of terraced houses in Byker. I know that sounds awfully snobby, but you know what I mean.'

'My sister lives in Gosforth in a detached house … her street is having a party,' said, Mari.

'Well,' said Beatrice, 'I suppose, if it's good enough for Gosforth, it's good enough for Jesmond.'

When her two friends had gone, Isa looked across the road at number thirty-nine and smiled. What would Mari and Beatrice have thought if they'd known number thirty-nine was a safe house? And that, she, Ms Isa Weddle, spinster of this parish, had of late, taken to sleeping with an automatic pistol under her pillow?

****

Before the trio went ahead with their idea of organising a street party, they took soundings. They asked people in the street they knew quite well for their ideas. One wag said: 'You can't have a 'street' party, in a 'grove'.' After laughing hysterically at the man's joke – Beatrice fancied she'd a way with men – Beatrice, certain she now had him in the palm of her hand, said: 'But you are in favour of us having a party?'

'Of course I am,' said the man. 'You liked my joke?'

'You should be on the stage.'

At a coffee morning hosted by Mari, the trio discussed forming a street party committee. Beatrice said she couldn't hold meetings in her house because her husband suffered from depression and he hated visitors. Mari said she had three children and keeping them quiet while her husband was away at sea, would be impossible.

'I will host the meeting,' said Isa, 'just so long as those attending don't mind Chippy. I'll not have my dog inconvenienced. The Queen, with her corgis, would understand that.'

'We don't want anyone on the committee we don't like,' said Beatrice. 'Put some folk on a committee and they will take over.'

'We want doers, not talkers,' said Mari.

'Don't forget the street party was our idea.'

'I think I mentioned it first.'

'Is that important?'

'I was just saying …'

'Would it help,' said Isa, 'if we made a list of jobs to do. For example, catering. Pratt the butcher lives at the top of the street. It might be useful to have him on the committee. If we were to have, say, a barbecue, he might provide us with cost price meat.'

'Pratt's a meanie,' said Mari.

'Mari's right,' said Beatrice. 'When I was selling flags outside his shop for cancer research, he put a penny in my collecting box and took two flags.'

'In my time in the civil service,' said Isa, 'I chaired many committees. I know how important it is to get the right mix of people on board.'

'I think Isa would make an excellent chairman,' said Mari.

'Hand on heart, Mari, I was not putting myself forward.'

'Mari, if I may say so,' said Beatrice, 'you are buying a horse before you have a stable. We don't yet have a committee. When we have one, it will be for the committee to select the chair. I am a member, as you know, of the WI. Last year I chaired the Victoria Sponge committee.'

'Not easy,' said Isa, smiling as she thought of the life and death committees she had chaired.

'It wasn't.'

'Did you come to blows?'

'Certainly not. The WI are not pugilists. Third place now refuses to speak to me. She claims I was having an affair with her husband.'

'Were you?' said Mari.

'We had a few kisses, that's all. Nothing serious. I need love, Mari. When Ken's depressed, I don't get any.'

'Every time John comes home from sea I have another baby. I can't keep him off me.'

'Lucky you.'

'Do you think so?'

'I do.'

'The middle names of our children help us remember the voyage he came home from when they were conceived. Charlie is Charles Magellan. Amy is Amy Panama. Bartholomew is Sargasso.'

'While I make us all an Irish coffee,' said Isa, 'why don't you two put your heads together and make a list of jobs to do and pencil in beside them the names of possible doers.'

Isa made the Irish coffee strong. She had her own ideas as to who should be on the committee and who should chair it. In her quiet way, Isa liked to be in charge.

Chapter 3

Later that week, Isa, Beatrice and Mari knocked on the doors of the people they deemed suitable to be asked to serve on the committee.

Keeping busy organising a party to celebrate a royal wedding took Isa's mind off her work as an MI5 operative. It brought her relief from trying to work out the game Desmond and 'TA' were playing.

Fussing over details such as who should be in charge of decorating the street took Beatrice's mind off Ken's incapacitating illness; depression or whatever it was. It gave her an excuse to get out of the house and meet people; especially, men.

Mari thought Isa and Beatrice bossy. They seemed to have forgotten the street party was her idea.

****

After many phone calls, false starts, changes of times and dates to keep people happy, Isa, one evening in March, warned Chippy to expect guests.

'We, my darling, are hosting a committee meeting. We are hosting the first meeting of the SPC. The Street Party Committee. Please be on your best behaviour. No growling. No sulking if someone sits in your seat. Tonight, Chippy, my darling, you must be like a child in Victorian England; seen but not heard.'

It had been agreed the meeting would start at eight. When her doorbell rang at seven, Isa wondered who was early. On opening her front door, she thought there was no one there and was about to close it when a figure slid out from behind a magnolia.

'Don't shut the door, Aunt Isa; it's me, Joan.'

'What on earth are you doing hiding behind my magnolia?'

'I wasn't hiding, I was looking at the house across the road.'

'Number thirty-nine?'

'Yes.'

'Come along in.'

The two women embraced. Chippy wagged his tail. He knew Joan. She'd once given him a biscuit. Dogs never forget.

'Joan,' said Isa, 'when we hugged I felt something under your jacket? I do hope it is not what I think it is.'

'It's my piece. I'm carrying.'

'You mean, you are carrying a firearm?'

'Yes.'

'Is it loaded?'

'Of course. No point in carrying it otherwise. You know I'm with Special Branch. I'm following in your footsteps.'

'Like father, like son.'

'Like aunt, like niece.'

'I suppose you'll be wanting a dry martini, shaken but not stirred.'

'Don't be silly. I'm on duty. A cup of coffee will do fine. You are pleased to see me?'

'Of course. Why should I not be?'

'You seem far away; you know … as if you have things on your mind.'

'I am pondering the reason you gave me for hiding behind my magnolia.'

'I wasn't hiding.'

'I know, you told me. Your gun won't go off, will it? You have the safety on?'

'Aunt Isa, I'm a professional; like you.'

'Like I used to be, you mean. When you get old, Joan, you start to worry about things you never used to worry about.'

'Believe me, Aunt Isa, my gun only goes off when I aim it at a bad guy ... some piece of filth that needs to be removed from our green and pleasant land.'

'Milk and sugar?'

'Black.'

Returning with the coffee and a pot of tea for herself, Isa said: 'Why are you interested in number thirty-nine?'

'My brief was to get to know it. I was told that you would explain why it was of interest to Special Branch. My boss hinted that you might be an MI5 sleeper. Aunt Isa, is that true?'

Isa found it shocking that after all these years her role of keeping a watchful eye on number thirty-nine was no longer a secret between herself and London.

'Yes,' she said, after a long silence. 'Number thirty-nine is a safe house and I am paid by MI5 to keep a watchful eye on it.'

'Wow! Aunt Isa, I never knew you were still in the spying game. You kept that quiet.'

'Your boss ... London or Newcastle?'

'Newcastle.'

'He knows we are related?'

'Yes. He asked me how old you were and if you used a walking frame.'

'Cheeky sod.'

'He's a decent enough bloke, Aunt Isa, just a bit old fashioned. He was grumpy, I think, because London were telling him what to do. He's a bit of a freelancer. He hadn't liked the way this London toff had spoken to him. I think they'd had words. My boss demanded that the instructions he was being given be put in writing. He doesn't trust anyone who lives south of the Tees. He told me what you have just told me … that number thirty-nine is a safe house. He asked me if I was fond of you. I told him you were my role model. I know you and Mam don't always see eye to eye but I've always admired you. It was your "pull" that got me into Special Branch. He let me read his instructions. They were on Home Office notepaper. I was impressed.'

'What did you read?'

'It wasn't complimentary. My boss thought it unprofessional. I think he let me read it because he knew I would tell you. He was sort of telling me to tell you to watch your back.'

'I'm waiting.'

'You won't like it.'

'Tell me.'

'London called you an "awkward supernumerary". Your nickname is the Witch. I am to tell you that from now on I will be receiving my orders from an agent you recently called an Ass-Hole. Does that make sense?'

'Sadly and worryingly, yes. The new London boss in charge of looking after number thirty-nine is an old acquaintance of mine from the years I spent in the Middle East. He has a warped sense of humour. I suspect that while playing the Eton wall game he received too many knocks to the head.'

'You don't like each other?'

'I detest him, and the feeling is mutual. Why has he involved you? What game is he playing?'

'This game he is playing, Aunt Isa, will it get me promotion? I am keen to move up the ladder. You won't believe this, Aunt Isa, but, in my last in-house appraisal the psychologist in charge made one of my targets to be "less enthusiastic". Can you believe that?'

'I think, Joan, you will not be happy until MI5 give you a suicide pill to hide in your bra just in case you are caught by some dastardly Russian agent who is going to torture you into revealing all you know about British Intelligence.'

'Did you have one in the Middle East?'

'No, I did not.'

'By the way,' she said, looking at her watch, 'I want to be off before your pals on the street party committee arrive. They are coming at eight, I believe?'

'How did you know that?'

'My boss told me. Don't ask me how he knew. I'd best be on my way. May I go out the back way?'

'If you want to look suspicious and draw attention to yourself, of course you can.'

'You know the rules of the game, Aunt Isa. Secret agents are tom cats. In case of an emergency, they must know their territory.'

Isa's back garden was the length of a cricket pitch. Its end fence, through which there was a gate, abutted a bridleway.

'I'll be in touch, Aunt Isa,' said Joan, at the gate. 'I wish my street was having a party.'

Chapter 4

The first members of the SPC to arrive were Angus and Morag. If they'd been birds, they'd have belonged to the wren family; both being below average height and very thin.

'Come in! Come in!' said Isa.

'A wonderful dog,' said Angus, patting Chippy on the head. 'It's because of you I sleep at night. What a guard dog. This is for you–' handing Isa a bottle of wine. 'I'll no have it said the Scots are mean.'

'There's no need,' protested Isa.

'I ken that. If there had been I wouldna' have brought it. Are we the first?'

'Yes. Whisky?'

'Is heather purple?'

'Morag?'

'If it's no too much trouble I'll have a wee G and T … not too much gin. I dinna want my wee head spinning when we're discussing such important matters as organising a street party to celebrate a royal wedding. Och! It's exciting.'

'We're here a bit early,' said Angus, 'to tell you, we saw someone leave by your back garden gate.'

'That would be my niece, Joan.'

'What's wrong with the front door?'

'She popped in to see me while she was out jogging.'

'She was na' dressed for the jogging.'

'She's young. You know what the young are like. I'll get the drinks.'

Before anyone else arrived, she asked them if they knew Dominic and Irene. Did they know who she meant?

'He lives at the top of the street. He's a teacher at a local primary school. A very good organiser. I know his mother. When everyone's here I'm going to propose him as our chair. Will you second him, Angus?'

'Beatrice won't like that,' said Morag. 'Beatrice likes to be boss. She once told me I was planting my daffodil bulbs upside down.'

'Were you?'

'Yes. But that is not the point. If, for whatever reason, you are trying to put a lid on Beatrice, I wouldn't bother. When a volcano wants to erupt there's no stopping it.'

Isa smiled, an enigmatic Mona Lisa smile.

'Angus, will you back me up,' she said, 'and second him? By the way, in case you don't know, Dominic's a MacTaggart.'

'Isa, you're a fly one. A Scot, is he? Then, he's the man for me.'

Beatrice and Mari were next to arrive.

'Don't ask me where Ken is,' expostulated Beatrice. 'Mari's husband has an excuse for not being here. He is seagoing. He can't be expected to fly from Valparaiso to attend a meeting to organise a street party; can he? My husband is in bed three doors away. I ask you?'

'Should Ken not see a psychiatrist?' said Mari.

'My husband,' said Beatrice, 'is not mad. What he needs to put him right is sex, but he doesn't want it. Down there I'm like a teddy bear.'

Angus, looking at Morag, then at the floor and then at the ceiling, said: 'Aye! It's going to be a good year for apples. Lots of blossom on my apple trees.'

Dominic and Irene were next to arrive. When Isa asked Dominic what he'd like to drink he said, 'Coffee', whereupon his wife said, 'I should think so too. You've already had a whisky.'

'In that case,' said Dominic, 'I'll have another one.'

'I should think so too,' boomed Angus. 'That's my boy! If you'd stuck to coffee I'd have said you weren't a MacTaggart.'

Isa was about to pour them their drinks when, once again, the doorbell ding-donged.

'Excuse me,' she said, 'that will be Jean and Harry. Dominic, Irene–' pointing at the drinks trolley– 'please help yourselves.'

Not being the sort to look a gift horse in the mouth, Dominic and Irene did just that.

Jean was a solicitor. Harry was in insurance. He worked the room as if he was on commission. After shaking hands with the men and hugging the women he said he'd have a beer. Jean said she'd have a G and T.

'I don't think we need to be too formal,' said Isa, when everyone was slurping. 'We all know each other … more or less … no need for introductions. Is everyone happy sitting, where they are, rather than at a table?'

'As long as I have somewhere to park my whisky glass,' said Angus, 'I'm as happy as a grouse before the twelfth of August.'

'We may be informal,' said Beatrice, 'but surely we should have a chairman?'

'Someone should be in charge,' said Irene, 'you know … to take notes of what we decide.'

'I have a clipboard,' said Dominic. 'I never come to a meeting without a clipboard.'

'I propose Dominic for the chair,' said Isa.

'I second that,' said Angus. 'It does my heart of Midlothian heart good to support a MacTaggart. As the African elephant said to the Indian elephant, Dominic, I'm all ears. What about putting me in charge of the bar. We are having a bar, aren't we? At the street party,

I mean.'

'Angus,' said Morag, 'shut up. Mr MacTaggart, Dominic, has the chair. This is not a council meeting. And you are no longer a councillor.'

'Aren't we putting the cart before the horse?' said Beatrice. 'What if Dominic doesn't want the job? It's not everyone who can chair meetings. When I was on jury service I was foreman. The judge was complimentary about the way I spoke and the questions I asked.'

'My husband is used to chairing meetings,' said Irene. 'Why shouldn't he be chair? Is it because he's a vegan? There's a lot of prejudice against vegans.'

'A MacTaggart who doesn't eat meat!' said Angus. 'The next thing I'll be hearing is that the earth is flat.'

'I am happy to chair the meeting,' said Dominic, 'unless, that is, any one objects.'

'Anyone object?' said Angus. 'No raised hands. Motion carried as far as I'm concerned. Dominic, you're in the hot seat. I suggest we talk about where the bar will be. I think it should be close to my front door.'

'Another whisky, Angus?' said Isa.

'Why not! Three fingers and two ice cubes.'

'Another G and T, Morag?'

'A small one.'

'Anyone else?'

As steam engines need water and coal to keep them going, the committee, to keep it going, needed alcohol. After everyone had been refuelled, Dominic showed he was 'Chair' by tapping his whisky glass with a pen. 'Beatrice,' he said, 'I believe it was your idea to have a street party.'

'Well, yes, I suppose it was … and Mari's'.

'And Isa's,' said Mari.

'Perhaps you would like to say a few words about the progress you, Isa and Mari have made in getting it off the ground. Before you launch forth, may I suggest we use a technique I have found useful when chairing discussions with children. To stop interrupters and butters-in you may only speak when you are holding this rosary–' taking one out of a jacket pocket and handing it to Beatrice.

'I've knocked on every door in the street,' said Beatrice, playing with the rosary, 'and ninety-nine per cent are in favour of a party. They understand that if we go ahead the street will be closed to motor traffic for most of the twenty-ninth of July. It's an inconvenience, I know, but, we can't be expected to pack up our picnic tables to let a lorry through, can we?'

'Or move the bar,' said Angus.

'I don't think I've ever seen a lorry come down our street,' said Irene.

'Irene,' said Dominic, 'you don't have the rosary and Beatrice didn't mean a real lorry.'

'What did she mean? She said "Lorry", I heard her. Beatrice, didn't you say, "Lorry"?'

'I was using "lorry" as a metaphor,' said Beatrice, 'for all traffic … here, you'd better have the rosary.'

'But people who don't live in the Grove,' said Irene, 'will still be able to come and go; won't they? Beatrice, don't answer until I give you the rosary. Rules is rules.'

Taking the rosary with a rictus grin, Beatrice said: 'Pedestrians will be allowed to come and go as they please.'

To show she wanted the rosary back, Irene fluttered her fingers.

'Don't speak until you have the rosary, Irene,' said Beatrice. 'Rules are rules!'

'What about cyclists?' said Irene, taking the rosary, clumsily, the way losers in a relay race exchange batons.

To show she wished to answer, Beatrice mouthed to Irene: 'Give me the bloody rosary.' Taking the beads, she said: 'The Grove will not be closed to cyclists. Cyclists will be expected to dismount and push their bikes.'

'I am more than happy to do the legal work to have the street closed,' said Jean.

'Jean, you haven't got the rosary,' said Irene, 'so you can't speak.'

'My wife's a solicitor,' said Harry. 'She's just passed a bye-law. She doesn't need a rosary to speak. She knows how to close a road to traffic. That's all that matters. Here, give me the worry beads. I'm in insurance. If we need insurance of any kind I'll be happy to give you a quote; no pro bono in insurance, I'm afraid; wish there was but, there you go.'

'Who in the street doesn't want the party?' asked Irene.

'Irene, does it matter?' asked Dominic.

'Dominic, you haven't got the rosary. You shouldn't be talking.'

'Nor have you. Let's forget about the rosary, shall we? As a means of keeping discipline with ten year olds, it works a treat. Clearly, it does not work with adults.'

'That woman I've seen with three children in number thirty-nine,' said Irene, making a face at her husband, 'I'll bet she'd object to a street party. I'm only saying that because she always looks so miserable.'

'She moved out weeks ago,' said Isa. 'I live opposite number thirty-nine. I see people coming and going all the time. We all know it's a rented property.'

'What if someone rents number thirty-nine and objects to the street being closed?'

'Irene?' said Dominic.

'What?'

'Nothing.'

'Dominic, you sounded quite sharp when you said that. I'm only thinking of other people. What if they want to move in when the street is closed? They won't be pleased if they can't get their furniture van to their front door. I know I wouldn't. What if they have a piano?'

'Irene, let's face such problems as and when they arise; shall we? At the moment number thirty-nine is empty.'

'I know this sounds awful,' said Mari, 'but I'm pleased the woman with three children has left. The children were out of control. I heard one of them tell the milkman to, you know … F-off.'

'I know who you mean, Mari. Not the sort of people we want in our street,' said Harry. 'If I'm any judge of human nature, and, I think I am … you have to be when you are in insurance … I've met people like her. She'd burn a hole in a pair of curtains and claim on the insurance to get new ones.'

'I don't think she looks happy,' said Irene, looking at her face in the mirror of a powder compact.

'That's because she didn't fit in,' said Beatrice.

'I don't mean the woman with the three children,' said Irene. 'I meant, Lady Di. I think she's been told to marry Prince Charles.'

****

By ten o'clock they had the bare bones of a plan. In the afternoon there would be a children's tea party and one for the elderly. To amuse the children there would be a conjuror. Isa volunteered to organise a game whereby children would fire arrows at balloons.

'Isa,' said Mari, 'you don't know children the way I do. We all know what happened to Harold at the Battle of Hastings. Please, no bows and arrows.'

In the evening there would be music and dancing for the adults. There would be a barbecue. A karaoke.

'And a bar,' said Angus.

Dominic said he would enquire about borrowing trestle tables from his church.

'What about a barrel of beer?' said Harry. 'I insure a brewery, don't you know? I'll talk to the manager. Cost price, minus five per cent because it's for a good cause.'

A date was agreed for the next meeting. Isa said she was more than happy to host it. In the meantime, who would like a hot sausage roll?

'Me,' said Angus, 'I've always said whisky and a hot sausage roll go together like a horse and carriage.'

'They are vegetable sausage rolls,' Isa explained to Dominic, 'cheese and onion and bread crumbs. I made them myself.'

'I've had them before,' said Angus; 'they are delicious.'

****

Dominic and Irene were the first to leave.

When Isa returned from seeing them out, Harry said: 'Dominic did a good job keeping us all in order. Pity about his rosary idea. Damn silly idea. I've seen him around but can't say as I know him. He mentioned something about ten-year-olds. What's his line?'

'Teacher,' said Isa.

'Private?'

'Council.'

'He's in the wrong job … should move into the private sector … that's where the money is.'

'Do you know anyone in the private sector who wants an accountant?' asked Beatrice. 'My husband's an accountant … that is, when he's at work.'

'Who's he work for?' asked Harry, gesticulating, airily, with the sausage roll he was holding between two fingers as if it was a cigar.

'Don't mind the crumbs,' said Isa, 'Chippy will hoover them up.'

'Don't encourage my man to be messy, Isa,' said Jean. 'Harry, there's more going on the floor than there is going into your mouth.'

'Who's he work for?'

'National Coal Board.'

'Ah! I see where you are coming from. Our Prime Minister, the "Divine Margaret" does not like the coal industry, right? She has a score to settle with them … and, as for that fellow, Scargill … have you seen him on television? Scary. A first-class debater. I'll bet you wouldn't fancy coming up against him in court, Jean? I've sold a bit of insurance to folk on the fringes of power. The rumour is that she calls the miners the "Enemy Within". If they take on this government, they won't win. She's not like Heath. She won't back down. What is at stake is our democracy. Who governs England? The Unions or Parliament? I'm all for her. She's going to change the face of England for the better.'

'I'm all for her as well,' said Beatrice, 'but I don't want Ken to lose his job. He's heard rumours that she'll not be happy until she's closed every coal mine in the country.'

'The NCB,' said Harry, 'is a typical nationalised industry. What it needs is a good dose of private sector realism. If it's cheaper to ship in coal from Australia, then let's do it. That's what I say. Take it or leave it. Lovely sausage rolls, Isa.'

'If that happens,' said Isa, 'the expression, "carrying coals to Newcastle" will become as redundant as the miners whose hard physical labour gave it, its original meaning.'

'You a leftie, Isa?'

'If I played for Newcastle, I'd be their centre forward.'

'Women can't play football.'

'Do help yourself to another sausage roll, Harry.'

'Don't mind if I do. They are delicious.'

****

By eleven o'clock Isa wanted them, every one of them, to bugger-off!

The men knew everything that was wrong with football managers. The women condemned the local primary school because it employed no male teachers.

They left at midnight.

'Night!'

'Night!'

'By-ee!'

Watching them disappear into their respective homes, she reflected on a casual remark made about streets like Chillingham Grove by a Hindu friend. An ex-lover. A senior civil servant in the Indian embassy in London. He had told her how strange he found it that English people could live cheek-by-jowl, yet not know each other.

'It would not happen in India,' he had said. 'In an Indian village, everyone knows everyone. It is not possible to keep secrets in an Indian village.'

Looking up and down the street she knew he was right. Who lived in the semi three doors down from number thirty-nine? Or, five or six doors up the other way? She knew their faces but did not know their names. What did they do for a living? She'd no idea. If she saw them in a supermarket she might nod at them and smile. If she lived in an Indian village everyone would know she was a spy.

Chapter 5

To drum up support for the party, Isa, Beatrice, Mari and Angus knocked on every door in the street. They found most residents more than happy to contribute to a street party kitty. Names were taken of those willing to make sandwiches and cakes for the afternoon tea.

Angus, very keen on Harry's idea of having a barrel of beer, had hit upon the idea of 'ATs'. Angus tokens. They were to be on sale to residents for a mere forty pence. On the night of the party you'd exchange your token for a pint of beer. Only folk with a token would be served a pint.

'Show me a public house where you can get a pint for forty pence,' he kept telling residents when he knocked on their front doors, 'and I'll show you a mermaid wearing a kilt. Forty pence for a pint is cheap.'

'Harry,' he boasted, at the next meeting of the SPC, 'I've sold two hundred ATs. I'm thinking we need another half barrel. There are some big boozers in Chillingham Grove.'

'I'll see what I can do, Angus. The price might have gone up. Supply and demand, you know.'

Dominic had drawn a map of the street on a roll of wallpaper. He used it to discuss where the stage should go, for the conjuror in the afternoon and the karaoke in the evening. Where the tables should go for the afternoon tea. Where the bar should go. He'd brought coloured pens. Permanent markers with centimetre-wide felt tips. With them, using different colours – he seemed fond of blue – he drew squares and oblongs on the map like a surgeon marking an abdomen prior to making an incision. By the time he'd marked in the position of everything, the map looked not dissimilar to that well-known ideogram of London's Underground.

'Will there be vegan food?' said Irene. 'I'm thinking of Dominic.'

'What if I see one of your children eating a chicken leg?' Beatrice asked Dominic. 'Do I turn a blind eye?'

'Eating a chicken leg will not send him to hell,' said Dominic. 'I would just ask you not to encourage them. I am well aware–' looking at his wife– 'that not everyone is as keen on not eating meat as I am.'

'Dominic,' said Irene, 'why did you look at me when you said that?'

'I am not stupid. You have been to the loo three times tonight. You do not have a weak bladder. You have not been diddling-off for a wee. You have been diddling off to eat the ham Isa has put out for you in her kitchen.'

'Anyway,' said Irene, breathing in deeply, 'you are only pretending to be a vegan to help you become a lecturer. How many times do I have to tell you? If I don't eat meat, I get dandruff.'

'It's going to be a good year for apples,' said Angus.

'Angus,' said, Morag, 'how'd you know?'

'Lots of blossom on my apple trees and the man on "Gardener's Question Time" said.'

'Angus! I sometimes wonder about you.'

****

Later, Isa came up with the idea of certain houses becoming tea-stations.

Mari and Beatrice thought this an excellent idea. They wished they'd thought of it.

'That way, anyone who wants a cuppa in the afternoon will be free to help themselves,' said Beatrice.

'Coffee at the "Tea Stations"?' asked Harry.

'No,' said Beatrice.

'It's just that last year Jean and I had a holiday in France.'

'I know you did,' said Angus, 'you showed us the photographs.'

'I've seen them too,' said Isa.

'Lucky you! I'll never forget the photograph, Harry, you took of your admission ticket to the Eiffel Tower.'

'I was just going to say,' said Harry, 'that when Jean and I were in Paris we got used to drinking coffee; that's all.'

'Harry,' said Beatrice, 'Chillingham Grove is not the Avenue des Champs Elysees. We are celebrating the marriage of the heir to the throne of the United Kingdom. Charles is not the dauphin. He is the Prince of Wales.'

'I'd be happy to be a "Tea Station",' said Jean, 'put a "TS" beside my house number. If Harry wants a coffee, I will make him one.'

Isa compared the meeting with those she'd attended in British Embassies in the Middle East. The ones called to discuss the assassination of suspected terrorists. The seriousness of their agenda, the killing of a fellow human being, had almost never stopped personal and interdepartmental rivalries, turning a tragedy into a farce.

Bidding the SPC good night, she looked across the road at number thirty-nine as she had done so many times over so many years. She saw an empty house. She saw a dead house. She saw a house without a soul. She also saw a threat. Looking at it made her shiver. As if sensing her mood, Chippy, who was at her side, growled.

Chapter 6

For the next few weeks Isa heard nothing from London. Outwardly nothing had changed. Every day she walked Chippy to the newsagent's to buy a Daily Telegraph. She met Beatrice and Mari for coffee. They talked about the street party; about the royal wedding. How many bridesmaids? How many page boys?

Always on her mind, hidden behind her smile, was the question: What are the posh boys up to? Once, in the middle of the night, she'd woken up, quite suddenly, from a nightmare. She'd been dreaming she was a clay pipe in a shooting gallery. The shooting gallery's customers, armed with air-rifles, were 'TA' and Desmond.

Then, Joan called to tell her aunt not to be surprised if she saw a 'Reed's Plumbing Services' van in number thirty-nine's drive. There'd be two plumbers. They'd be wearing white boiler suits.

'Of course,' said Joan, 'they're not real plumbers. They're MI5 boffins. They are there to bug number thirty-nine. MI5 want to eavesdrop on the house's next guests.'

'Do you know who these next guests might be?'

'Aunt Isa, I'm a foot soldier. Back at the office I'm the tea girl. When the big-wigs have a pow-wow they send me out to buy bacon sandwiches. I know my place. Oh and one more thing, you are to find a gardener for number thirty-nine. My boss told me that this new guy in London who keeps telling him what to do is concerned that, as the house has been empty for a while, its gardens must need attention. My boss calls this guy from London who keeps pestering him, the "Fairy". London wants number thirty-nine to look the same as all the other houses in the street. You are to find a gardener.'

This puzzled Isa. 'TA' should know she was paid expenses to keep number thirty-nine's gardens tidy. Why did he not know?

'So,' she said, looking up from scratching Chippy's ears, 'I'm to find a gardener, am I?'

'Why don't you ask that cousin of yours, Malcolm? He does your garden. He might want a bit of extra work.'

'It may interest you to know, Joan, that Malcolm is already paid to look after number thirty-nine's gardens.'

'Is that why they look untidy?'

'Tut! Tut! Do not be so critical. On the whole he does a pretty good job.'

'Who pays him?'

'I do. I claim his wages as expenses.'

'Does London not know that?'

'They should.'

'From what I've heard about your cousin, he's a bit of a rogue.'

'We are all of us made up of good and bad.'

'What are my bad bits, Aunt Isa? Do I have any?'

'Your idealism, Joan, scares me. Your trust in authority scares me. You are young. You think everything is black and white. You do not see the many shades in between. You trust your superiors. I don't. I put it to you that London is using you as a go-between. The question we must ask is … why? What are the posh boys up to?'

****

As soon as her niece left, Isa had a long conversation with Chippy.

Why, she asked the dog, did 'TA' not know she employed a gardener to cut number thirty-nine's grass? Had a bureaucratic slip allowed this aspect of her supernumerary work to be forgotten? Was it not on her file that she claimed expenses to pay a gardener?

Had someone doctored her file? Or, had she simply been forgotten, like a mug of coffee allowed to go cold under a pile of papers in an untidy office? She had been keeping a watchful eye on number thirty-nine for a very long time. If you lived next to a railway line for a long time you stopped hearing the trains. But, she wasn't a train. She was Ms Weddle. Marksman. To keep her country safe, she had killed bad guys.

Desmond had not had the manners to tell her he was leaving until after he'd gone. His dubious gift of a Glock and accompanying letter, needed a lot of thinking about. Without his input she'd still be racking her brains trying to put a name to the mysterious caller who claimed to know all about her and to have worked with her in Beirut.

How much had Desmond told 'TA', about her role? What if 'Mr Wonderful' had knowingly omitted to mention the role she played in looking after number thirty-nine? What if, on taking over responsibility for looking after the safe house, 'TA' had not an inkling she was its 'watchful eye'? If that was true, it must have come as a shock to him to learn that he was once again working with Ms Isa Weddle.

'When he phoned me, Chippy,' she asked the dog, 'was he trying to frighten me? The heavy breathing. The faux anonymity. Am I a threat to him, Chippy? Is that why Desmond sent me the Glock?'

Chapter 7

In June a letter popped through Isa's letterbox. As usual she gave it to Chippy to mouth-carry into the kitchen where, as he'd been trained to do, he dropped it onto a chair.

The quality of the cream-coloured foolscap envelope told her at once it was not junk mail. It looked legal. As if it might contain important documents from a firm of solicitors who used expensive stationery to show they meant business. Its postmark told her it was from the House of Lords.

On a sheet of paper, bearing the House of Lords' logo, she read:

'Dear Ms Weddle,

I wish you to ring the number at the bottom of my billet doux. You may ring at any time between 8am and 7pm; Saturday and Sunday, not excepted. Ask for Jeremy. The switchboard have been told to expect a call and will put you straight through. IMPORTANT. DO NOT RING ON YOUR LANDLINE. USE A PUBLIC TELEPHONE BOX. Destroy this note. Memorise the number. There must be no evidence of contact between us. Tell, no one! Especially Joan.

*You will know that my credentials are bona fide when I tell
you I am a friend of Desmond. I know number thirty-nine is
a safe house. I know Tony Adder is in charge of running it.
Need I say more? Please ring.*

No signature.'

Of course she would ring. Of course she would tell no one. She was
used to keeping secrets. She was a professional.

'Chippy, why can I not use my own phone? If it's bugged, I'll be
furious.'

****

The telephone box smelt like a urinal. The number she'd been told to
ring had been easy to remember. It was her age to the power three.

The phone rang twice before a female voice said: 'How may I
help?'

A switchboard operator? A discreet exchange somewhere in
Whitehall?

'May I speak to Jeremy, please?'

'Who is calling?'

'My name is, Weddle. Ms Isa Weddle.'

'One moment, madam.'

'Ms Weddle, thank you for ringing,' said an RP voice. 'I'm
Jeremy. And how is Chippy?'

'You know I have a dog?'

'Yes. I mentioned Chippy for the same reason I used House of
Lords notepaper for the note I sent you. To impress you. To let you
know I am not a charlatan. We have not met for over twenty years.'

'We have met?'

'Not officially. At the time I was very junior and wore a uniform.'

34

'Jeremy? I can't recall a "Jeremy" in my life. Is Jeremy your real name?'

'It is one of my names. I wish most urgently to meet with you. On Thursday of this week I will be fishing the Tweed. On my way up from London I will stop off at Newcastle. May I offer you breakfast at the "County Hotel"? Would that be possible?'

'Do I have a choice?'

'You would like an alternative date?'

'I mean do I have the choice of refusing to meet you?'

'Of course. I am not in the business of replacing habeas corpus with interdicting. I hope you will. An inducement. I was in the restaurant when Yuri was killed and you were badly wounded.'

'What time?'

'Eight-thirty. Tea or coffee?'

'I beg your pardon?'

'When we meet, do you want tea or coffee? Once went out with a girl who wanted Ovaltine. My club didn't have it. Since then, I like to know.'

'Tea, please. English breakfast tea.'

'Kippers? The full English?'

'Toast would be nice.'

'Bring Chippy. He won't be allowed into the breakfasting room. Hygiene, you know. I often sleep with my own dogs. The doorman will look after him for you. One more thing. Tell no one about this conversation. By "no one" I am, of course, referring to your niece Joan and Tony Adder.'

'Are they not on our side? You are MI5, aren't you?'

'I am internal security, Ms Weddle: "quis custodict ipsos custodies".'

'Who watches the watchers? Juvenal.'

'Just so. I spy on spies. For reasons of security, I keep well away from the British Secret Service. One more thing, do not be late. Our meeting is not a wedding. You are not a bride and I am not a bridegroom. In the afternoon I am fishing the Tweed with my old school chum, his Grace, the Duke of Northumberland. If I was late he'd be vexed and so would I. Pip-toodle.'

Thinking, when in Rome, Isa replied: 'toodle-pip'.

Chapter 8

To meet the mysterious Jeremy, Isa rose early. She wanted, time to put on her face. When she met the enigma, she wanted to look stunning. Men had always liked her and she liked them.

The day was forecast to be a scorcher. From an extensive wardrobe she chose a peach-coloured, lightweight linen trouser suit. To stop the sun bleaching her hair she wore a straw trilby feminised by two pheasant feathers.

Many years ago she'd shot the pheasant with a machine gun. At the time she'd been on a 'weapons familiarisation' course hosted by the Coldstream Guards at Redesdale, the British army's firing range in the wilds of north Northumberland.

She left home with Chippy on his lead in plenty of time. The walk to the 'County' would take twenty minutes. She gave herself thirty. If 'Jeremy' had a fishing date with his 'Grace', she'd better be on time. It was one thing to keep him waiting, quite another to be the cause of him keeping a duke dithering in a bothy.

****

The County Hotel's doorman wore a tailed coat, the colour of a ripe tomato, a green waistcoat with gold buttons, black trousers and a top hat that made him look seven feet tall.

She wanted to ask him if the pink carnation in his buttonhole was real or if it squirted water, but held back, well aware that doormen like policemen are not renowned for having a sense of humour.

He looked a very serious kind of doorman. The sort of doorman who, if it had been pouring with rain and she'd said: 'Lovely day?' Would have replied: 'Do you think so?'

'He won't bite,' said Isa.

'You sure, madam?'

'He's licking his chops because he can smell meat. The parcel you have in your hand is dripping blood.'

'It's liver, madam. Mr Jeremy said I was to give him liver. He said I was to keep my eyes open for a lady with a dog what looks like a wolf. We don't see many wolves in Newcastle. You might in Wolverhampton. Ha! Ha! But not in Newcastle. I take it, madam, you are Ms Weddle?'

'I am she,' said Isa. 'And what is your name? If you are looking after my dog, I must know your name.'

'You mean before I changed it by deed poll to Horatio?'

'Yes.'

'Derek, madam,' doffing his top hat, 'Derek Nelson.'

'Derek, my dog is called Chippy and he is not a wolf. He is a German Shepherd with a dash of husky. And, even if he were a wolf, you would not have to worry.'

'And why would that be, madam? I'm keen to know. The things folk tell me makes me a whizz at pub quizzes.'

'Because, Derek, you are not a sheep. Wolves do not eat doormen. They eat sheep. Now, which way to the breakfast room? Chippy is having liver. Mummy is having tea and toast. Do not give him the liver all at once. Cut it up into little pieces. Before you give him a piece, ask for his paw.'

'Madam, I am not a butcher.'

'But you are a doorman who knows how to please. I know you are.'

'Yes, madam.'

'Now, direct me.'

'Straight up the stairs, first right. Follow the aromas. That's what I tell the paying guests.'

'Stay! Chippy.'

****

Would she recognize him? Beirut was a long time ago. People change.

When she'd been blown up, shot and invalided out of the service, she'd been in her mid-fifties; the age, as the saying goes, when policemen start to look young. At that time there'd been lots of young men working for British Intelligence in Beirut.

The door into the 'Breakfast Room' was opened by a bell-boy, with one arm – at least that's the impression he gave, because his other arm – if he had one and hopefully he had – he kept folded behind his back.

In the breakfast room a bowing maître d'hôtel said: 'Please to follow me, Ms Weddle.'

How did he know her name?

At the far end of the room, at a table for two, in a window alcove, sat a tall man, wearing a green Harris Tweed suit, with a matching waistcoat, a checked Barbour shirt and a Coldstream Guard's tie.

He'd a mop of fair hair and looked like someone who might own a farm in Sussex. A white scar disfigured an eyebrow. One blue eye didn't look right.

Before introducing himself, he bowed and kissed her hand.

'Good morning, Ms Weddle. I am Jeremy. Please do take a seat.'

She sat down.

'Thank you, Ken,' whereupon the maître d'hôtel who'd pulled out a chair for her disappeared the way an ice cube melts in hot water.

39

'I might remember you,' she said, after staring hard at Jeremy in an attempt to place him. 'SAS? Am I right?'

Jeremy nodded. 'Funny thing was, I and my team were in the café to protect you. You didn't know that. Two of my team were killed. I was lucky. I only lost an eye.'

'I, too, was lucky, so the doctors tell me.'

'Tea and toast for Ms Weddle, sir,' said the maître d'hôtel, unloading those items off a tray and onto the table with the speed and self-assured aplomb of a snooker referee replacing the black.

'Thank you, Ken.'

'My pleasure, sir. More liver for the wolf, madam?'

'Well?' said Jeremy. 'He is your dog. I would not dare to presume.'

'Why not?'

'More liver for Chippy, Ken.'

'It's as good as done, sir.'

'Thank you, Ken.'

'THANK YOU, SIR.'

Once again Ken, melted away.

'I don't know how you do it,' said Isa. 'I mean, how you get waiters to tie your shoelaces and squeeze toothpaste onto your toothbrush.'

'I am used to servants. A horse won't move if it knows its rider can't ride. Servants know me and I know them.'

'How?'

'Osmosis.'

'Jeremy, we live on different planets.'

'Do we?'

'Yes.' Then, knitting her brow and giving him a quizzical look: 'I like you. Don't ask me why.'

'In the nick of time you a have stopped the guillotine chopping off my aristocratic noddle.'

'Something like that. Before my toast gets cold ...'

'If it does Ken will bring you some more.'

'Thank you. Why am I here?'

'Excuse me,' as if he was about to stifle a sneeze, Jeremy removed his dead looking eye, sucked it the way a child sucks a gobstopper and, in the most unaffected way, popped it back into its socket, saying: 'Sometimes it gets awfully itchy. I do hope I didn't embarrass you? Once, or so I'm told, my great grandfather while dining with the late king at Windsor took out his false teeth to remove a piece of grouse. Perhaps getting to grips with prosthetics is a family failing. But, as they say, that is by-the-by. You are here, Ms Weddle, in order that I might take you into my confidence. What I am about to tell you, and I assure you no double entendre is intended, makes us bedfellows.'

'I am too old for what my mother called…"that sort of thing".'

'But still very attractive.'

'Jeremy, do cut to the quick. I am susceptible to flattery.'

'You are here, Ms Weddle, because you and I are the victims of a certain person's treachery. I lost an eye. You lost the man you loved and almost your life. I do wish you would try the kippers. I eat them Scottish style with toast and marmalade.'

'Tony Adder?'

'You have heard rumours?'

Isa nodded.

'Rumours, gossip, has destroyed many an intelligence network. I sometimes think our secret service should be called the "Colander Service". Only a small number of people know about number thirty-nine. I wonder how many know, who should not know. Never mind. Time will tell. MI5 keeps a number of "safe" houses. Costs the taxpayer millions. I call them: "fire engines". They might never be needed but, when they are you realise the money spent on keeping them in a state of prepared readiness has been money well spent. For the last few months, our mutual acquaintance from days of yore, Tony Adder – from now on I shall refer to him as "TA" … as I know you are wont to do – has been put in charge of looking after number thirty-nine. In many ways the poor chap is nothing more than a glorified landlord. He pays its utility bills. Spying, as you and I know, Ms Weddle, is not as glamorous as non-spies think.'

Isa buttered a slice of toast.

'To cut to the quick. Quite soon a vodka salesman will be renting number thirty-nine. He is a Russian KGB officer. No doubt he will sell some vodka to make his cover look good. His real purpose is to meet with representatives of the National Union of Mineworkers. Communist Russia wishes to show solidarity with England's underground workers. He will be giving CIU clubs loans to buy vodka. In reality it is hard cash to be put in a war chest, ready to be used by the miners in their next fight with the government of the day. Make no mistake, Prime Minister Thatcher will not allow her government to be trashed by the miners the way they trashed Ted Heath's government.'

'I worry when people tell me their secrets. It makes me complicit. I am not your agony aunt.'

'I have, of course, heard of "agony aunts" but, I never read them. Your tea will be getting cold.'

'Are you surprised? What you are telling me has made me forget it was there.'

'What I am going to tell you next may make you, also, forget your toast. "TA" is a traitor. His superiors in London are giving him rope. The case against him is a jigsaw with very few pieces missing. 'TA' is confident he has persuaded his superiors that Leo – that is the Russian vodka salesman's name, by the way – might be persuaded to betray Mother Russia. With the help of MI5, 'TA' is helping a KGB agent set up business in the UK as a commercial traveller, selling vodka. The peripatetic nature of Leo's business will enable 'TA' to meet him here, there and everywhere … not, of course forgetting number thirty-nine. It is through Leo that MI5 know about the Kremlin's plan to give financial support to the NUM. That is the red meat the Russians have thrown our way.'

'To show that Leo is a reliable source of information?'

'Yes. For money, 'TA' is telling Leo everything he knows about the British Secret Service. The information he will be able to give them will be priceless. To legitimise 'TA's' contact with Leo, the Russians are more than happy to throw Arthur Scargill to the wolves. They know the Home Secretary is as keen as mustard to get his hands on any information that will blacken the miners; make them look unpatriotic; be able to call them communists. I know 'TA' told the Russians about your meeting in Beirut, who in turn told the terrorists who blew you up.'

'And, killed Yuri,' said Isa. 'The explosion in which you lost an eye.'

'I also lost my stutter. Before I was blown up and lost an eye I had the most frightful stammer – always avoided saying a word like "frightful"; now, I don't. "Frightful". "Frightful". Not a trace of a stumble on the "F".'

'Now you can say, "Fuck off".'

'As a matter of fact, yes. Not a phrase I would use in front of a lady. You are a refreshingly forthright woman, Ms Weddle. I do believe my mother would approve of you. May I count on your assistance in this matter?'

'To put 'TA' behind bars?'

'Yes.'

'You are salting my desire for revenge.'

'For justice, Ms Weddle. For justice. Revenge is not a pickled herring. The butter on that finger of toast has quite melted. May I? Talking skulduggery gives me an appetite.'

Jeremy, Isa knew, was giving her the 'Risotto treatment'. He was eating the toast slowly to give her time to think. He was giving her time to think, the way you added stock, a little bit at a time, to risotto rice. You had to give the rice time to absorb the stock. He was giving her time to chew over what he'd told her.

When he judged the rice, as it were, ready to absorb more stock, he said: 'At the moment your role of keeping a watchful eye on number thirty-nine is very much "hands off". I want you to be "hands on". Are you willing?'

'I loved Yuri. We were meant for each other. If what you are telling me is true, 'TA''s treachery has ruined my life. Why should I ruin his?'

'To protect other agents. To remember that democracy is a better form of government than communism.'

'What do you want me to do?'

'In a corner of number thirty-nine's front garden, there is a small rockery, yes?'

Isa nodded.

'If you go up close to the rockery you will find a red star stencilled on one of its stones. Underneath that stone the boffins 'TA' has dressed up as "plumbers" …'

'You know about them, do you? Are they your men or 'TA''s?'

'For the moment, I will not answer that question. As I was saying, 'TA' or a member of his team, will leave the keys to number thirty-nine under the stone marked with a red cross. When the vodka salesman arrives to take possession of number thirty-nine, the keys will not be there. You will have them.'

'Will I?'

'Yes, your wolf … I do hope Derek is looking after him.'

'Do you know the names of all the staff?'

'Just the ones I need to make use of. As I was saying, you will tell Leo that your dog, while chasing a cat, in a fit of doggy madness, charged into number thirty-nine's garden and dug them up. When you give him the keys that will be your story. When he arrives and can't find them – the keys, that is – he will be, to say the least, irritated and, probably, more than a little unnerved. Remember he is a KGB agent. He is not here to sell vodka. He is here to spy. He will be on edge. He will wonder why 'TA' has not kept his word. 'TA' had assured him they'd be there and, they are not. You will be watching for him coming.'

44

'How do I know when he will be arriving?'

'I will tell you. He is flying into Newcastle airport from Oslo. As soon as I know he is on a plane and heading your way I will let you know.'

'How?'

'As Asquith said: "Wait and see". When you see him wondering what to do because he can't find the keys, you take your dog for a walk and ask him if you can help. He will probably refuse but you will tell him you know the house is rented out and, is he perhaps looking for keys? You are asking because your dog found some in the garden. Encourage him to think you are a busy-body. Offer him a cup of tea. You and I, Ms Weddle, are playing a dangerous game of chess with the Russians. I repeat, according to 'TA', Leo is on the brink of becoming a double agent. It is through Leo that MI5 know about the Kremlin's plans to give financial support to the NUM. For lots of money, 'TA' is selling our secrets to the Russians. The Russians will do everything they can to protect him. To have a mole high up in your enemy's secret service is every spy's dream. To keep 'TA' safe they are prepared to make sacrifices. Much of what 'TA' tells the Russians will be humdrum stuff but, from it, the KGB will be able to build up a picture of the organisation of which, I am proud to say, I work. Oh dear! Does that sound too patriotic for an Englishman? You know, a little over the top?'

'Yes, it does, rather. On the other hand, Jeremy, we are the good guys.'

'Democracy is better than communism.'

'In a communist country, Chippy would not be fed liver.'

'We are singing from the same hymn sheet.'

'But, in different registers, Jeremy. You are, Basso profundo. I, a light weight, mezzo-soprano.'

'I think, Ms Weddle, you are more, much more, a coloratura soprano.'

'When Chippy flatters me with a kiss I give him a bone. When you flatter me, I wonder what you want. If I was a character in a Jane Austin novel I'd be on the verge of a swoon. Dear me, Jeremy, you are quite the lady's man, aren't you? Are you married?'

'To my work?'

'I meant, do you have a wife?'

'I know what you meant. This is a business meeting and we have work to do.'

'Are you giving your fag a rap on the knuckles?'

'No. Best, Ms Weddle, I remain a man of mystery.'

'Like the Scarlet Pimpernel?'

'I am more than happy to accept that comparison. The "SP" was a toff and a spot-on good egg.'

'His heart was in the right place. I'll give you that. He was rescuing aristocrats. You are hunting one down.'

'A bad egg.'

'OK. Fair enough. Two questions about the matter in hand. Number one: why involve me with the keys?'

'Psychology, Ms Weddle. Psychology. The story of your dog digging up the keys is plausible. Just. When 'TA' hears about it he will have to decide if it is true. He already thinks you are an overpaid busybody.'

'Does he, indeed?'

'It will make him question your involvement. It will give him something more to worry about. 'TA' is a spy close to breaking point. He drinks too much. There have been times in the last year when he has been indiscreet to the point of foolishness. I do believe he is close to absconding to Russia and not coming back.'

'Why does he betray his country?'

'He likes Impressionist paintings. He is manic, quite manic, about collecting them. I am sure there is a noun for such a fetish. One of our English words that end in "ology", no doubt. I call it, "greed". 'TA' spies and betrays his country for money. His motives are straightforward. No moral issues are involved. No unswerving belief in an ideology. Your second question?'

'Your answer to my first question puzzles me. The psychology of my dog digging up the keys I find, implausible. I think you want me to find the keys for another reason. And please do not remove your glass eye to disconcert me and give you time to think.'

'I was told you were clever.'

'And the real reason?'

'For the moment it is best you do not know.'

'An honest answer. Do you find telling the truth difficult? As a kleptomaniac cannot stop stealing, I sometimes think a spy cannot stop telling porkies.'

'Your second question?'

'When 'TA' was given responsibility for running number thirty-nine, was he told of my involvement?'

'No.'

'Why?'

'That is a third question. Our bargain was for two.'

'Why?'

'Because I wanted to use you to give 'TA' a scare. I have told you. A frightened spy makes mistakes. If on a visit to number thirty-nine he'd spotted you sitting in your front garden he might have spontaneously ignited like that chap in "Bleak House". Do you read Dickens?'

'How did he find out about me?'

'I've heard on the grapevine it was his pal Tobias Lacy who tipped him off. He knows your pal Lucy Miller. Perhaps she gave him your address. I don't know. Once upon a time I believe you were all pals. In the spying game gossip can get a man killed. Still, all in all, I'm not sure it wasn't for the best.'

'You have put me in the line of fire, haven't you? I am a doormat. One of those disposable ones. When you are finished with it, you throw it out.'

'I'm afraid, Ms Weddle, domestic metaphors are wasted on me. I've always had servants. If you are a doormat, may I make the bold assertion that you are the most attractive doormat upon which I have ever had the pleasure of wiping my boots. Unless my sensory radar is playing tricks on me, I further assert that, despite your display of ruffled feathers ... we warm to each other.'

'Do we?'

'Yes, we do.'

'I do hope you are not going to propose?'

'Don't be a silly-billy–' looking at his watch– 'I know it's early but, what about a glass of champagne? I am thinking our joint venture needs anointing. Dear me, that makes catching a traitor sound religious and that, it most certainly, is not. But, we are on Tyneside where they used to build ships. Whoever launched a ship without cracking a bottle of fizz across its bow?'

By a system of signalling, undetected by Isa, Ken appeared at the table with a bottle of Moet.

'I'll pour, Ken.'

'As you wish, sir.'

'And, Ken–' handing that good man a hip flask– 'fill her up, will you.'

'The usual, sir?'

Over the second glass of fizz, Jeremy said: 'Newcastle has a magnificent railway station,' then, as if remembering the business he was about, which he'd never forgotten in the first place: 'How is the street party progressing? I hear you are on the SPC.'

'How did you know that?'

'Will there be jelly for the children? Years ago, Mummy and my nanny had a row about how I should be allowed to eat jelly. Nanny was a progressive. She wanted me to learn by sucking and squeezing. Mother was all for the spoon.'

'Who won?'

'Nanny. Nanny Baton, she was called. A wonderful woman. I loved her. We still keep in touch.'

'Noblesse oblige?'

'Nanny Baton was my best pal. In the big house in which I was brought up we were both private soldiers … everyone else, especially the butler, were officers. I had to know my place. It did not pay to step out of line.'

'If I may say so, you are suddenly very free with information about yourself.'

'It's the champagne.'

'Or, Jeremy, you are letting your hair down for a reason. You are a professional spy. Everything a professional spy does is premeditated, or should be if he or she wishes to stay alive.'

'I have allowed you a peek into my private life by way of a quid pro quo.'

'What do you want?'

'For their street party in the evening, I wish the residents of Chillingham Grove to wear fancy dress.'

'Champagne-inspired or premeditated?'

'Premeditated.'

'Why?'

He shook his head.

'You cannot tell me. You are giving me an order?'

'Do your best, Ms Weddle, to see it happens. It will greatly facilitate a plan I am working on.'

'How much have you not told me?'

'Quite a lot. May I top you up?'

'I have a weakness for champagne.'

'I know. It's in your dossier. You may have gone to a comprehensive, Ms Weddle, and I to an altogether posher establishment, but, I fear, we both have a weakness for the best money can buy.'

'Top me up, Jeremy.'

'My pleasure, Ms Weddle.'

****

Walking home through Newcastle – the shops all decorated in red, white and blue in readiness to celebrate the coming royal wedding – with Chippy breaking wind and making bad smells because of all the liver he'd eaten, Isa kept wondering how Ken had known when to bring the champagne.

She remembered her friend Lucy. A medical doctor who worked for Médicins sans Frontières in Beirut. She had mentioned in a letter that she'd bumped into Tobias Lacy.

Jeremy was right. Gossip was dangerous. Would she ever get used to toffs? Not if she lived to be a hundred.

Chapter 9

Over the next few days Isa mentioned the two words 'fancy dress' to any resident of Chillingham Grove she happened, by chance, to bump into; that is, as long as they were not on the SPC.

She did not know why Jeremy wanted the evening bash to be fancy dress. Until she did, she thought it wise to distance herself from the idea. When you were a spy, guilt, through association, was always a danger.

After having sowed 'fancy dress' seed she was therefore not in the least surprised when chatting to Jean and Harry, Harry said: 'Because folk in the street know I'm on the SPC they keep telling me they think the evening bash should be fancy dress. What do you think, Isa?'

'If that's what folk want; fine by me. Best ask Dominic and Beatrice. Dominic's in charge and Beatrice would like to be.'

'I like the idea,' said Jean. 'When you dress up as another person you become that person. It makes one forget one's worries.'

'You haven't got any,' said Harry. 'We're not in debt and we have a car.'

'I was thinking of Beatrice.'

'Her husband? His depression? Awful thing, depression. I'm surprised I don't suffer from it. Selling insurance is not a walk in the park. But, there you go. If I bump into Dominic I'll tell him everyone wants a fancy dress party. We'll discuss it at the next SPC.'

****

The next, and last, meeting of the SPC took place three weeks before the big day. Isa, as host, was, as usual, generous with drinks and nibbles. Since working together over the last few weeks its members had come to more or less accept each other's funny little ways.

Dominic and Irene always bickered. Angus had been observed picking his nose. Harry always tried to sell them insurance. Beatrice was always on the starting blocks to stage a coup to become Chair. Dominic was over-the-top proud of the map of Chillingham Grove he'd drawn on wallpaper. If you did not want detention, you did not smirk at his map.

Sitting back in comfy chairs, they now watched him pull the map out of a cardboard tube.

'It protects it,' he explained, 'the way a hat box stops a hat getting squashed.'

'Where'd we be without your map, Dominic?' said Harry, winking at his wife.

'Irene!' snapped Dominic, as the map coming out of the tube as a scroll refused to lie flat when it was laid out, 'I thought you were holding it.'

'You didn't tell me to. You know I'm pregnant.'

'What's that to do with holding down the map?'

'I was thinking of the baby.'

'Are you having another baby?' said Beatrice.

'Planned?' said Mari.

Irene shook her head. 'The rhythm method let us down. NFP doesn't work.'

'NFP?' said Angus.

'Natural Family Planning.'

'I used to work in 'Town and Country Planning',' said Angus. 'Believe me, I know how difficult planning can be. You submit your plan in all good faith and along comes someone with clout who objects to this and that. Before you can sell a haggis to a Campbell, the straight road you pencilled in has become a dog's hind leg.'

'Angus,' said Morag, 'we are not talking about cycle tracks and how wide a pavement should be. We are talking about a real baby. I sometimes wonder about you.' Then, patting her husband's hand, 'Angus and I can't have children. My fault. You are lucky to be so fertile, Irene.'

'Like the bloody River Nile, if you ask me,' said Angus. 'Oops! Sorry, shouldn't have said that. How many do you have now? Children, I mean. I've seen them playing in the street.'

'Six,' said Irene, 'the one in here,' patting her tummy, 'will be number seven.'

'Irene,' said Dominic, 'put your finger there!'

'Alright! No need to raise your voice. I'm not deaf.'

'Just pregnant,' said Angus.

'Dominic's in a mood because he's not a vegan anymore. Dominic, it's not my fault you are back to eating red meat. The professor of Education who inspired his veganism is leaving to work in Canada. His replacement hunts, shoots and fishes. We've started buying the "Shooting Times". Dominic has paid for a year's subscription. It's cheaper that way. What the "Shooting Times" costs us we'll save in me not having to buy shampoo to get rid of my dandruff.'

'Irene! Your finger! Take it away. Isa has brought paper weights. Thank you, Isa.'

'Dominic! You weren't half so bad tempered when you were a vegan.'

'Your better half, ambitious, is he?' whispered Angus.

'He has to be with all the mouths he has to feed.'

'I suppose it's not your fault you are the River Nile.'

'Is everyone paying attention?' said Dominic, tapping his whisky glass with a pencil. '"TS" on the map means that house is a "Tea Station". On the map, Angus, when you stop whispering to my wife, I have marked where the bar and barbecue will be.'

'Dominic,' said Harry, 'a refresher course on what the different colours on the map mean. If you don't mind.'

'Green cross means a tree. A yellow dot is a lamppost or telegraph pole. Red is for the afternoon activities. Blue is for the evening activities. You will please take note that in blue I have written: Fancy dress, with an exclamation mark. I have had people knocking at my door telling me they think that in the evening we should have a fancy dress party.'

'What a good idea,' said Isa, 'I like to dress up.'

'Dominic likes dressing up,' said Irene. 'Last year he played "Widow Twankey" in the school pantomime.'

'You a cross-dresser, Dominic?' said Harry.

'The boy playing the part of "Widow Twankey" took stage fright. I had no choice but to stand in.'

'We believe you,' said Angus, 'you know, wink-wink, nudge-nudge. What about moving the bar closer to my front door; then, I'll be able to pop into my house and get ice. Folk like ice in their drinks. I know I do.'

'I've been thinking,' said Beatrice.

'I thought I could hear the clock ticking,' said Harry. 'How's your hubby, by the way?'

'He's back at work.'

'Terrible thing, depression. Not like a broken leg when you come out of hospital, plastered.'

'If you went in hospital with a broken leg, Angus,' said Morag, 'you'd go in plastered and come out sober.'

'If it's going to be fancy dress,' said Mari, who so far had said little – her previous attempts at making a contribution having been nipped in the bud by the robust behaviour of the other participants

– 'I'll come as a sailor. As you all know, my husband, George, is in the merchant navy. I have one of his uniforms in a wardrobe. I think this is exciting. That's me sorted.'

'The uniform won't fit,' said Beatrice. 'George is a lot bigger than you.'

'I will use safety pins.'

'What would you come as, Harry?' said Isa.

'Off the cuff? As a pirate. I've always thought selling insurance was akin to making clients walk the plank.'

'I've always wanted to be a fairy,' said Jean. 'I could come as a fairy.'

'Strict rules,' said Angus, 'you will only be served at the bar if you are in fancy dress. Going to the bar in mufti would be like a nudist wearing a jock strap. When in Rome and all that.'

'What will you come as, Dominic?' said Isa.

'You have a Santa Claus costume,' said Irene, answering for her husband. 'You could come as Santa Claus.'

'Irene,' said Harry, 'you could come as "Snow White".'

'Could I?'

'Yes, dress up your tribe of kids as dwarfs.'

'Snow White had seven dwarfs. I only have six children.'

'You come as "Snow White and the six dwarfs with one in my tummy". Get it?'

'Harry?' said Jean.

'What?' said Harry.

'How much have you had to drink? Isa, you are too good a host.'

'I think I'll come as "Cleopatra",' said Irene, 'you know, fertile as the Nile.'

'I know a joke shop where you can buy rubber snakes,' said Angus. 'If you are "Cleopatra", you have to have a snake. Dominic, you're a Scot. Why not come wearing a kilt and a Santa bonnet? Start a new fashion. It's my view you can never have too many Scots at a party. Dominic, you play the pipes?'

'Tell me about it,' said Beatrice, 'I live next door to Dominic and Irene. When he plays, my windows vibrate.'

'Aye,' said Angus, 'the pipes are for the Highlands and the wild lands. They are no for suburbia. Chillingham Grove is not the Great Glen. I'm thinking. What if you were to play, "Auld Lang Syne"?'

'It's not New Year's Eve,' said Irene.

'I know that. I'm thinking, Dominic, you could play it to bring the party to an end. It would be a fine ending with everyone in the street joining hands. Dominic, write it on the map: "GRAND FINALE. Auld Lang Syne". Everyone who thinks it a good idea, raise a hand.'

Every hand went up. In blue ink Dominic wrote on the map: "GRAND FINALE. Auld Lang Syne".

****

As she bid the SPC goodnight, Isa wondered what they would have thought if they'd known the idea to have a fancy dress party was the brainchild of a senior member of the British Secret Service. A man who fished with the Duke of Northumberland. A man who used Alnwick Castle as a B&B.

She looked up and down the street. Lots of lit windows. Only number thirty-nine showed no sign of life.

Chapter 10

A week before the royal wedding Isa watched a 'Reed's Plumbing Services' van, through binoculars, reverse up number thirty-nine's drive. Two men, wearing white boiler suits, climbed out. They looked lean and fit. The sort of guys you might expect to see guarding the president of the United States of America. These would be the men Joan had told her to expect. On the backs of their pristine white boiler suits, she read: Reed's Plumbing Services.

Who were the two people who climbed out of the back of the van? The van's gull-winged doors had let her see only their legs.

****

Half an hour later a van with a yellow banana, as big as a surfboard, on its roof, drove up and stopped outside her house. In green letters on the banana, she read: 'MISTER CHUCKLE'.

A man dressed as a clown got out. Preparatory to walking up her path, he stopped to stare at number thirty-nine.

He was wearing baggy trousers, a double-breasted pin stripe jacket, an orange wig and on the end of his nose, a red plastic golf ball.

'Mr Chuckle,' said the man, when she answered his ring, 'children's entertainer. Street parties my speciality. No chuckle too small. My card. I come highly recommended. Issy!'

Very few people called Isa, Issy.

'My god!' said Isa. 'Tobias Lacy!'

'Aren't you going to invite me in? I'll put your hesitation down to the shock of seeing me and not, heaven forbid, to disdain. Your niece tells me you make a nice cup of coffee.'

'Did she? In that case, you'd best come in. It's your lucky day. I've no rat poison. If I'd known you were calling I'd have popped out and bought some.'

'No need to be like that, Issy. Once upon a time, we were friends.'

'I don't think so.'

'I disagree, but never mind. So,' he said, looking around her lounge, like an estate agent, 'this is where agents who take early retirement end up. I hope to god it never happens to me. You will not be surprised when I tell you, Newcastle is not my idea of heaven. Lots of books, I see. "Mathematics for the Millions". You always were a clever little bugger, Issy. Me? I got into Cambridge because of my daddy. You got there because of your brain. Dear me, you do cast your net wide. The "Collected Poems of Thomas Hardy". Do you read that stuff or, is it there to impress? The way in my youth I used a briefcase to carry my sandwiches. Before you answer, it is my duty to warn you that I've been trained to tell when a person is lying. I've made you smile. Where is the bedroom?'

'I always thought you were homosexual.'

'It depends on my mood. I'm not fussy. I'm the sort of chap who eats a bacon sandwich without bothering to remove its fat.'

'Why are you here?'

'For a cup of coffee.'

'Bullshit.'

'I am here, my dear Ms Weddle, to offer my services to your street party. I believe you need a children's entertainer. I can, when I have to, don't you know, pull a rabbit out of a hat.'

'Dominic, the chair of the street party committee has seen to that.'

'Has he, indeed?'

'Yes. He has. Your popping up out of the blue has given me quite a jolt!'

'Made your heart beat fast, have I?'

'You should be so lucky.'

'Do I get coffee or, before you make it, do you want to pop out and buy some rat poison?'

'I'll make you a coffee, Tobias. Sit down. And do take off that silly clown's nose and wig. I live in a respectable street, not a Big-Top.'

'Where's your dog?'

'How do you know I have a dog?'

'Tony told me. I'm not keen on canines. Snakes are more my cup of tea. Such fun watching an adder eat a mouse.'

'Is that why you are so friendly with 'TA'?'

'His surname?'

Isa nodded.

'Your surname is Weddle. Does that mean you meddle?'

'In Beirut, you, me, 'TA' … we were paid to interfere.'

'We did rather stick our noses into the affairs of the Middle East.'

'In my opinion … not our finest hour.'

'Are you not a patriot?'

'I will not deign to answer that question. Unlike some toffs I know, I pay my taxes. I do not have millions stored in an off-shore bank account.'

'Are you, perchance, referring to me?'

'I am assuming you have an off-shore bank account. Toffs like you always do. A nanny, a man servant and an off-shore account.'

'Do not forget the butler.'

'I would not be surprised.'

'My man servant pays tax.'

'But you don't.'

'Through my largesse to my man servant, I make a significant contribution to the economy.'

'If you didn't have a man servant the UK would have fewer nurses and doctors … is that what you are saying?'

'Swings and roundabouts, Issy … swings and roundabouts.'

'Stop smirking.'

'I wasn't smirking. I was thinking. It must be hell being poor. Do you have ginger snaps? I like a ginger snap with my coffee.'

'Like we did at Uni?'

'You have remembered. Fond memories.'

'If you say so.'

'Oh, but I do. One sugar. No rat poison.'

At the back of a cupboard Isa found a packet of out-of-date ginger snaps. What did a few weeks matter when you'd not seen someone in years?

She served the coffee and ginger snaps on a tray.

'You'd look good dressed as a waitress,' he said. 'Short black skirt and a little notebook, swinging from your belt. I'll bet you come from a long line of waitresses. When you are as brainy as you are, it must be all too easy to forget your true station in life.'

'And you, Tobias? You come from a long line of rulers? Would you like me to anoint you with the coffee, or would you prefer to drink it?'

'I'll slurp if you don't mind. Oh, goody, ginger snaps. May I dunk?'

'Why have you been messing with my curtains?'

'You have noticed.'

'In retirement I have become a house frau. I space my collection of Toby jugs five centimetres apart. I know when one has been moved. My curtains. I do not like them pulled that far back.'

'It lets in more light.'

'Why did you pull them back?'

'I was waving to Tony and Joan. I assume you did see them go into number thirty-nine?'

'Joan and Tony Adder are in number thirty-nine?'

'You sound surprised. Tony was certain you'd be watching. He's taken your niece under his wing. She has a good brain. She knows more about "bugs" than I ever will … more than Tony, as well … though, he'd never admit it. But then, Tony's like me, isn't he? Got into Cambridge because he had "pull".'

'You've done very well on a third-class degree.'

'The establishment trusts people like me.'

'Silly old establishment. I have never trusted you. At uni I was always careful to be chaperoned. Because of posh boys like you and 'TA', we girls at Cambridge had to protect our virginity by going around in herds, like gazelles.'

'Or … cows.'

'Do not be vulgar.'

'Awfully sorry. I always fancied you, but you knew that, didn't you?'

'You had an alpha male reputation. If it wears a skirt …'

'Buy it a box of chocolates. These ginger snaps are soft. How long have you had them?'

'I bought them in Beirut.'

'Touché. Beirut. That was a long time ago. It may interest you to know that I am still gainfully employed in that neck of the woods. Spying is like prostitution, don't you think? No matter how hard the moralists try to stamp it out, it still goes on.'

'Lucy told me she'd bumped into you.'

'She did, did she? I wondered if you kept in touch. Isa, Lucy, Tony and Tobias. We were the four musketeers, were we not?'

'I don't think so. Your memory is making roses out of weeds.'

'Is that a quote from one of the Persian poets you were always quoting in our halcyon days?'

'It might be.'

'You know … this ginger snap,' holding one up to peer at it as if looking at it through a magnifying glass, 'has seen better days. So soft, I do believe I will not have to dunk.'

'It is more than you ever gave me at Cambridge. You did not woo with flowers and chocolates. You and Tony were smash and grab. Your sense of entitlement made you blind to the needs of others. You had a reputation for meanness.'

'I was a student. Short of money.'

'Not that short. Your father, I seem to remember, owned a factory. You had a sports car. I had a bicycle.'

'My E-type Jag? I loved that car. Best fanny-magnet I ever had. Interesting that you should remember it after all these years. Tempted you, did it? Got your juices flowing?'

'Swapping my virginity for a ride in a sports car never seemed a good idea to me.'

'I could have opened doors for you.'

'And closed them whenever you fancied. You enjoy having power over people, don't you, Tobias? Please, never forget, you do not have power over me. I am a free spirit and will not take kindly to having my wings clipped.'

'Ms Hoity-toity. My dear Issy, like you, I am a humble servant of the state. HMG is my master. I do whatever I can to make this green and pleasant land a safe place in which to dwell. It is because of me that plebs like you sleep, safely, in their beds at night. I make sure the bad guys don't kill you. When you pick up a cauliflower in a supermarket there is no dirt on it. Its florets are lily white. Do you know why? Because someone like me, and like you used to be, has chopped off its dirty roots.'

'Do you get a hard on, when you think of the queen?'

'I say, that's a tricky one to answer. Is patriotism an erotic experience? Mrs Thatcher turns me on. She is a very sexy woman. I wouldn't say she and I were this close,' crossing his fingers, 'but, I know I'm in her good books.'

'You have met her?'

'Many times.'

'You are that high up?'

'Yes.'

'I'm impressed.'

'You should be. She is a very formidable lady. My brief for this job is to be thorough. Leave no stone unturned.'

'And what is this job? I still have no idea why you are here. Is your motive personal? Please don't say I'm flattering myself.'

'I do believe, if you keep knocking on a door, it will open,' he said, walking over to the room's large bay window.

****

In retrospect Isa found it difficult to remember the chronology of what happened next. She remembered hearing a gun shot. She was all too familiar with that sound. Yes, she'd definitely heard a gun being fired. And she definitely remembered a big hole, like a snowflake seen under a microscope, suddenly appearing in her lounge window. And she definitely remembered Tobias lying on his back. And she definitely remembered the blood; the blood pumping out of his double-breasted jacket, as if the bullet which had hit him, had hit a red oil-well.

Through the hole in the window she remembered someone shouting: 'Open the front door! Open the fucking front door!'

She let three men into her home. Two of them were the 'plumbers'; unmistakable in their white boiler suits. The third man, though she'd not seen him for years, was Tony Adder. Without a by-your-leave the two 'plumbers' ran into the lounge.

'No need for you to see more than you've already seen,' said 'TA', closing the lounge door. 'Out of sight out of mind, eh? Where's your dog?'

'I don't know. He doesn't like bangs. He could be upstairs under the bed. Tony, what the hell is going on? What has happened to Tobias? Has someone shot him? Are your colleagues medics?'

'Make me a coffee and I will tell you.'

'What about Tobias?'

'My men are seeing to him.'

'They are plumbers. Tobias's problem is not a dripping fifteen-millimetre compression joint. He is bleeding to death.'

****

Over coffee in the back garden, 'TA' asked Isa: 'Any chance of a bicky? I like a bicky with my coffee. Tobias liked ginger snaps.'

'I have dog biscuits.'

'But I'm not a dog, am I?'

'If you were, Tony, you'd be an Afghan hound. Sleek and ever so snooty.'

'What about a retriever? Desmond. Remember him? Desmond's a wonder with dogs. He points into the heather and, off his dogs go, searching for the bird he's shot.'

'Sir,' said one of the 'plumbers' coming into the garden, 'bad news. Mr Lacy is dead. Usual routine, sir?'

'Of course.'

'Leave it to me, sir.'

'Believe me, Thompson, I will.'

'Tobias is dead!' said Isa. Wide eyed. Not believing what she was hearing. 'Tony, what the hell is going on?'

'Bad news for your niece, Joan.'

'Joan? What's she got to do with Tobias being shot?'

'She shot him.'

'What?'

'It would seem your niece has shot dead a senior member of MI6. She will tell you she was told the weapon wasn't loaded. I wonder who will believe her. What if, in a court of law, a witness was to hint, just hint, mind you, that she was having an affair with Tobias and was jealous of his relationship with another woman. You take my point? Murder? Manslaughter?'

'What do you want?'

'At the Battle of Copenhagen, Nelson said, he saw no ships. He turned a blind eye. If you see me popping in and out of number thirty-nine, may I suggest you do the same.'

'Why?'

'To stop Joan going to jail. I do believe I hear your doorbell ringing. If it's a neighbour asking about the bang, tell them it was a car, backfiring. That's how people who live in ghastly suburban streets like Chillingham Grove explain a gun shot. I see no reason to be inventive. Your neighbours wouldn't know a cliché from a soufflé.'

'And the broken window?'

'A meteorite?'

****

The neighbour at the front door was Mari.

'Did you hear a bang?'

'Yes.'

'It was awfully loud.'

'It must have been a car backfiring.'

'Do you think so?'

'I can't think what else it could be.'

'What happened to your window?'

Looking over Mari's shoulder, Isa logged the fact that the van with the banana the size of a surfboard on its roof had gone.

'It was Mr Chuckle,' said Isa, shaking her head, 'the man in the van with a banana on its roof. He was cold calling to be hired as the street party's children's entertainer. While juggling with cricket balls he tripped and sent one through my window.'

65

'We don't want him.'

'We certainly don't.'

'What's happening across the road?'

'Number thirty-nine? The workmen there came across to ask me if I needed help with my broken window. They're plumbers. They are installing new radiators.'

'Does that mean new tenants?'

'I did ask them, but they said they'd no idea.'

'Isa, if you don't mind my saying so, you look, well, a bit shocked. Let me treat you to a coffee. My place in fifteen minutes. I'll ring a glazier for you, if you want.'

'No thanks, I know someone who will fix the window. If you don't mind, I'll take a rain check on the coffee.'

She found 'TA' in the lounge. No sign of Tobias. Where he had fallen, a two-metre square of carpet was missing. Her feet crunched on broken glass.

'Where's he gone?'

'Tobias?'

'Of course that's who I meant.'

'To an MI5 mortuary. One of our specials. Frightfully sorry about the carpet. No matter how hard one tries, it is impossible to remove blood stains. He did bleed a lot. HMG will recompense you. I will get you a claim form.'

'Your concern terrifies me. Now, will you please go?'

'I know when I'm not wanted–' looking at his watch– 'for the moment, Issy, adieu.'

'And don't call me "Issy". That's what Tobias used to call me.'

'I will if it annoys you. I enjoy annoying people like you. It makes a change from shooting pheasants. May I remind you, Issy, from now on, as far as number thirty-nine is concerned you are the three wise monkeys. You see nothing. You hear nothing. You say nothing. You and Joan owe me.'

'Otherwise?'

'Joan, dear, overenthusiastic Joan, so young, so naïve, will face a charge of manslaughter. Furthermore, I will personally see to it that your dog goes, prematurely, to doggy heaven.'

'You wouldn't dare.'

'Wouldn't I? You said before, Issy, I do not have power over you. I do now.'

'Blackmail?'

'An ugly word. If you are a sensible pleb you will accept my control. You are no longer a bucking bronco. You have been broken in.'

'Where is Joan?'

'In number thirty-nine, in a state of shock. In Beirut, Issy, you and I were often shocked. Murders. Assassinations. I seem to remember that the famous British stiff upper lip helped. As for Joan. She's in a spot of bother. Isn't she? I will let myself out.'

****

The arrogant bastard strutted back to number thirty-nine as if he was the man who'd broken the bank at Monte Carlo.

She wanted to go across and comfort her niece. She knew how MI5 worked. Number thirty-nine would be a crime scene. A senior officer had been killed by friendly fire. Whose fingerprints were on the rifle? Who had loaded it with live ammunition? Joan would have to make a statement.

Chapter 11

Alone, Isa talked to Chippy about what had happened.

The 'Boss's tone of voice puzzled the dog. She sounded sad. She wasn't happy. He rubbed his big head against her legs.

'To whom do I owe loyalty, Chippy? To you, my old friend–' stroking his head– 'yes, definitely. In defending me you would lay down your life. I know you would. In the pecking order of loyalties … who comes first … who comes last? Do I put my country before my love of family? Can I trust Jeremy? Do I go running to him like one of his gun dogs with a pheasant in its mouth, barking: 'Do you know what happened this morning, Jeremy? My niece shot dead Tobias Lacy. Tony Adder is blackmailing me.'

Years ago, in Cairo, 'TA' had told her not to put on airs and graces. 'Ms Weddle, your father was a bricklayer. At Cambridge you thought a bidet was a loo. When you had a cold, you emptied the contents of your nose into a serviette. And then, there's your mummy, stitching buttons onto my Pa's colonel's uniform. You are not one of 'us', Ms Weddle. To me and my class, you are loo paper.'

'How often have I seen the "old-boy" network, Chippy, promote a "good-egg" above his level of competence.'

Hearing his name, Chippy opened an eye and just as quickly shut it. He wanted to put his nose between his paws and have a snooze. Empathy was a sprint, not a marathon. There was only so much he could do to help the boss.

'A "posh" boy is blackmailing me. He is blackmailing Joan. Who can I trust?'

Looking through the hole in her front room window she saw that the Reed's Plumbing van had gone. Had the men in white boiler suits and 'TA' taken Joan with them? In handcuffs? Heaven forbid!

To replace the broken window she needed a glazier. Her cousin, Malcolm, was not a glazier but he was good at DIY. He was one of those men, who, as the saying goes, was good with his hands. He lived a ten-minute drive away. He was also family. She'd known him all her life. Metaphorically speaking she thought of him as a pillow. Their bond was a shared childhood. He took her back to a time when she had no worries. No doubt she did the same for him.

He was not privy to the fact she had killed for her country. He was not her confidant. She could not tell him, for example, that number thirty-nine was a safe house. When he cut its grass and she paid him, he thought his cousin was acting on behalf of the rich bugger who owned it and had bought it as an investment.

If he asked how the window came to be broken, she'd bounce him off the subject or make something up.

****

If the good folk of Chillingham Grove thought it a bit out of the ordinary that a lady like Isa – a lady who, when she was dressed for a party, looked as if she'd walked off the front page of 'Vogue' – should have a dog that looked like a wolf for a pet, instead of a poodle or an Afghan hound, they thought her choice of car way over the top.

Her Mercedes was one of those where you pressed a button and its roof folded into its boot.

She drove to Malcolm's with the car's top down. Driving, al fresco, made her feel alive. As usual, Chippy sat beside her in the front passenger seat. As far as he was concerned, driving, al fresco, with the 'Boss', was doggy-heaven.

****

Malcolm lived in, what is called, a Tyneside flat. One family upstairs. One family downstairs. There was always trouble with the neighbours 'doon' below who were always complaining that the folk who lived upstairs made too much noise.

He'd bought the flat with his redundancy money. When the pit at which he'd worked closed, he'd started a new life as a jobbing gardener. Feeling wind and sunshine on your face when you were working was something he would never tire of enjoying.

It was to help him that Isa paid him to look after her garden and number thirty-nine's. He lived alone and was fond of three things: women, nicotine and alcohol; in that order.

As always, he was pleased to see her.

'Yuh alreet, Isa? Have you brought me a cake?'

'No, I've brought you work.'

'Oh, dear me, that's bad news. Will I get paid?'

'Yes.'

'That's alreet, then. Cup of tea? What aboot the dog? Does he still fart a lot? Last time he was here he dropped one like a friggen stink bomb. A nearly sent you the bill for the air freshener.'

'Chippy will have water. I will have tea.'

'Can I give him a custard cream?'

'No. Custard creams give him flatulence.'

'Flatulence, eh? Divent come your airs and graces with me. (In an RP accent) Oh, do excuse the pong, my dog has flatulence. Ha! Ha! You're a funny one, you are, Isa. I'll put the kettle on. Why don't you just come out with it and say, me dog's farted?'

He poured the tea from a battered aluminium tea pot. If it had been a boxer, the referee would have stopped it pouring. The mugs into which he poured were chipped and cracked.

'It looks weak,' said Isa.

'Aye, the tea leaves have gone on strike. They usually do when they've been used before.'

'Like you did?'

'Aye, and the buggers still closed the pit.'

'And Mrs Thatcher is wanting to close more.'

'So they say. Nowt to dee with me now. I'm finished with the pits. I'm self-employed. I'm not on the "King Coal", like some of the blokes a used to work with. Sad. Very sad. One of them topped himself last week ... jumped in front of a train ... silly bugger ... didn't nar what to dee with himself when he couldn't gan to work. A hate the fucking Tories. Nivva mind. I'm deeing alreet. I can still afford me tabs–' lighting a cigarette, then blowing smoke rings out of his nose. 'Clever that, eh?'

'Do you like smoking?'

'What sort of a friggin question is that? A wouldn't dee it if I didn't like it, would I?'

'It's bad for you.'

'So is gannin doon a coal mine. Do yuh think that's good for you? Howay, Isa, there's a bonny lass, nee lectures. Am a in your bad books?'

'Why should you say that?'

'When you come and see me yuh always bring me a cake. Not today. Is something up?'

'My front room window is broken.'

'Oh, is that aal?'

'Can you come and fix it for me?'

'Course I can. It'll cost, mind. Insurance job?'

'Sort of.'

'I can milk it?'

'Feel free.'

'How'd it happen?'

'If I told you, you wouldn't believe me.'

'Try me.'

'It's best you don't know.'

'You're a dark horse, you are.'

'And you make a nice cup of tea. May I use your loo?'

'Oh, my god! (RP accent) I'm going to the loo for a poo. Folk around here call it the netty. Yuh nar where it is … and, divent forget to flush.'

'I don't need it.'

'Eh? Why did yuh ask, then? Yee taking the Michael?'

'I wanted to see how you'd react when I called the toilet a loo.'

'Did I dee what yuh thought?'

'Yes.'

'Yuh set a trap for me and I walked straight into it. You're a clever bugger, you are, Isa … divent get too clever, like that bloke, Liquorice, what flew too close to the moon. That's classical biology, that is. Am always shown off me learning. Am boasting, aren't I?'

Isa studied her cousin. He was looking at her, straight faced, through the frosted glass of a cloud of cigarette smoke. Not for the first time, she wondered who was teasing who.

She'd used the word 'loo' as a diversion to bounce him away from asking too many questions about the broken window. It had worked. His riposte, though, reminded her, he was no fool.

'I have a neighbour,' she said, in an attempt to create a second diversion, 'who is always boasting about her farts.'

'Now, ya talk'n. Heh! Heh! To think that folk in Jesmond talk like that. Makes yuh think. Come on, let's gan and have a look at that window of yours. In any case, you'd better be ganin. You've been here an hour. It usually takes an hour for the word to spread there's a posh car in the street. A car without wheels is like an out of work pitman. Nee good to anybody.'

'What about your car?'

'They wouldn't dare. They nar who I am. And, I nar who they are. Off you go. I'll get me tools. I'll be with you in less time than it takes a pissing cat to put out a fire.'

Chapter 12

Isa drove home wondering how her niece could have done such a silly thing as to aim a loaded rifle at another human being. She was a professional. What she'd done was against all the rules.

She'd not be surprised if Joan's killing Tobias brought on her eczema. For some reason it always attacked her ankles, as if it was a viper and, from the ground, could reach no higher.

It was years since she'd been in a life and death situation. Driving home, she deep breathed. She struggled to remember the training she'd received on how to handle trauma. It was like learning, she'd been taught, to live with a lion in a cage. If you wanted to survive you had to let the lion know who was boss. The lion, when he roared, had to know that if he attacked you, he'd feel pain.

While she was driving, Chippy licked her hand. His affection let her know that in her needy-time, he was there to help.

Again and again she asked herself why Joan had pointed a loaded weapon at Tobias. Had she meant to kill him? That this might be a possibility made her heart beat fast. It made the metaphorical lion in the metaphorical cage growl.

Chippy lay against her like a bolster full of hot water bottles. She didn't mind that his weight was interfering with her driving. If she'd a minor accident she was insured. A bashed car was easy to fix.

What was not going to be easy to fix was Joan's mental anguish.

In a friendly fire incident, there were two casualties. The victim and the perpetrator. Tobias was dead. He was out of it. Nothing could hurt him now.

Joan, on the other hand, would be going through hell. Feelings of guilt and remorse would be overwhelming her. She was responsible for the death of a fellow officer.

****

On reaching home Isa found Joan's car blocking her drive. Folk who parked in such a way as to stop an owner parking off-road, in her own drive, were thoughtless. They were selfish. They thought of no one but themselves.

It was no good excusing Joan by pleading she'd just shot someone dead and had a lot on her mind. She'd done it before. It was one of her bad habits. Circumstances did, however, encourage mitigation. Joan did not need a reprimand; she needed tender loving care. She would need counselling.

Where was she? She wasn't in the car. Was she in number thirty-nine? If so, why? Looking across at the safe house and seeing no sign of life, she walked up her drive, all the time clucking disapproval at her niece's thoughtless parking.

Before opening her front door, she paused to look at the hole the bullet had made in her lounge window. She feared any explanation she offered a neighbour as to the cause of the breakage would be greeted with scepticism.

On the other hand, if she told the truth they would think she was telling a fairy story.

It was Chippy's growling at the hole that made her pause. Her awareness that something was amiss prepared her for the shock of seeing a hand waving to her through the broken window.

'Don't worry, Aunt Isa,' shouted Joan, 'it's only me. I'll let you in.'

I do have a key, thought Isa. It is my home; not yours.

Meeting inside, they did not hug. They were too shocked for intimacy. Isa was wondering how Joan had gotten into her home without a key. Joan had been crying. Her mascara had run a marathon.

Isa drew a curtain across the shattered window. It was her home. Joan's trespass made her wish to assert her ownership.

'How did you get in?' she asked her niece, as the shuddering curtain she'd pulled alternately lit and shaded the room. 'Has Special Branch taught you to pick locks?'

'Are you not pleased to see me?'

'Of course I am.'

'You know what I've done, don't you?'

Isa nodded.

'Mr Adder gave me the key to your front door.'

'He did what?'

'Did you not know he had a key?'

'No, I did not.'

'Oh! I'm in big trouble, Aunt Isa … aren't I? He keeps telling me, I owe him.'

'Tony?'

'Is that his first name? I always call him "Sir".'

'I've known him a lot longer than you. Would it surprise you to know, if it had not been for the "old boys' network", he'd have been kicked out of Cambridge?'

'What did he do?'

'Lots of naughty things. He was investigated for the murder of a male prostitute found dead in a public lavatory. Tony and Tobias were, it was rumoured, more than good friends.'

'Homosexuals?'

'They were very close.'

'And I've gone and murdered my boss's lover, is that what you are saying?'

'In those days homosexuality was a crime. We knew it went on. We just didn't talk about it.'

'Aunt Isa, it was Mr Adder, who assured me the rifle wasn't loaded. He told me to aim at Mr Lacy.'

'He was egging you on to murder his lover. Why would he do that?'

'Maybe Mr Lacy had found someone he liked better.'

'You are suggesting Tony used you to settle a lovers' quarrel?'

'I don't know, Aunt Isa. All I know is, I'm in big trouble. If Mr Adder can't sweep this under the carpet, I could go to jail for a very long time. Aunt Isa, it was an accident! I was assured the rifle wasn't loaded. Mr Adder knew I liked guns. The rifle, Aunt Isa, was a real high-class piece of kit. Mr Adder had borrowed it from the SAS. Its telescopic sights were out of this world. The best sniper's rifle in the world, Mr Adder told me. He opened a window for me and told me to aim at your bay window. "What do you see?" he asked me. I fine-tuned the sight and told him I could see a man. "I want you to imagine that the man you have in your sights is an enemy of England," he said. "Aim for the middle of his chest. I order you to kill him." I thought it was all a game. There was no one more surprised than me when the rifle fired. I was expecting to hear a "click", not a "bang". When I looked around for Mr Adder, he'd disappeared.'

'He was at my house, Joan; shouting at me through the broken window to be let in.'

'When I realised what I'd done I nearly fainted. What stopped me was the fresh air coming into the room through the window Mr Adder had opened for my target practice. I can't believe I'm responsible for the death of another human being. Mr Adder told me the gun wasn't loaded … not even with blanks. I knew I hadn't fired a blank because I could see, Aunt Isa, that your front room window was shattered. I'm a marksman. I knew I hadn't missed. The man I'd fired at, had to be dead.

'I fear, Joan,' said Isa – who during her niece's resume of events had been pacing the room – 'that you have been set-up. 'TA' … as I always call the bastard … has taken advantage of your youth and your love of firearms.'

'You think Mr Adder knew the gun was loaded?'

'Almost certainly.'

'He used me to "take-out" Mr Lacy?'

'I know that's difficult to believe but, yes, that's what I'm thinking. What did he tell you about the man you'd shot? Did he seem upset?'

'Just the opposite … rather jolly, in fact. He told me not to worry. He told me that for a cock-up like this I'd be promoted … just so long as I did as I was told. The idea of being promoted for killing someone by accident seemed a flippant thing to say … don't you think so, Aunt Isa?'

'I'm afraid, Joan, many a bungling idiot owes his promotion to "bungling". There will be an official inquiry into what you have done. A friendly-fire incident is a serious matter.'

'He kept telling me, I owe him. I'm in the shit, Aunt Isa; aren't I?'

'Yes, I'm afraid you are. Who carried Tobias out of my lounge? Did you see? He was a big man. Do you know what they have done with the corpse?'

'Mr Lacy's body? I've no idea. When I realised what I'd done I went to the loo and cried. Until Mr Adder came back and dragged me out, I was incommunicado.'

'Who were the men in the white boiler suits?'

'They were there to bug number thirty-nine. I was helping them. You know I have a degree in electrical engineering.'

'Who do they work for?'

'They did what Mr Adder told them. He was their boss. They obeyed him.'

'Big blokes,' said Isa, thinking aloud, 'they'd have no bother carrying Tobias.'

'Why was Mr Lacy dressed as a clown?'

'He told me he was a children's entertainer. He was here to lobby for the job of entertaining the children at the street party. Before he told me the real reason for his visit, you shot him. Joan, please, pull yourself together. Tears never have, and never will, bring the dead back to life.'

'It's because you said … "shot him" … god! What have I done?'

'You've killed a bloke … that's what you've done,' said a voice from behind the drawn curtain. 'Put the kettle on,' said Malcolm, pulling the curtain out of his way to enable him to poke his head into the room, 'and open the front door. A cannit climb through the window. If I do I'll die the death of a thousand cuts.'

'Hello, Joan,' he said, coming into the lounge and bringing with him a smell of cigarette smoke. 'Yuh, alreet? Long-time-no-see,' then, pointing a pretend rifle at her, 'Bang!'

'Malcolm!' said Isa.

'What?'

'How much did you hear?'

'Enough to nar why you couldn't tell me how your window got smashed.'

'Tell me.'

'But you already nar.'

'I want you to tell me so I know how much you know.'

'Eh?'

'Tell me what you heard.'

'Joan fired a rifle … "smashing piece of kit" … right? At a bloke dressed as a clown. She shot him from number thirty-nine. Oh, dear me. What's happened to your carpet?'

'The missing bit was bloody; it had to be cut out.'

'Oh, dear me, that's arful … that is. If someone cut a chunk out of my front room carpet I'd give them a reet bollicking.'

'MI5 will pay for the damage.'

'A government job, eh? Yuh nar, like the window?'

'Malcolm, forget about the "friggin" carpet, will you?'

'Hoy! Friggin's my word.'

'Well, it's my friggin word now and I'm friggin well going to use it if I friggin well want to.'

'You're a tea-leaf, you are, Isa.'

'Shut up and listen.'

'Hoy! Divent tell me to shut up.'

'Malcolm,' said Joan, 'do you know what this is?'

'Oh, dear me,' said Malcolm, looking at the Glock Joan was pointing at him.

'Shall I shoot him, Aunt Isa?'

'No, just tell him to shut up and listen.'

'Malcolm, shut up and listen.'

'Is that thing loaded?'

'Of course it's friggin loaded. What's the point of carrying a friggin empty gun? When I point a gun at some piece of filth ... I shoot to kill ... that's what I've been trained to do.'

'Oh, dear me! Divent yee friggin start.'

'Malcolm,' said Isa, 'I don't think you understand how serious this is. I want you to forget everything you heard.'

'Keep me gob shut, eh? That'll be easy ... I mean, can yuh imagine me ganin into the club and tellin me mates ... "Did I tell yuh, I have this relation, Joan ... she works for Special Branch ... carries a gun in a shoulder holster ... did a tell yuh, she shot a bloke dead in Chillingham Grove ... oh, and by the way, the bloke she shot was on her side and, when she shot him, he was dressed as a clown. A mean, howay! Come on! They'll think I've lost me marbles. They'd call me a liar and give me a Chinese burn ... that's what the committee did to a bloke in the club last week. I need a tab.'

'If you want to smoke, you'll have to go outside.'

'What'll yuh do, if a just light up?'

'Joan will shoot you.'

'Aye–' looking at Joan– 'a believe she would as well.'

'Out you go. While you are smoking, if you don't mind and it's not too much trouble, you can measure my broken window for a replacement pane. We can talk through the void.'

'The what?'

'The hole in the glass.'

In between the time it took Malcolm to walk outside and get to the window, Joan said: 'Can we trust him?'

'I don't think we have a choice. He is family.'

'Your side … not mine.'

'Pull the curtain back, Isa,' shouted Malcolm, through the broken window. 'Am ganna take oot the broken glass. And watch out. Keep oot the way. Glass is dangerous. Catch those sharp edges the wrong way and there'll be blood all ower the place. Any more blood on that carpet and there'll be nowt left to cut oot. Stand back.'

He removed the shards with pliers; like a dentist pulling teeth.

'I've been watching you,' Isa told Malcolm, when he'd finished.

'Oh, aye! That's nowt new to me, Isa. Women are always looking at me. Fancy me, do yuh?'

'I was admiring your gentleness. You could have been wiping a baby's bottom instead of removing shards of glass.'

'Hi! A can be gentle when a want to be, yuh nar. Gloria, she's me latest, says am like one of them crocodiles she's seen on the telly carrying its bairns in its jaws. Give's some money and I'll gan to the glaziers and buy the glass.'

'I'll get my purse.'

Returning, Isa handed Malcolm a bundle of notes.

'It won't be that much.'

'Keep the change. Out of choice, Malcolm, I would not have involved you in any of this. Your eavesdropping has made you an accessory to a murder. From now on, whether you like it or not, you are on the payroll.'

'Whose payroll?'

'The British Secret Service.'

'Oh, dear me! Me, a secret agent. Hi! What do I have to do for it?'

'Keep your mouth shut and your eyes and ears open.'

'Will a get a gun, like Joan?'

'No.'

****

As soon as Malcolm had gone – his van started after three tries and left a trail of smoke as it sped off down the street – Isa's thoughts, as if hitherto they'd been on a piece of stretched elastic, snapped back to Joan. What do you say to someone who has accidently killed another human being?

'Open a tin of dog food,' Isa told her niece. 'I think you need to be kept busy.'

'Aunt Isa, I can't do it.'

'Pull yourself together. Going to pieces never solved a quadratic equation. Because you have accidently killed someone should not stop you opening a tin of dog food. Do you want Chippy to starve?'

'Aunt Isa, I don't know how your tin opener works. I've never seen one like that before.'

'You do it like this, see–' demonstrating by opening the tin herself.

'How much do I give him?'

'The whole tin. He's a big dog. He's as hungry for dog food as I am to know how you got into my house.'

'Mr Adder gave me the key, I told you. He said: "It will surprise your aunt when she comes home and finds you there. I like giving her surprises.'

'How come he had a key to my front door?'

'I don't know, Aunt Isa.'

'I will, of course have the locks changed. Another job for Malcolm.'

'Will I go to jail, Aunt Isa?'

'I don't know.'

Joan began to cry. The full works. Heaving shoulders. Sobs and sniffles.

'For goodness' sake, Joan; pull yourself together.'

'I'm not a pair of curtains, Aunt Isa.'

'Ah! That old joke. Not so down you can't joke. A good sign. Well done. Things are looking up. Chippy will be relieved. Dogs can smell stress. I wonder what it smells like … never mind. Stroke his head. Play with his ears. It will make you feel better.'

'Sorry, Aunt Isa,' said Joan. 'I've rather let the side down … haven't I?'

****

Joan left. Malcolm walked up Isa's drive carrying a pane of glass.

Through the unglazed window she asked him if he would like a cup of tea.

'Aye, gan on, then. Three sugars and I'll have it oot here, where a can smoke.'

****

She brought the mugs of tea into the lounge on a tray. To her surprise and delight, she found he had the new pane in-situ and was scrolling lumps of putty around its perimeter with the dexterity of a classical pianist playing a toccata with a thumb.

In lieu of not being able to serve him through the 'void' she took the tray outside, putting it, in the absence of a table, down on the bonnet of her Mercedes.

She liked watching men work.

'What's that you are using?'

'Putty knife.'

She admired how he used it. How, in one fell, downward swoop with its diagonal blade, he changed bumpy putty into a smooth bevel.

'Isa!'

It was Beatrice, shouting from Isa's garden gate.

'I've been scrounging,' said Beatrice, holding up a carrier bag in which Isa saw rolls of red, white and blue metallic paper. 'Gratis. From the wool shop. I'm going to make bunting out of them. You getting a new window?'

'Replacing a broken pane,' said Isa, walking down her path to meet her neighbour.

'How did that happen?'

'I did it,' said Malcolm, coming over to join them, a ball of putty in one hand and a putty knife in the other. 'I threw Chippy's marrow bone through it.'

'Temper?'

'It slipped oot me hand.'

'You do Isa's garden … don't you?'

'Aye … and number thirty-nine's. Duh yuh want your garden deeing?'

'No, I do not. I don't want my windows broken. It seems to me you are onto a good thing if you break a window and are then paid to replace it.'

Never one to miss a chance to impress a good-looking woman, Malcolm, said: 'Watch!'

After sucking hard on his cigarette and looking up at the sky as a cockerel is wont to do prior to letting rip a cock-a-doodle-do, he blew smoke rings out of his nose.

'Not many folk can dee that.'

'Not many people would want to,' replied Beatrice.

'Would you like to see me waggle me ears?'

'No.'

Beatrice was not a fan of workmen. She would not dream of offering a blue-collar worker a cup of tea.

'Did you hear a "bang" this morning?' she said when Malcolm, in the huff, knowing he'd failed to impress, had gone back to glazing.

'A "bang"?' said Isa. 'Yes, I think I did hear something. I thought it was someone letting off a firework they'd bought for the big day.'

'At that time in the morning?'

'People are very excited about the wedding. Patriotism, Beatrice, makes folk do silly things. Do you think we should have fireworks at the street party?'

'No, I do not. They will scare my hedgehogs.'

'How many do you have now?'

'Five. Last week the ice-cream man ran over "Puddles".'

'Was he dead?'

'Are you stupid? Of course he was dead. A hedgehog's spikes are no match for an ice-cream van's Goodyear tyres. Isa, I apologise for my brusqueness. I didn't mean to call you "stupid". After me, you are the most intelligent person in Chillingham Grove. I know you are. "Puddles'" death has upset me. I'm still not back to normal; think how you would feel if something happened to Chippy. I have to have something to love. When he's depressed, Ken won't even give me a peck on the cheek. In my youth, an admirer told me I was a very loving woman. I still am. My hedgehogs mean everything to me. They are all I have. They love me and I love them. I don't wish to be nosey but what was that yellow van with a banana on its roof doing outside your house? It said "Mr Chuckle" on its side and that he was a "Children's Entertainer". You haven't forgotten, Dominic's booked a children's entertainer.'

'Mr Chuckle was an old friend,' said Isa.

'Was?'

'Is an old friend. He knows I am on the SPC. He was touting for business.'

'How'd he know you were on the SPC?'

'I must have mentioned it to friends he and I have in common.'

'Would they be the plumbers doing work at number thirty-nine?'

'What makes you say that?'

'Because he left your house with them. A man wearing a ginger wig?'

'It couldn't have been him,' said Isa.

'Why not? Clowns have legs, don't they? Anyway, it's not important just so long as you haven't forgotten Dominic has booked a children's entertainer. We don't want to double book ... do we? I never know from one day to the next how he's going to be ... Ken, I mean. His depression seems to get worse when he sees people enjoying themselves. He thrives on disasters. If a "Titanic" was to sink every day he'd cheer up no end; and, yours truly might get a loving kiss off him; even a peck on the cheek would be something. I'm going to ask Mari if she'll help me make the bunting. When you are cutting and sewing, it's nice to have someone to talk to.'

'Would cutting and sewing not be therapeutic for Ken? I'm not medical, so, I don't know. Excuse me, I think Malcolm wants me.'

'Good luck with that one. I wouldn't let him near my dahlias.'

'He is family.'

'You can pick your friends but, you can't pick your family ... is that what you are saying?'

'Under Malcolm's gruff exterior, there beats a heart of bronze. For years he looked after his poorly mother. Once a week he bought her a frozen dinner from Iceland.'

'You'll never convince me. I don't like the way he's playing with that hammer. I get the impression he'd like to throw it at me the way that Indian in the western I was watching last night threw a tomahawk at a rancher.'

'If you need any help with the bunting, let me know.'

'I will and good luck with the sex maniac.'

'I beg your pardon?'

'Malcolm! I know men. Bye ... ee!'

Why had Malcolm butted in and claimed he'd broken the window? Drat him! She'd told Mari a different story. Come to think of it; what did she tell her? She was getting too old for the spying game. When Beatrice and Mari meet for a chat, they'll wonder what's going on. Working with an overenthusiastic amateur was going to be uphill work. When you told lies, if you did not want to be found out, you had to have a good memory.

****

Washing putty off his hands at Isa's kitchen sink, Malcolm said: 'Does she have a skivvy to wipe her arse? We does she think she is? She needs a bat across the gob, she does.'

'Beatrice is my neighbour. She is like the monsoon in India – you get used to it.'

'Eh?'

'A beer and a bacon sandwich?'

'Aye! Gan on then. Have you got beer in?'

'How could I offer you beer, if I didn't have some in?'

'I didn't think yuh drank beer, that's all.'

'When I hosted the "SPC", I got some in for the "boys".'

'SPC?'

'Street party committee.'

'Oh, dear me! A thought yuh meant the RSPCA. Yuh nar, cats and dogs on the pop. "Snobby-Gobby's" hubby on the committee?'

'Beatrice wouldn't like you calling her that.'

'She's a snob.'

'Her husband is not on the committee. He suffers from depression.'

'Am not surprised … married to her. Mind you, she's a good looker. She's the sort of woman who attracts men who like kissing tigers … nar what a mean?'

'No, I do not know what you mean.'

'When you had your heeds together, did she tell you she fancied me?'

'Just the opposite. She thinks you are a sex maniac.'

'Takes one to recognise one.'

'Please yersell.'

'I'll grill the bacon. It is more healthy that way.'

'Oh, dear me, you're health-mad, you are, Isa. It won't make yuh live forever, yuh nar. You've got to die of something.'

While the bacon 'grilled', Isa poured two beers.

'Two?'

'One's for me.'

'A thout yuh didn't drink beer. Last time a seen that many bottles of red wine–' nodding at a wine rack– 'was in a pub on the quayside.'

'Would you have preferred wine?'

'Never touch the stuff. Bad for your health.'

'It might interest you to know that when I worked in the Lebanon, I drank a lot of beer. Chilled beer … not lukewarm English beer.'

'Was that because it was hot? I've never been to Lebanon. Is that in South America?'

'No …it is not … and you know it isn't … stop teasing. I drank beer because I was mixing with a group of alpha males who drank beer … a lot of beer. Malcolm … I want to tell you a secret.'

'If it's aboot your love life … I hope it's not dirty? Ha! Ha! I divent want me cousin Isa making me blush.'

'We all know about the birds and the bees.'

'Aye, that's true.'

'What I am going to tell you will not make you blush. Stop fidgeting. Please, smoke, if you wish.'

'You mean, in the house? I don't have to gan outside?'

'Yes.'

'Oh, dear, me! Now, a am worried. Things must be bad when you're letting me smoke in the house.'

'Have you ever been scared?'

'Oh, aye! Plenty of times, doon the pit.'

'Joan and I are scared. A member of Her Majesty's Secret Service is blackmailing us.'

'Eh?'

'When I worked in Lebanon? I killed for my country.'

'Eh? Oh, aye! Why you telling me?'

'To get it into your thick head that what you overheard Joan and I talking about is not a game.'

'A thought you were a civil servant?'

'That was my "cover". My real job was working for the British Secret Service.'

'I had heard rumours, like,' said Malcolm, sucking hard on a cigarette, 'from me mother. She and your mother used to do a lot of chin-wagging. You were like a secret agent, eh? When a was blasting out coal, underground, my nice cousin Isa was blasting bad guys to kingdom come. Are you kidding?'

'No.'

'Yuh nar how to use a gun?'

'As well as you know how to use dynamite. I am a "marksman" … so is Joan.'

'When she shot that bloke … there was nee chance of her missing?'

'None whatsoever. She was the victim of a sting.'

'She killed "Mr Chuckle"?'

'That was her target.'

Malcolm shook his head. To help him think he lit another cigarette. He needed nicotine.

****

'Bacon tastes better when it's fried,' said Malcolm, tucking into the bacon sandwich Isa had served him, 'but, this is alreet. Very tasty.'

'Malcolm?

'What now? If I was a doorbell, I'd be worn out.'

'In the next few weeks, I may need your help.'

'Will a get danger money?'

'I'll pay you in home-made cakes.'

'That's alreet, then. What do I have to do?'

'Keep your mouth shut and your eyes and ears open. I am now going to tell you something few people know. Number thirty-nine is a safe house. Do you know what a safe house is?'

'Sort of … but tell me.'

Isa explained.

'Are you listening?'

'Why aye … course am listening. Can a give Chippy a piece of bacon?'

'No.'

'There you are, Chippy. A bit of bacon never hurt anyone.'

'Malcolm!'

'Hi! I'm a secret agent. I've a licence to give Chippy bacon. Good, eh? You bribe me with homemade cakes. I bribe Chippy with bacon.'

'Touché.'

'A nar what that means. The three musketeers say it when they are sword fighting.'

'Malcolm, you need a fright.'

'Boo! Ha! Ha!'

'Chippy! Guard!'

At once Chippy snarled and barked at Malcolm.

'Alreet! Alreet!' said Malcolm, when the dog had him backed into a corner. 'Am listening.'

'Down!' said Isa.

Backing off, the dog whined.

'He always gets a treat when he's threatened someone. It keeps him on his paws.'

'A thought he was a nice dog?'

'He is. Are you listening?'

'Cross me heart and hope to die.'

'Sometime soon a Russian vodka salesman will be arriving at number thirty-nine. When you cut its grass, I want you to keep your eyes and ears open. One more thing.'

'Oh, dear, me! Holy mother of god! You're ringing the doorbell again. What now?'

'I want new locks on my front door. The man who is blackmailing me has a key. He's in for a shock if he thinks he can walk into my house any time he likes. We'll talk about money later.'

'Eh? We'll talk about money now. There's nee tick at Gedney's.'

'I don't care how much it costs. Just change the bloody locks. Money is not a problem.

'It might not be to you, cousin Isa, but it is to me.'

'I'll give you more than you need.' Taking out her purse she handed him a substantial sum. 'Keep the change. Off you go.'

'Hi! Are yee pushing me out?'

'I want the locks changed before sunset.'

'A rush job? Oh, dear, me! I've got a lot on today. What about me other customers?'

'Malcolm, just change the fucking locks. Charge me what the fuck you like.'

'A never thought I'd hear me cousin Isa … who went to a posh university and lives in Jesmond, use that naughty word. Oh, dear me! Things must be bad!'

****

To help her stay calm, while Malcolm was away buying the locks, Isa plumped cushions. She removed imaginary dust from chair legs. Multiple scenarios raced unbidden through her mind. Jeremy must be told about what had happened. Might he already know? How much 'rope' had he given 'TA'? She needed time to think. She'd put off ringing Jeremy until tomorrow.

****

An hour later Malcolm arrived back, whistling and looking as if he'd backed a winner.

'Did you get the locks?'

'Oh, dear, me! You're ringing me doorbell again. A got a tin of blue paint.'

'Out of my money?'

'Nar! Nar! What duh yuh think I am? The paint is oot of a skip. When a went to get the locks … a went skipp'n as well … yuh, nar … looking in skips. Oh, dear me! This is hard work. When you gan shoppin, Isa, yuh look in shop windows … cos you've got money. When Malcolm gans shopping he looks in skips … cos he's got nee money.'

'You did get my locks, though?'

'Course a got your friggin locks. Is ya finger not sore ringing me doorbell? Yuh nar–' lighting a cigarette and looking thoughtful– 'am thinking, my front door would look nice painted blue. Blue's me favourite colour.'

'I didn't know that.'

'Nor did I … until a fund that tin of blue paint. HA! Ha! Ha! Oh, dear me! Life is full of surprises.'

While Malcolm smoked, drank tea, dreamed of painting his front door blue and fitted the locks, Isa decided to do a bit of 'skipp'n' herself. Why not? She rather liked the idea of looking through other people's rubbish. It was like looking in your neighbour's shopping trolley. Who would have thought Jean bought baked beans?

She'd ring London on the contact number she'd used to contact Desmond. MI5 was a skip full of posh rubbish. Why not rummage around in it? Who might answer? Was 'TA' still on Tyneside? Had he gone back to London? If he'd flown back by helicopter and landed on the roof of GCHQ, he'd have had time. But not by train or car.

She'd ring on the pretext of demanding recompense for the hole in her carpet. She'd play the irate house frau. If a minion answered, she or he might let slip a bit of information indicative of what was going on. In other words, she might find a tin of blue paint.

Picking up the phone in the hall, she blew Chippy a kiss. He was watching Malcolm poke a chisel into a mortise joint, no doubt keeping his paws crossed that sometime soon a contraband custard cream would come his way.

Listening to the phone she'd clamped to an ear, she prepared herself for verbal action; like an actor waiting in the wings for her cue.

Why was no one answering?

In the past when she'd rang, her call had been picked up on the first ring. The girls working MI5's switchboard were professionals. They knew the person ringing might be in a life and death situation.

At last.

'Hello! My nail varnish is coming off.'

'I beg your pardon.'

'Sorry, madam. I wasn't talking to you. I was talking to my friend, Freda. We work the switchboard together. I'll be with you in a mo-mo. Hello, are you there?'

'I'm here. Are you?'

'Sorry about that. We're very busy at the mo-mo's. I mean … minute. When me and Freda are slack we make up words … you know … to pass the time. How can I help? I'm here to help … that's my job.'

'Tony Adder's office, please.'

'Adams?'

'No, "Adder".'

'Like the snake?'

'Yes … like the snake.'

'I'll bet an adder is good at sums; you know, two plus two? I've just thought of that … wait till I tell Freda. When we're slack, we have a good laugh. You have to laugh, don't you? Least, that's what I think. How can I help?'

'If it's not too much trouble, put me through to Mr Adder's office. Have you been drinking?'

'Why should you think that?'

'I have no idea.'

'Well, if you haven't ... why should I?'

'Mr Adder's office ... if you don't mind.'

'First I've heard of a "Mr Adder" and I've been working here for six years ... hang on a mo-mo ... I'll ask Freda. Freda, you heard of a Mr Adder? That's right, the same as the snake. Freda's worked here longer than me and she says she's never heard of a "Mr Adder" and, that's nothing to do with her not liking snakes. Freda thinks you've got the wrong number. You're not one of those animal rights people, are you? You know ... going on about snakes.'

'You are switchboard?'

'Ladies' lingerie.'

'"Heaton and Jarrow",' said Isa.

The British Secret Service employed 'fronts'. Ladies' lingerie was a new one. No one could ring MI5 and expect a switchboard operator to sing out: 'MI5 speaking. Department, please? Assassination? Dirty tricks?'

'Fronts' were disguises, like false noses and stick-on beards.

'Eton and Harrow?'

'No! Heaton and Jarrow.'

'What you on about, madam?'

'Heaton and Jarrow.'

'Madam, unless, Eton and Harrow are a new line in ladies' lingerie, I haven't a clue what you are on about. Would it help if I put you through to cosmetics?'

'You really are Ladies' lingerie?'

'Why shouldn't I be? Why should I say I'm Ladies' lingerie if I'm not?'

'I think I have the wrong number.'

'You don't need help, do you? I mean, going on about "snakes" and posh schools, like, what is Eton and Harrow. Nurse is very nice. I mean, you wouldn't like me to put you through to "medical", would you? Nurse is used to dealing with folk, you know, who are, well, you know …'

'No thank you. Sorry to have bothered you.'

What fun 'TA' must have had transferring her Desmond contact number to a department store.

'You bastard!' she said, putting down the phone.

'Hoy!' said Malcolm. 'What have a done now?'

'Not you!'

'Thank god for that. A thowt me days was numbered. I've changed your locks.'

'I've been hung out to dry.'

'Oh, aye! Like wor mothers used to hang oot their washing?'

'Across a back lane?'

'Aye, that's reet.'

'And, when the coalman came in his lorry and tooted his horn, they would rush out and take in their washing, to let him pass.'

'Aye, that's reet. Me granda used to say: "Sailors take in sail when it's windy … housewives take in their washing to let the coalman's lorry through". You had to watch the coalman.'

'You mean, count the bags as he emptied them into the coalhouse?'

'Oh, aye! Yuh just had to blink and he'd charge you for ten when he'd put in nine. That's how a learnt to count.'

'Counting the bags of coal?'

'Oh, aye! A never knew there was a number bigger than ten until a was seventeen and started counting me girlfriends. Ha! Ha! They were the days. Good days them. Aye!' he said, lighting a cigarette. 'It's the poor what gets the blame … the rich what gets the pleasure and the cat what gets the gravy. Duh yuh remember that cat me mother had? It loved gravy?'

'Talking of food,' said Isa, 'will you let me cook you something?'

'Will a be able to smoke?'

'Yes.'

'At the table?'

'Yes.'

'Oh, dear me! Things must be bad.'

'These are exceptional circumstances.'

'Are they?'

'Yes, they are.'

'What's on the menu? Mince and dumplings? A like mince and dumplings. When a used to gan poaching a got a liking for duck. Nivva had duck for years.'

'I'm going to take you to Italy.'

'Oh, aye! On a jet plane?'

'No, in a saucepan.'

'Not a chip pan? Are wuh not having chips?'

'No, pasta.'

'Eh, what's that?'

'Wait and see. It's very good for you ... healthier than chips.'

'But a like chips.'

'You only think you do.'

'Do I?'

'Yes.'

'Why is everything a like bad for me?'

'Eavesdropping is bad for you. It could get you killed.'

'Aye! So you keep saying.'

'While I make the carbonara ... have you had it before?'

'Carbonara? A nar aboot carboniferous coal seams. Is it like black pudd'n?'

Shaking her head at her cousin's ignorance – or, was it wit? – Isa said: 'Go and play with Chippy in the garden. I'll give you some dog biscuits. You hide one and tell him to find it. He's good at sniffing

95

things out.'

'Oh, dear, me! What a day! Forst … a hear aboot a murder … then … me cousin's a spy … then a fix a window … then a fix two locks and now am told to gan outside and play with a wolf.'

'Stop moaning. You could still be down the pit.'

'Aye! That's true.'

****

Isa served the carbonara, in a tureen. Malcolm could help himself.

'What's this for?' he said, picking up a napkin. 'It's as big as what the barber puts round me neck when I gan for a haircut.'

'You know fine well what it is for… stop teasing.'

'How do a eat this? A nar how to use a knife and fork, yuh nar … the knife's for the gravy and the fork's for the big bits.'

'Shall I be mum?'

'Eh? Oh, aye.'

'Hold out your bowl.'

'Hi! Am not Oliver Twist.'

'Say when.'

'That's enough worms for the minute. I had worms when a was a bairn. Me mother put a slug pellet up me backside.'

'A suppository.'

'Is that what it was?' Looking at his loaded plate. 'I've had spaghetti out of a tin, but this looks different.'

'You eat it like this,' said Isa, spinning her fork into the spaghetti on her plate until, like a combine harvester, she'd turned a portion of it into a bale.

Malcolm ate the 'anacondas' as he called the long strings of spaghetti, by cutting them into mouth-size worms.

'Very tasty, this,' he said. 'Very canny. As a said to Mary … she's me latest … when she gave me a kiss, last neet: "I'll have some more of that".'

'Help yourself.'

'Nar, nar. You do it. A like been waited on. This is what the Italians eat, is it? They're not daft, the Italians.'

'Better than the peanut butter sandwiches I know you like?'

'A wouldn't say that.'

'Don't talk with your mouth full.'

'Oh, dear me! Yuh canit help yasell, can yuh?'

'Doing what?'

'Ringing me doorbell. Nagging. Shall a finish off what's left or is that for the wolf?'

'Chippy has mince.'

'Just a minute! Hoy! The dog gets mince and a get worms ... that can't be right.'

'The worms are good for you. You can play games with them.'

'Can yuh?'

To show him what she meant she put a string of spaghetti into her mouth, then sucked it in. We called it "Sucking Shoelaces".'

'We?'

'The team of assassins I worked with in the Middle East.'

'Eh! Assassins? Oh, aye! And me mother nivva used Parish money.'

'When we'd taken someone out ...'

'Like on a date?'

'No, Malcolm. When we'd killed a bad guy, we needed to unwind. Another game we played was "Dracula". Watch!'

Sucking hard on his fag, Malcolm watched Isa hang a string of spaghetti out of the corners of her mouth ... as if she had fangs.

'Oh, aye, very funny. Yuh nar, a never nar when you are having me on. You're a dark horse, you are, Isa. Did yuh really work with the SAS?'

'Do you not believe me?'

'After what's happened today? A divent nar what to think.'

'Tell no one about number thirty-nine.'

'Aye! Mum's the word and aal that. How'd yuh do that with the spaghetti? Let me have a try. Am thinking … if a did an impersonation of "Dracula" at the club, somebody might buy us a pint.'

'Or, pour one over your head.'

'Aye–' sucking hard on his cigarette and narrowing his eyes– 'a never thought of that.'

****

As soon as he'd gone, to rid the house of the smell of cigarette smoke, Isa opened her downstairs windows. If only memories were as easy to blow away. Tobias Lacy and Tony Adder were bad smells that had first made her nose twitch, when she'd been in her twenties.

Tobias was dead; like an unburied, rotting corpse he was making a stench that was weaving itself into the very fabric of her being.

To her surprise she found she could not be bothered to make herself a cup of tea. She felt like a car in a scrapyard. A car without a battery. A car with its reusable parts removed. A car waiting to be put into a hydraulic crushing machine. A machine powerful enough to turn a car into something the size of half a dozen shoe boxes, stacked together to make a cube or, like an oven in a crematorium, powerful enough to turn a human body into a few tablespoons of ash.

Sensing her abjectness, Chippy became her shadow. Wherever she went, he followed.

Dragging herself – reluctantly, it must be said – out of a comfy armchair and onto a hard chair with a hard back, she gave herself, what she called, 'marching orders'. If Joan could make a joke out of 'pull yourself together', then she, Ms Isa Weddle, a lady with years of spying and espionage under her poke bonnet, could surely stiffen the sinews and find the energy to fight back. She was not a nobody. She was Ms Isa Weddle, a supernumerary employee of Her Majesty's

Secret Service.

To keep busy while trying to make sense of events, she emptied a kitchen drawer of its accumulated rubbish. She found a tin opener with a wooden handle. It had belonged to her mother. Through years of use and washing, its handle had split. It looked the way a tree looks when it has been struck by lightning. She was about to bin it when she changed her mind. She was fond of relics.

Was she a relic? Why had 'TA' ordered Joan to assassinate Tobias? Could she trust Jeremy? Would she ever hear again from Desmond, aka Mr Wonderful? Might Joan, in her distressed state, do something silly? Might she park her car on a level crossing and wait for an express train to smash it and her into more bits and pieces than there are stars in the Milky Way?

Her niece needed her help. She'd not let her down.

Isa was a social animal. Her mental well-being demanded she had someone with whom to talk, argue, chat, kiss and cuddle. Chippy was a ten out of ten empathiser; sadly, though, he was a dog. In the world of realpolitik, he had limitations. She did not often feel lonely – she was used to living alone – but she did now.

She badly needed someone with whom to have a chat. Though she and her sister, Dorothy, did not see eye-to-eye, Dorothy, like Malcolm, was kin. It was not Isa's fault that if she said 'black', her sister would say 'white'.

She'd not spoken to Dorothy for weeks. It was time to get in touch. She also wanted to know Joan's telephone number. It occurred to her that in view of recent events she might need to contact her niece.

Of course, she could not tell Dorothy her daughter had killed a high-ranking member of the British Secret Service. If she had done, she'd have broken the Official Secrets Act. But she could ask her for Joan's telephone number. They could talk about the weather. They could make polite conversation. They could pretend to like each other.

How could two sisters be so different? Isa liked cats and dogs. Dorothy disliked all animals. And Isa couldn't stand Dorothy's husband, Ivan. He managed a sewage works. Behind his back, she called him Mr Turd.

When anyone asked Ivan what he did for a living, he was fond of telling them: 'Jesus turned water into wine. I turn excrement into drinking water. I do a very important job. Where would society be without me?'

All Dorothy knew of her sister's working life was that her clever sister had worked abroad and had a 'bloody good pension'. She knew her sister must have a good pension because she bought expensive clothes. Isa always had to have the best. And then, there was that car! A car, like that, for a woman of her age? Ridiculous! Ivan said that when he retired from killing germs and making the world a cleaner place, on the pension he expected to get, he'd never be able to afford a car like that. Did Dorothy know how much a car like that cost? Folk thought his job a joke … well, it wasn't … and another thing … he was sick of folk holding their noses when they saw him. If he and his mates went on strike … like them bloody miners were always doing … there'd be turds coming out of taps instead of water.

Putting the phone to an ear, preparatory to punching in her sister's number, Isa heard deep breathing. The inhalations jolted her, physically, as if she'd done an emergency stop in a car. Her phone was tapped. And for some reason the eavesdropper wished her to know it was tapped. Why?

The invasion of her privacy made her feel dirty. It made her, angry. It made her want to scream. Was this 'TA's' doing? Was he reminding her of their bargain? That if she failed to keep her mouth shut about his proposed visits to number thirty-nine, Joan would go to jail for a very long time? If so, he'd played the wrong card. How right Jeremy had been to tell her to use a public telephone when she'd rang his London number.

'Fuck off!'

'Who is that?' said Ivan. 'Don't you go telling me to ... fuck off. If this is another dirty phone call because I manage a sewage farm ... I'm telling you now ... I'm sick of them. My work is important.'

'Ivan ... it's me ... Isa.'

'Why'd you to tell me to fuck off?'

'I wasn't talking to you.'

'Who were you talking to?'

'A wasp.'

'What do you want? If it's money, I haven't got any.'

'Can I speak to Dorothy?'

'It's not convenient. She's doing what a wife should be doing, she's making her husband's dinner. My dinner. Is it important?'

'Can you give me Joan's telephone number?'

'Hang on.'

Isa did not write the number down. She remembered it as eight to the power five.

'I'll tell Dot you rang. Dealing full time with sewage makes a man hungry. I may be old fashioned but, when I come home I like my dinner on the table.'

'Good night, Ivan.'

****

Only on the third try, rings separated by gaps of an hour, did Joan answer Isa's call.

'Where have you been? I've been worried about you.'

'Oh, hello, Aunt Isa.'

'Are you alright?'

'I'm fine. As well as can be expected under the circumstances. I've been on the firing range. Mr Adder said it was important for me to keep my hand in. He said that what happened this morning, you know, the accidental shooting, was like falling off a horse. When you fall off a horse it was important for your self-confidence that you climbed straight back on again. He said it was important for me not to lose confidence in my shooting. I did as I was told. Mr Adder is very persuasive.'

'Did the therapy work?'

'I'm still a marksman.'

'A sharp eye and a steady hand.'

'And a desire to do what is right for my country, Aunt Isa. Patriotism.'

'You sound like a Girl Guide, learning to tie a reef knot.'

'Are you not a patriot, Aunt Isa?'

'After what I have seen and done, I am a "limited company" patriot.'

'I'm not sure what you mean by that. I don't think Mr Adder would approve. He is always going on about how patriotic he is. A real flag-waver, is Mr Adder.'

'Mr Adder will be pleased to hear that.'

'Are you going to tell him?'

'I don't need to. He is listening in. Joan, be careful what you say. We are speaking on a bugged phone. I think we should meet somewhere we can talk in private.'

'Bloody hell! Does MI5 trust no one?'

'In the spying game there is no such thing as trust. What about the "Sediment"? You know where I mean?'

'Yes.'

'People listening in,' said Isa, 'Mr Eavesdropper, do you know where the "Sediment" is?'

The eavesdropper replied by playing 'God Save the Queen'.

****

In bed, Chippy in his basket guarding the bedroom door, Isa went over, 'Why?' and 'What if?' scenarios.

Why had 'TA' picked Joan to execute Tobias?

What if Tobias knew his long-term pal, Tony, was a traitor? What if Tobias was working for Jeremy? What if he was part of the 'rope' MI5 were giving 'TA'? Tobias and 'TA' had been pals for a very long time. What if they were both traitors? What if the posh boys were setting her up? What if she was becoming paranoid?

At three in the morning she found out how 'TA' had got his hands on her front door keys. Downstairs she had a hall stand. In one of its drawers, she kept a spare set.

Coming down the stairs in the middle of the night with Chippy wondering what the hell was going on, she found, not the keys in the drawer, but a note.

'Hope you didn't mind my boys borrowing the keys to your front door. Love the pyramid fob. I'm going to keep it. Why? To annoy you. We all have memories of Egypt, don't we? Tony.'

Chapter 13

Next morning, to contact Jeremy, Isa walked Chippy to the telephone box she'd used previously. The one smelling of urine. To get to it she took a roundabout route. The bugging of her phone had made her cautious. Every time Chippy stopped to urinate or sniff a wall, she used the time it took him to do doggy-things to check she was not being followed.

She'd an intimate knowledge of the area. She knew its cul-de-sacs, its one-way streets, its alleyways built to let through nothing wider than a sedan chair. Its intricacies reminded her of the suburbs of Cairo, without of course that city's noise, heat and stench.

Emerging, at last, onto a main road and within a dozen yards of the telephone box, she paused.

She'd been right to be cautious. The man she could see inside the telephone box was wearing a white boiler suit. The van parked next to the kiosk was the Reed's Plumbing Services van she'd last seen parked in number thirty-nine's drive. The bastards had stolen her front door keys and given them to 'TA'. She approached the kiosk at the speed of a quick walk like a horse cantering before it breaks into a gallop.

Pulling open the kiosk's door she told Chippy, 'Guard!'

On cue the dog snarled and growled; straining on his lead he jumped upwards and forwards.

To whom was the 'plumber' talking? Was it a personal call or was he reporting in?

The 'plumber' in the van seemed amused at his colleague's predicament. He was shaking his head as if to say: this should not be happening.

'Tell the wolf to behave,' the 'plumber' in the phone box told Isa.' Do you know who I am? I'm MI5.'

'In that case, we are on the same side. If my dog bites you it will be friendly fire. Kneel!'

'I'll get my overalls dirty.'

'Kneel! And turn around.'

Being a sensible fellow and not wishing to give Chippy a pound of his flesh, he did as he'd been told.

When he was on his knees and with his back to her, Isa told him to give her the phone.

To use it and stay outside the kiosk she stretched its cord to breaking point. Putting it to her ear she heard: 'Thompson, are you there? What the fuck is going on? You don't have a hard job to do … keeping tabs on Weddle. She isn't going to snap the elastic … Thompson? '

'Good morning, Tony. Ms Weddle speaking. Can you hear me?'

'Yes.'

'Fuck you!' she said, dropping the receiver and letting it swing on its cord.

'He doesn't like dogs,' shouted the 'plumber' through a wound-down window in the van.

'And fuck you as well,' said Isa.

'Now, now. No need to be like that. Mr Adder said you are one of us. It's just you've gone AWOL.'

'Do you always do what Tony tells you?'

'Is that his first name? You are more familiar with him, Ms Weddle, than I am.'

'Are you not going to help your colleague?'

'Not when the wolf is looking at me as if I'm a pork chop.'

'You are not as stupid as you look.'

'Ouch! Mr Adder said you had a way with words.'

'What class of shot are you?'

'I don't do weapons. I'm technical.'

'And you?' to the 'plumber' in the phone box?'

'Same as my mate … technical.'

'It may interest you to know, I am a marksman.'

'Like Joan?' said the 'Plumber' still on his knees in the phone box.

'Yes,' said Isa, 'like Joan. And, like my niece, if I ever have you in my sights, I assure you, I won't miss. You–' to the 'plumber' in the phone box– 'get back in your van and piss off.'

The 'plumbers' did not 'piss off'. From the safety of their van, they introduced themselves.

'I'm Bryan.'

'I'm Ted.'

'We do what Mr Adder tells us,' said the one called Bryan. 'Isn't that right, Ted?'

'We don't like what's going on,' said Ted.

'What is going on?' said Isa.

'We know a bit more than you do, Ms Weddle,' said Bryan, 'but, not much. You know how MI5 works.'

'Are you really a "marksman"?' said Ted.

'Yes. Do you think I shouldn't be because I'm a woman?'

'When you were out in the "field", you know, on active service, did you ever, you know …'

'Yes,' said Isa, 'I have killed to keep my country safe.'

'Looking at you,' said Bryan, 'you'd never think you were a paid assassin.'

'Appearances, gentlemen, can be deceptive. A word of advice from someone who, many years ago, worked with your boss: never forget his surname.'

'England's only poisonous snake,' said Bryan.

'Ms Weddle, as a matter of interest, would you have let the wolf bite me?'

'Definitely.'

'I don't believe you.'

'Heel, Chippy.'

****

Isa knew she was out of touch with the technology now available for surveillance. She'd read that computers were making possible things which, in her day, would have been thought impossible.

The phone box the 'plumber' had been using was close to her home. What if he'd been fitting a device to it that would enable 'TA' to listen in to anyone who might be using it? Had 'TA' expected her to use it? Or, had the 'plumber' been using it, quite simply, to keep 'TA' up to date?

By their accents the 'plumbers' were not local. If they were not from around here, where were they lodging? They had to sleep somewhere. Why hadn't they gone back home? Had they more technical work to do on number thirty-nine before the Russian arrived? Or, were they on Tyneside to keep a watchful eye on her, just as she kept a watchful eye on number thirty-nine?

'TA' would have a departmental budget. If he wanted funds to keep her under twenty-four-seven surveillance, he'd have to justify the expense to his superiors.

For MI5 the prospect of recruiting a spy inside the Kremlin would be a high priority. If they were not generous, he might suspect they did not believe his story that he was on the verge of recruiting Leo. How much hanging-rope was MI5 giving him? He would know from experience that the agency was tight fisted.

On the balance of probabilities, she concluded that he would not have been given unlimited resources. She'd bet that the only agents he had at his disposal were her niece and the two 'plumbers'. And they were foot soldiers. They would be told no more than they needed to know. It was possible the 'plumbers' felt ashamed at intimidating one of their own. Did they make faces at 'TA' behind his back? Did they know he was a traitor? Was it possible, 'TA' was also blackmailing them?

****

Back home she thanked Chippy for his help by giving him a slice of ham.

She wrote a letter to her friend Lucy. Lucy would be interested to hear that Tobias was dead.

Lucy lived in Beirut where she worked as a doctor for Médicins Sans Frontières. They exchanged news and gossip about twice a year. They'd met at Oxford. They'd clicked. Her father was a teacher in a run of the mill comprehensive. Her mother was a nurse.

Isa could not tell Lucy how Tobias had died. What Lucy read between the lines was up to her. She knew that in the Lebanon, Isa and Tobias had worked for MI6. In the letter, Isa pulled no punches. Lucy and Isa's memories of Tobias Lacy were unpleasant.

She would post the letter at Newcastle's main post office. At the same time, she'd ring Jeremy from one of the public telephone kiosks in its main entrance.

Chapter 14

A crisis was no excuse for not looking one's best. Before going into town one always put on one's 'face'. The day was warm and sunny. To keep cool she changed into a blue linen trouser suit. To protect her hair from the sun she wore one of those straw hats that girls at private schools wear, with an all-round upturned brim. Sunglasses protected her eyes.

She told Chippy where she was going and that he was to stay at home and guard the house. When she closed the front door on him, he whined. Although she had never had a husband, she was sure dogs were like husbands. If she and Yuri had married, would Yuri have whined if she'd told him to stay at home and wash the dishes while she went shopping?

Coming out of her front door she looked across at number thirty-nine. The 'plumbers' were back. They were carrying a box the size of a coffin into the house. When they saw her, they put it down and waved.

Were they saying they had forgiven her for letting Chippy intimidate them? If so, why? Big guys don't forgive. They fight back. Were they taking the piss? She gave them the sort of minimal nod a Prime Minister, when he is leaving number ten, might give to the policeman guarding its front door.

She'd take a bus into town. Deep in thought as she set off down the street, she did not see Beatrice and Mari chatting outside Beatrice's garden gate.

'A penny for them?' shouted Beatrice.

'Sorry,' said Isa, 'I didn't see you. I was deep in thought.'

'We could see that, couldn't we, Mari?' said Beatrice.

'I'll bet you were thinking about the street party,' said Mari. 'I think about it all the time.'

'I have every confidence in the SPC,' said Isa. 'We are well organised.'

'Do you know the 'plumbers'?' said Beatrice.

'They seem to like you,' said Mari. 'It's good to keep in with tradesmen.'

'I don't know them that well. They came to help when Mr Chuckle broke my front room window.'

'Your cheeky gardener chappy told me he broke it,' said Beatrice.

'Isa told me Mr Chuckle broke it,' said Mari.

'I think when Malcolm claimed responsibility, he was flirting with you, Beatrice.'

'That's a funny way to try and win a girl's heart.'

'He has a warped sense of humour.'

'I think it's the royal wedding,' said Mari, 'it's making everyone feel romantic.'

'It's not making Ken feel romantic,' said Beatrice, pulling a face.

'Oh dear,' said Mari, 'is he still not enthusiastic about the street party?'

'I've told you before, Mari, my husband's depression always gets worse when he thinks people are enjoying themselves. His illness is most perplexing. He's in bed at the moment. Doesn't want to get up. And, when he does get up, he'll go to the fridge and drink three glasses of white wine.'

'Would it help if you borrowed Duncan's videos of the "World at War"? Duncan's in the middle of the Indian Ocean at the moment.'

'Anything about Dunkirk cheers him up.'

'What about that film about the sinking of the Titanic? I think it was called, "A Night to Remember". It made me cry.'

'Anything about the Titanic cheers him up. I do believe he'd be happy if the Russians started a third world war.'

'I'd better go,' said Isa. 'I have a letter to post. I'm going into town.'

'There's a post box round the corner,' said Mari.

'I know there is. I need a stamp.'

'The post box is next to the post office. The post office sell stamps, you know,' said Beatrice.

'I'm going into town to shop.'

'Is that why you are not taking Chippy?'

'It doesn't seem right,' said Mari, 'you not having your dog with you.'

'Dogs are not allowed in shops.'

'Guide dogs are,' said Beatrice.

'Chippy, is not a guide dog.'

'Are you going to dress him up for the street party?' said Mari.

'I can see him with a red, white and blue bandana tied round his neck,' said Beatrice.

'Such a pity he's not a bulldog.'

'I wonder if anyone will come to the fancy dress as John Bull … with a bulldog?'

Isa glanced at her watch.

'That's the watch your boyfriend gave you, isn't it?' said Beatrice. 'The one who was blown up by a terrorist when you worked abroad.'

'Yes,' said Isa, 'but that was a long time ago.'

'I remember you once showing it to me. It was on the anniversary of his death. You were quite emotional. You smoked a cigar.'

'That's right. On the anniversary of his death, I always smoke a cigar. The smell reminds me of him.'

'How romantic,' said Mari. 'Is it a Rolex?'

'It is the real thing, isn't it?' said Beatrice.

'Yes … for what it's worth … it is,' said Isa.

'Ken bought one off a street vendor in Greece. He thought he was getting a bargain. It quite cheered him up when he found it was a fake. It confirmed his low opinion of human beings. That was the time our plane had to turn back because of engine trouble. I was wetting myself. Ken, on the other hand, claimed the scare gave him a new lease of life. Funny thing, depression.'

'The bulldog is a symbol of British grit … isn't it?' said Mari.

'What are you on about, Mari?' said Beatrice.

'Symbols.'

'Symbols,' said Isa, 'are like dogs. They take a lot of looking after. If they are not cherished and loved, they lose their power to inspire.'

'This ring,' said Beatrice, holding up her left hand and displaying the gold band on her second finger, 'is a symbol of my marriage to Ken. I will tell you this. I am sick of cherishing it. Believe me, Isa, you are lucky you are not married. You have no worries. Lucky you. You don't know you are born. Believe me.'

'Yes,' said Isa, 'I have no worries. I'd best be off before Chippy eats an armchair. He dislikes being left on his own.'

She left them talking about the 'plumbers'. Was number thirty-nine having a new bathroom installed? They'd heard rumours.

****

Newcastle's General Post Office looked like a Greek temple. As if the letters delivered there should be written on tablets of stone rather than on paper, and that, to deliver the mail, postmen should carry hods on their shoulders instead of sacks.

Under the shelter of its portico, fitted into an alcove as wardrobes are in a bedroom, there stood a row of public telephones in booths the size of broom cupboards. To shut out the wicked world while a user was conversing (if the user so wished) each booth had its own concertina door. All were dusty and dirty.

It was from one of these that Isa rang London. Someone answered on the second ring.

'How may I help?'

'May I speak to Jeremy, please?'

'Do you have a code?'

'Heaton and Jarrow.'

'Where is Jarrow?'

'It is a town on the bank of the River Tyne.'

'North bank or South bank?'

'South.'

'And "Heaton" is?'

'A suburb of Newcastle.'

'Hello,' said Jeremy, 'I take it you have a problem?'

'Tony Adder is intimidating me.'

'In what way?'

'He stole the keys to my front door.'

'Change the locks.'

'I have. He has bugged my phone and made sure I know about it.'

'Has he indeed?'

'He is also blackmailing me and my niece Joan, who, as I'm sure you know, works for Special Branch.'

'How is he blackmailing you and your niece?'

'Do you not know?'

The ensuing silence made Isa certain she'd asked him a question he did not want to answer. Posh boys were never lost for words.

The kiosk was hot, stuffy and cob-webby. Her hat brushed dirt off its sides. The mottled mirror above the phone made her look as if she had a skin disease. From biting her lower lip she'd smudged her lipstick.

'Sorry about that,' said Jeremy, at last. 'I had to remove a fly from my glass eye. Glass eyes attract the little blighters like fly paper. I still use it. Fly paper, I mean. My people tell me I'm old fashioned. I

113

tell them, it works. Now, about your question … for the mo I must leave it unanswered.'

'You sounded like Desmond when you said "mo". One of the derring-do's speech characteristics.'

'Was it, indeed? That was careless.'

'In what way?'

'All will be revealed, Ms Weddle. In time, all will be revealed.'

'Do you know Desmond? '

'We were at school together. Desmond and I are old friends.'

'Surprise! Surprise! Which comprehensive?'

'I don't think so, Ms Weddle. I don't think so. At the mo … Ha! Ha! At the moment, you are collateral damage.'

'I am disposable. Like an old tank used for target practice. After all my years of service, am I to end up with a bullet in the back of my head? Thank you, Isa. As you are no longer of use, piss off and join the angels. Bye! Bye!'

'Tut! Tut! Most definitely not. You have my word on that. You will come out of this smelling of roses.'

'What about the carpet in my lounge?'

'Please explain.'

For better or for worse she told him about the assassination, or killing, or accidental murder, or whatever you wanted to call it, of Tobias.

'So,' he said, when she'd finished, 'you think Tobias is dead?'

'I don't think he is dead. I know he is.'

'Quite! Just so! Have you met the 'plumbers'?'

'Bryan and Ted?'

'You know their names, do you?'

'They are 'TA's' stooges.'

'For the sake of the greater plan, Ms Weddle, you must assume that they are, indeed … as you so eloquently put it … 'TA's' stooges.'

'You are playing your cards close to your chest, Jeremy. You'd make one hell of a poker player.'

'I don't play poker. That is for rich Americans. Bridge is my game. It is best I keep certain things privy to myself.'

'Knowledge is power.'

'That is true. I am, however, not a politician hoarding power for personal advancement. Believe me, it is best, for the mo ... for the moment, you know nothing of ... how shall I put it? Of what is going on backstage.'

'In your opinion.'

'Yes, Ms Weddle. In my opinion. Believe me when I tell you I have told you no lies. I have been as honest with you as I deem national security allows.'

'But you have been less than forthright.'

'I ask you to remember, why?'

'To catch a spy with his trousers down.'

'I know what you mean. Of course, I do. But, to take what you have said literally. 'TA' would have been easier to find evidence against if he had been into questionable sexual practices. He buys his Impressionist paintings by proxy. I think it would be difficult to have sex by proxy. Though, I'm sure someone has. Do you not agree?'

'It is not something I lie awake at night thinking about.'

'Unlike your mutilated carpet?'

'I hope MI5 will pay for a replacement.'

'I will make a note. You will be reimbursed. I give you my word.'

'Wait, I have to put more money into the telephone.'

'You have change?'

'I came prepared–' pushing an assortment of coins into the slot marked 'Coins'. 'What do you want me to do?'

'Nothing.'

'Nothing?'

'Take your dog for a walk and keep your eyes open.'

''TA' doesn't want me reporting to London any of the comings and goings I see at number thirty-nine.'

'Do as he says. I have other ways of knowing what is going on.'

'And the vodka salesman?'

'What about him?'

'When is he arriving?'

'You will be told.'

'How? Carrier pigeon?'

'I had thought of that.'

'You are joking?'

'Of course. How and when you will be advised of the vodka salesman's arrival will depend upon circumstances. I can tell you now he is not now flying into Newcastle. Moscow likes to change their agents' schedules. It keeps me and my team on our toes. He will be flying into Heathrow. More than that, I cannot tell you. Believe me, I do understand your desire to know everything that is going on but ... you of all people know how we spies do business ... no one must be told more than they need to know. I fear you do not trust me.'

'Not one hundred per cent.'

'Was I not right to advise you to contact me on a public telephone, because I feared ... rightly as it has turned out ... that yours might be compromised?'

'You were.'

'I am not Iago, Ms Weddle. I am what I say I am.'

'I can hear you saying that to all your agents.'

'My agents have no choice but to trust me. I do my best not to let them down but, sometimes ... as my distant relative, Harold Macmillan, is famous for saying ... "Events, dear boy! Events!" In our long careers in the spying game we have both survived the unexpected. The best laid plans of mice and men and all that.'

'The forgotten open window that gives the burglar access as if he'd been given a key to the front door.'

'Quite. Just so. What's that banging?'

'An old lady with a walking stick wants to use the phone. I have been on a long time. I'd better go before she breaks the door down.

Goodbye.'

'Au revoir.'

Outside the kiosk Isa adjusted her straw hat and checked her trouser suit for cobwebs.

'I know you,' said the old woman.

'Do you?' said Isa.

'Yes, I do. You're the woman with the big dog. Looks a bit like a wolf. I live in your street.'

'Do you?'

'Yes, I do. Right at the top. That's how you don't know me. But, I know you. I'm coming to the street party. Look!–' showing Isa the contents of a shopping bag. 'I've bought a flag. It's fancy dress, isn't it?'

'That's right.'

'I'm coming as Britannia. I love the royal family. When the Queen got married, I camped out all night on the Mall. It was wonderful. She gave me a wave, you know.'

'Do you not wish to use the phone?'

'No, why should I?'

'You were banging on the door with your stick.'

'That's because I recognised you and wanted to show you my flag. What are you going as? The fancy dress?'

'I've not decided.'

'There's not much time. Don't you dare go as Britannia, mind? I'm Britannia and I don't want anybody stealing my thunder. You wouldn't know a shop that sells plastic forks, would you?'

'Cutlery will be provided for those sitting down for the afternoon tea.'

'And a pastry fork for the Victoria sandwich cake?'

'Of course.'

'Union Jack serviettes would be nice. When I said "forks", my dear, I did not mean cutlery. I meant the fork Britannia holds. A shield in one hand. A fork in the other. I do hope I will be strong enough to hold a shield if I am holding a fork. I only have two hands and I will need one for my walking stick.'

'I think what you are looking to buy is called a trident. The "fork" is called a trident.'

'Don't you think I don't know that? I like to call it a "fork" because that is what it looks like. A big fork.'

'What about a garden fork?'

'Too many prongs and too heavy. I'm old you see. No strength in my arms. What I'm after is a lightweight plastic fork. By the way, what's your name?'

'Isa.'

'Isa?'

'Short for Isabel.'

'Is a bell necessary on a bike? I like a joke. I'm Mary.'

'Hello, Mary.'

'Let me give you a piece of advice. You are not married, are you? I've never seen you with a man. If you want to catch a man, make sure your lipstick isn't smudged. Men don't mind smudging your lipstick when they are kissing you but, before they kiss you … they like your lips looking like roses. Britannia's hat is the problem.'

'Is it?'

'Kept me awake three nights until I solved it. The full moon helped. I'm going to put a colander on my head. Its holes are just the job for elastic. For the chin strap. I don't want it falling off when I'm dancing. That would make me look silly. Britannia should look dignified. You'd make a good Britannia. When I see you in the street, I always think you look regal.'

'Thank you.'

'The smudged lipstick spoils the image, but, that can be put right, can't it? I'll bet you are true blue. Like me. I've heard rumours there are one or two socialists in Chillingham Grove. I'm not happy about that. Mrs Thatcher will sort the country out. I think she's wonderful. It's about time we had a woman in charge. Where's your dog? I've never seen you without your dog.'

'At home.'

'I like geckos. If I had my way, I'd put a picture of a gecko on the Union Jack. Do you think putting a gecko on the Union Jack's a good idea?'

'Mary,' said Isa, 'please excuse me. Chippy will be missing me.'

'Chippy?'

'My dog. The wolf. He dislikes me leaving him.'

'A gecko wouldn't.'

'You can't take a gecko for a walk like a dog.'

'You can. You can get gecko leads. You shouldn't take them out for a walk when it's cold but, in the summer, you can.'

'Perhaps a shop selling gecko leads might also sell forks. Could be worth a try. Now, if you'll excuse me, I must fly. See you at the street party.'

'Look out for Britannia.'

****

Isa walked home. Northumberland Street was busy. Everywhere there were poster-sized photographs of Charles and Di. Newcastle city council had wrapped pythons of red, white and blue bunting around lampposts.

Looking at a dress in a shop window, Isa did not see the dress; she saw Jeremy; heard Jeremy; saw him remove his glass eye and clean it the way a spectacle wearer removes his spectacles to give them a good polish. Inside her head their telephone conversation bounced and spun like a ball, looking for a number on a roulette wheel. He'd kept a lot back.

A man with one eye seeking revenge on the man who was more than likely responsible for its loss was a man on a mission. If it was proved beyond doubt that 'TA's treachery had been responsible for the death of Yuri, would she too be on a mission? She'd loved Yuri.

119

Whoever was responsible for his death had ruined her life.

How much did Jeremy know about the murder of Tobias? What had he said? If only she'd been able to tape record the phone call.

In a shop doorway she took out her compact. She removed the smudge that silly old woman had brought to her notice. It was while doing this she remembered she'd forgotten to post the letter she'd written to Lucy. Her conversation with Jeremy and Mary had made her forget all about it.

Almost home, she went into her local post office. The one Beatrice had reminded her about.

An overweight, thirty-something woman, on a swivel stool behind a glass screen, weighed the letter and told Isa how much. Isa thought it expensive, but paid up.

When the counter assistant, swivelling on her stool like a weather vane in gusts of wind, sailed the air-mail letter in the general direction of a mail bag hooked to an iron ring and missed, Isa said: 'Do you mind if I wait until I see you pick my letter up and put it in the post bag? I don't want it getting lost.'

'First time I've missed today,' said the overweight, thirty-something woman behind the glass screen, still swivelling like a weather vane on her stool. 'It's because I'm thinking of my boyfriend. Love makes me spin–' this time doing a complete circle on her stool, like a weather vane unscrewing itself. 'It's Jamie what makes me make errors. Jamie's my boyfriend. He's lovely. At least I think he is. He's got big lugs, like Prince Charles. My best friend, Maureen, doesn't like him. I think she's jealous because when I'm going out with Jamie, I'm not going out with her.'

'My letter please. Off the floor and into the bag if you don't mind.'

'No prob.'

Next door to the post office was the newsagent's shop at which, every day, Isa bought her Daily Telegraph. A sandwich board on its forecourt held a poster-sized photograph of Charles and Lady Di. The shop's front was a blaze of red, white and blue bunting. Isa had heard the expression: 'Deck the hall with boughs of holly' but never: 'Deck the newsagent's with red, white and blue bunting.'

Drifting out from a loudspeaker inside the shop – its door was wedged open – Isa heard Mendelssohn's Wedding March. The music made her want to cry.

Back home, Chippy was, as usual, thrilled to see her. Number thirty-nine looked empty. No sign of the 'plumbers'. What bugs had they planted? The street looked urban and sleepy; it looked the way Pearl Harbor must have looked in the days before it was attacked by Japan.

Chapter 15

The next day Isa received a most pleasant surprise.

'Donald,' said the young man at the door. He'd blue eyes like Paul Newman and a dimple in his chin. '"Jesmond Carpets". My boss says you want a carpet fitted. Front room. No expense to be spared. It's all been paid for by a gentleman called–' looking at his clipboard– 'Jeremy.'

'Come in,' said Isa.

From the range of samples he showed her she found one she liked. She'd seen him around. "Jesmond Carpets" was close to the newsagent's.

'Our order book is full,' said Donald. 'I suppose everyone wants their home looking its best for the royal wedding. Your carpet will be fitted tomorrow. How you've jumped the queue, I don't know. This Jeremy ... got "pull", has he?'

Isa smiled.

'You don't have to say anything. I can see I've hit the nail on the head. See you tomorrow. I'll be here early.'

'I'll have the kettle on.'

'Tea. Three sugars. That dog of yours looks like a wolf.'

Jeremy was letting her know he was a man who kept his word. A man who could be trusted. It made her feel coddled. Living alone, she missed having someone to make her a cup of tea.

****

Isa likened the approach of the royal wedding to the many parachute jumps she'd done. You jump out of the aeroplane. At first the ground below you looks like a map. It doesn't change much. Then, suddenly, it's charging up at you.

After all the SPC meetings the royal wedding was days away. In less than a week Prince Charles and Lady Diana would be man and wife. And good luck to them. She and Yuri would never be husband and wife.

There were times when she felt Yuri's loss as a physical pain.

Before going to bed that night, she stood at her front room window and checked out number thirty-nine, the way a nurse on night shift checks a comatose patient to see if he is still breathing. No lights shone from its windows. An empty house. A safe house for people in fear of their lives. A safe house for a traitor who thought it a safe place from which to sell his country's secrets.

When would Jeremy tell her the vodka salesman was arriving? In his plan she was a walk-on part. A spear carrier. She wasn't happy about that.

****

The next day, Donald, as good as his word, arrived with her carpet.

He rang her doorbell at eight am.

'You look tired,' she told him. 'I'll put the kettle on. Tea with three sugars?'

'Yes, please. I need the sugar. I'm not surprised I look knackered. I've been up all night. I've had to drive to Kidderminster, to get your carpet. My boss told me your job was top priority ... "Think you're working for the queen," he told me. "Chillingham Grove's posh," I told him, "but, it ain't Windsor Castle." Now, if you don't mind, your majesty, I'll lay the carpet before I fall down. And keep the wolf

THE LADY WITH THE WOLF

out of my way. He doesn't bite, does he? What do you feed him on?'

'Postmen.'

'A joke?'

'An attempt.'

'Very funny. How does he feel about carpet fitters?'

'Loves them.'

'I'll bet. Nice doggy. Now, if you don't mind, I'll press on.'

****

Isa was in her kitchen making red pepper and lime soup when Donald poked in his head and said: 'There you are, ma'am. All finished.'

'"Ma'am"?' said Isa.

'You are the queen, aren't you?'

'A joke?'

'An attempt.'

'Very funny.'

'Someone once told me if I ever got tired of laying carpets, I should try the stage. Stand-up comedian.'

'Did you believe them?'

'No.'

'Very wise.'

'Here, this is what I found under the carpet–' dumping a rubber bone – one of Chippy's toys which had been missing for months – and a black box the size of a matchbox, down onto the kitchen table– 'your dog's been hiding things.'

'Has he?'

'See for yourself. I'm off to bed. This bloke, Jeremy … he has a lot of "pull". I've never known my boss pull out so many stops for a rush job. Must have cost your pal a bob or two. Thanks for the tea.'

****

The black box had to be a bug. She might not be familiar with the latest technology available to MI5, but she knew a bug when she saw one. Its aerial – a five-inch length of plastic-coated wire – made it look like a mouse. She yanked this out with the animal rage of an infantryman removing his bayonet from the abdomen of an enemy.

What was its range? For how long was it able to keep transmitting before its battery died? What secrets had it already transmitted to its receiver? Were there any other bugs in her home? To find out she let Chippy smell the 'mouse'.

'Search!' she told the dog.

Tail wagging, happy to be sent on a mission at the end of which he knew he'd be given a treat, Chippy, escorted by the 'boss', sniff-investigated every room and cupboard in the house. Would he find a matching scent? When he did not, Isa told him: 'You have put my mind at rest. Here, my faithful friend.'

The Cumberland sausage the 'boss' gave him made Chippy feel the way a PAYE employee feels when, on opening her pay packet, she finds she has been given a bonus.

The Cumberland sausage placated Chippy, but to assuage her anger at knowing MI5 had violated her private space – had made her home feel dirty – first by tapping her phone, now, with a 'mouse' bug – Isa needed fresh air. If she didn't feel the sun on her face and a breeze ruffling its fingers through her hair, as Yuri had used to do, she'd smash plates and scream four letter words.

'How dare they! How dare they!' she kept telling herself.

****

To vent her anger, she took Chippy for a walk.

A good walk for a dog is when the dog, on returning home, wants to lie down and go to sleep. When Isa returned home from her 'venting-walk', that's how she wanted to feel; weary but not exhausted; tired but not so tired she couldn't make herself a cup of tea. Most important of all, she was hoping the walk would put an ice pack on the bruise of her angst.

It was years since she'd walked so fast. The pace, though, suited Chippy just fine.

Quite involuntarily she found herself subvocalizing the mantra: How dare they! How dare they!

Rage, anger and a sense of being let down by those in power had put a spring in her step. They had given the worm a backbone. Though, in truth, it must be said, Isa had never, ever, felt like an invertebrate.

Walking past the newsagent's she wanted to tear down its bunting. His patriotism was commercial. She had killed for her country.

'How dare they! How dare they!'

She peered into the window of a bespoke tailor's. Alfredo made her trouser suits. He'd some gorgeous-looking summer jackets on display. If she went in and bought one, would it make her feel better?

'How dare they! How dare they!'

By default she found herself circumnavigating, at the speed of a quick march, the spirogyra-infested lake of the nearby Exhibition Park.

At its green edge, three boys, aged about nine, were fishing the green stuff out with nets on wire hoops stuck into bamboo canes. She saw them look at Chippy.

'Gan on, ask her,' said one of the boys, egging-on one of his pals to do the dirty work.

In the Lebanon, she thought, they'd be looking after goats.

'Mrs, is your dog a wolf?'

Children were so unlike spies. They came straight out with what they wanted to say.

'My dog is a cross between a husky and an Alsatian,' she explained.

'My aunty Doris has a dachshund,' said another of the boys. 'I take it for walks. She gives me twenty pence a walk. I'm saving up for a goldfish.'

'Is he a good dog?'

'Would he protect you if you were attacked?'

'Chippy! Guard!'

On cue, Chippy barked and snarled.

Like monkeys climbing a tree to get out of the way of a hungry leopard, the boys shimmied up a nearby children's climbing frame.

'It's a wolf! It's a wolf!' they shouted, making a drama out of the situation the way a desk-bound MI5 operative who'd never fired a Glock in anger might, out of boredom, make a drama out of a burst tea bag.

The last boy to reach the sanctuary was told by his mates: 'Jack's shit his pants. Shitty pants! Jack's a shitty pants.'

Isa wondered if Jack really had shit his pants. In the Lebanon she'd seen that happen to adults. When you were on a life and death assignment, you always packed spare knickers.

****

Her walk was successful in helping her control her anger at being the target of an MI5 bugging operation but only to the extent that if she'd been an electric hot plate a red 'H' would have been flashing to indicate that though it was switched off, it was still hot.

Back in Chillingham Grove she saw more and more houses decorated with red, white and blue bunting.

Union Jacks the size of tablecloths hung from the front windows of Pratt, the master butcher's house. In the middle of his lawn, a Union Jack fluttered from a flagpole. At his front gate a sandwich board advertised: 'Pratt's famous Royal Wedding Burger. Buy three get one free.'

Further off down the street she saw a gypsy caravan. One of those shaped like a barrel and painted all the colours of the rainbow.

A man was walking beside it, pushing what looked like a wheelbarrow. A black Labrador sitting very alert on the driver's box made it look as if the caravan was being driven by a dog.

When the gypsy put down his wheelbarrow and disappeared up a front path, the horse stopped. When the gypsy came out, picked up his wheelbarrow and trundled it to the next house, the horse followed him.

When she passed the caravan, the gypsy was up a drive, knocking on a door.

Close to, she saw the wheelbarrow was in fact a portable grinding wheel. The last time she'd seen one like that had been in an Egyptian souk. A gypsy who sharpened knives. At least he wasn't selling double glazing. If he knocked on her door she'd humour him by seeing if he spoke Romany. She knew a few phrases, one of which was: 'Your horse has haemorrhoids'.

Passing close to the caravan she saw that what had looked like a horsewhip from a distance was in fact a radio aerial. Another hint that the gypsy might not be what he seemed was the Labrador's cushion. The dog was sitting on a scattered pile of Spectator magazines.

In her time Isa had heard of some shocking cases of disguises failing because of cultural ignorance. Take the case of the posh boy disguised as a pleb. Or so he thought.

Trailing a member of the IRA, he'd sat on the beach at Scarborough wearing a bespoke Panama hat instead of the improvised working-class man's sunhat made from a pocket handkerchief knotted at four corners.

The silly fellow had thought Scarborough beach, on a Bank Holiday Monday, was Henley-on-Thames during regatta week. His sense of entitlement cost him his life. On the credit side it earned him a posthumous OBE. On the debit side it cost the Scarborough rate payers a small fortune. The IRA man who murdered him put the corpse in a sewer. As a piece of grit is the starting point for a pearl, the posh boy became the starting point for a fat-berg.

Why would a gypsy trying to earn a living by sharpening knives own a pile of 'Spectator' magazines? 'Horse and Hound'? Possibly. 'Fur and Feather'? Maybe. The 'Spectator'? No! How many gypsy caravans had radio aerials?

Back at home she watched him from her front room window. Would he knock on her door? She was certain that he would. And, when he did, she was certain he would not be asking her if she had knives she wanted sharpening.

He certainly looked like a gypsy. Perhaps too much like one. A stereotype, rather than the real thing.

He marched up her drive like a soldier on parade. The pheasant feather in his trilby was OTT; like a bishop sticking an 'I BELIEVE IN GOD' fridge magnet in front of the cross on his mitre.

She opened the door before he rang.

'Hello, Jeremy, would you like a cup of tea?'

That Ms Weddle had seen through his disguise, shocked Jeremy. To give himself time to get over his disappointment, he took out his glass eye. His world was in danger of falling apart. Last week his London club had run out of steak and kidney pud. Never happened before. One knew there was a first time for everything. But, all the same. Worse. One couldn't blame the socialists. Margaret Thatcher was Prime Minister. The Tories were in the driving seat.

'I say … how'd you suss me?'

'The horse whip is a radio aerial. Your dog is sitting on a pile of "Spectator" magazines. Your trilby may look old and battered but that is a posh boy's trilby. You bought it from the shop in London where MI6 paid for me to be fitted out with a bespoke shoulder holster. Your dog is not a gypsy's dog. It is a gun dog. Your shoes are hand-made.'

'Clearly, all your knives are sharp, Ms Weddle.'

'But you will sharpen some anyway in case anyone is watching. You have to have a reason for talking to me while you tell me, face-to-face, what it is you have come to tell me. As the fox said to the chicken when he knocked on her front door … "My visit is not social".'

'Aesop?'

'No. I just made it up. A knife to sharpen and a cup of tea, I think?'

'Business first. 'TA' has told MI5 Leo will be arriving on the twenty-eighth. At the moment he is in the Russian embassy in London. Probably drinking too much of what he is supposed to be selling. Can't stand the stuff, myself. Whisky's my tipple.'

'Is that a hint?'

'Very kind, I'm sure. Being under the influence while in charge of a horse-drawn vehicle wouldn't look good on my CV. Do you like the horse? It is from her majesty's Windsor stables.'

'Really?'

'I kid you not–' giving the horse a glance the way a spiv looks with pride at a new pair of shoes, then– 'Leo will be driving north in a red Volvo estate. Big car. Lots of room for his samples. Diplomatic number plate. The Russians are making no bones about letting us know he is more than a vodka salesman. It makes 'TA' seem to be a good and faithful agent.'

'But you still don't think he is?'

'Innocent until proven guilty but the facts are against him.'

'In case anyone is watching us chatting like old friends, I will go and get you a knife to sharpen.'

'If I may, I will bring my wheelbarrow into your drive.'

'Of course. What woman would dare come between a gypsy and his grinding stone?'

'Quite!'

'Would your horse like a carrot and your dog a bowl of water?'

'Esmeralda has a nose bag and Lola will have a bowl of water. Thank you. Your concern for animals tells me you would have made someone a wonderful wife.'

'Yourself?'

'Me? I'm a confirmed bachelor.'

'I wasn't proposing, Jeremy, I was asking if you would like a drink.'

'Tea, with a slice of lemon, Ms Weddle, would be very nice.'

'I think I have lemons–' then, out of the blue, looking at him the way a wicket keeper looks at the setting sun wondering if light should stop play: 'Jeremy, I find your glass eye erotic.'

The comment was below the belt. It was off limits. It made Jeremy jerk back his head as a baker does when he opens the door of a hot oven and receives, full in the face, a blast of too hot air.

To further discomfort him – Isa took a wicked pleasure in taking men out of their comfort zone – she licked a finger and wiping its wetness down one of his sunburnt cheeks, said: 'Checking your sunburn is real and not that sprayed-on stuff you buy at the chemist's. Do forgive my fussing. Sometimes playing the mother hen appeals to me. I will get your lemon tea. I will have the same. It will remind me of the Lebanon. In those days we all drank lemon tea. Why, I wonder, do workmen love sweet tea? Three heaped teaspoons of sugar seems to be the norm. That was Donald's fix. The carpet fitter. By the way, thank you for the carpet. Such a pity it would be inappropriate for you to come in and see it.'

'I don't want to blow my cover–' fiddling with a brass earring the size of a hoop.

'Jeremy, a ridiculous question but … you are up to sharpening knives? I mean, you can do it?'

'Ms Weddle, the British Secret Service does not disguise an agent as a sharpener of knives without sending him on a training course. Each course has a bespoke training module. Course leaders try to think of everything. We all know what happened to the agent at Scarborough. If Calais was incised into the heart of Queen Elizabeth the first, the story of the agent who wore a Panama hat on Scarborough beach is burned into the psyche of every public schoolboy who joins the British Secret Service. Ms Weddle, do, pray, for the benefit of prying eyes, bring out a knife for me to sharpen. It is not good for the health of my disguise for us to be seen to be familiar. While you pop inside for a knife, I will put a nosebag on Esmeralda, and give Lola a treat.'

'Shall I bring out my tongue to sharpen?'

'That part of your anatomy, Ms Weddle, is already sharp enough. Indeed, I would say … attach it to a syringe and it would make an excellent hypodermic needle.'

'That's a very pointed comment.'

'Touché, Ms Weddle.'

'I will go and get a knife for you to sharpen. I like putting men's noses to the grindstone.'

'I refuse to bite. You are, Ms Weddle, a verbal duellist.'

'I also make lemon tea.'

'Go on, then. Off, you go. Know your place, woman.'

'Don't be cheeky! I don't know why, Jeremy, but I like you. You are like the grill in my oven. It takes a lot of warming up but, when it gets going, it does everything the brochure promised.'

'Ms Weddle, a knife for me to sharpen. We have work to do. Do you know how much it is costing MI5 per day to hire a gypsy caravan? The firm charges by the hour. They are worse than lawyers.'

'Lucky me there was enough left in the kitty to pay for my carpet.'

****

She brought out a carving knife for him to sharpen. Not as big as a sabre, but curved like one. A family heirloom. Blunt. Years ago used by her father to carve the Sunday roast.

On a tray she brought out two mugs of tea and the bug found by Donald when he'd been laying her new carpet. She'd used the bug as a paperweight to stop the note she'd written for Jeremy, flying off down the street and ending up goodness only knew where. Gardens in Chillingam Grove were like African elephants; they had big ears. Who knew who might be listening behind the beech hedge?

Taking his mug of tea off the tray, Jeremy read: 'Is this what I think it is? I have removed its aerial. Please write your reply. Gardens in Chillingham Grove have EARS!'

Using the pencil provided, Jeremy wrote: 'Standard KGB bug. Dated technology. You have stopped it transmitting. Well done. May I have another slice of lemon in my tea, PLEASE?'

These upper class toffs were all the same. Within five minutes of you letting them put their foot in your door, they had you running around after them as if you were their nanny and they were still in nappies.

Returning with a slice of lemon, held in tongs, it seemed to Isa, Jeremy's enthusiasm for playing the role of a gypsy knife sharpener knew no bounds. When sparks flew off the knife he was sharpening, he exclaimed: 'Bejeebers!'

The bug had disappeared off the tray; confiscated, she assumed, by Jeremy. No doubt he would hand it over to Military Intelligence. Spoils of war. A boffin would take it apart. Put it under a microscope. Find out how it had been put together. Where it had been made. The frequency on which it transmitted. Its range. Its sensitivity. All would be measured and evaluated. The findings put on record for future use.

She wanted to have a proper conversation with him. As a legitimate reason for allowing him into her home, she said, in a voice loud enough for an eavesdropper to hear – anyone might be hiding behind the beech hedge: 'Yes, you may use the facilities.'

'Thank you, lady,' said Jeremy, saluting her by raising his trilby, 'but I have an Elsan in my caravan.'

Did the chump not know her question had been rhetorical? A way of getting him into her house so she could have a proper conversation with him without the neighbours talking?

'Bejeebers!' he said, handing her the knife he'd sharpened. 'The sparks is flying today. And every spark a Tipperary fairy. That'll be an English pound, lady.'

'I'll get my purse,' said Isa, continuing the charade. A good spy had to be a good actor. If you were not a good actor you could not be a good spy.

When she came out to pay, she found Jeremy ready for the off. Like a lot of modern spies, he probably had a lot of paperwork to do. There he was, sitting, as aloof from reality as a bishop in a pulpit, high up, very regal, with Lola beside him, on the driver's box. His grinding wheel was hanging off the back of the caravan. It would be pulled along like a trailer.

Esmeralda was stamping her hooves. She wanted to be off. It was as if she'd read Jeremy's mind and with her hooves was impersonating pistons being revved, in a petrol engine, by an impatient car driver stuck at traffic lights.

Lola and Chippy were looking at each other the way two dukes look at each other when they are wondering if they are sharing the same mistress.

When Isa paid him, he whispered to her (ignoring the fact overfamiliarity with a client would be giving the game away) 'Tom the tinker from Tipperary. I've given a lot of thought, don't you know, to the fellow's character. I played him as a practical fellow with just a hint of the fortune teller about him. Like a dash of Tabasco sauce with scrambled eggs. I'd give myself ten out of ten.'

'Would you?'

'Yes, dash it, I would. Wouldn't you?'

'No, I would not. I think you'd best trot off. We shouldn't be seen talking like this. People will assume we are familiars. I've spent years living in this street, cultivating the image of a respectable spinster.

Respectable spinsters do not chinwag with gypsies.'

'Latcho drom,' said Jeremy. 'That, by the by, is Romany for pip-toodle.'

'I know what it means. You are forgetting, Jeremy, I speak many languages.'

Chapter 16

As a public house, it didn't know what to make of itself. It was not in the town. It was not in the country. It existed in a kind of no-man's land. Its closest neighbours were a sewage works and a cemetery.

The cemetery brought in a good trade in funeral teas. Mourners didn't feel so bad when they saw the dismal surroundings the deceased was leaving behind.

The employees of the nearby sewage works also kept it commercially viable. It was where these essential workers celebrated birthdays, promotions, retirements and Christmas.

Its beer garden was a holly bush in a barrel. Enthusiasm for the royal wedding was shown by a Union Jack flag hanging from a clothesline alongside a bra and a jock strap.

Its customers that afternoon were a handful of topers with red noses and sunken cheeks. They'd been in since opening time and would leave at closing time. Their intoxication coming not from swigging, but from sipping. As if their pints were saline drips.

Isa arrived at the 'Sun Inn' – called by locals, the 'Sediment' or, 'Sed' – without, Chippy. The public house was not dog-friendly.

Entering, she spotted Joan at a corner table facing the door. A good seat for a spy. Tucked away in deep shade, she could see who was coming in before they saw her. No one could shoot her in the back. On the other hand, goodness only knew what she might catch from the cream and plum patterned flock paper on the wall behind her. It looked as if it had ringworm.

Joan was with her mother and father. This took Isa by surprise. Had Joan invited them, or had they invited themselves? By the look on Joan's face? Probably the latter. Did they know their daughter was a murderer? If she'd told them about number thirty-nine she could be had up for treason. The official secrets act was very clear about what and to whom one could and should share information. 'Blabbings' were like the fart a courtier let rip in the presence of Queen Elizabeth the first. Never forgotten by those in power.

'You know why we are here?' said Joan's stepfather, Ivan.

'To buy me a drink,' said Isa.

'That'll be the day. With all your money.'

'And brains,' said Dorothy.

'Mam!' expostulated Joan. 'Don't be so horrid to Aunt Isa. She is your sister. Sisters should love each other. I wish I had a sister. Someone with whom I could chew over my worries.'

'You can talk to your mam and me,' said Ivan. 'We are here to look after your interests.' To Isa: 'Where you going?'

'To buy myself a drink.'

'I'll get you one,' said Ivan, 'you know I was only joking.'

'She's in the huff, Ivan,' said Dorothy, 'you and your little jokes. Isa, let Ivan buy you a drink.'

'I'll buy you a drink, Aunt Isa,' said Joan. 'Come to the bar with me and tell me want you want.'

At the bar Joan ordered her aunt an orange juice.

'Put it on my tab, Joe,' she told the barman. 'Loos, Aunt Isa. We need to talk.'

The ladies' toilets were down a twisting flight of stairs. So far underground that during the Second World War they'd been used as air raid shelters.

'It's a man's pub,' said Joan. 'The Gents is next to the bar. Very convenient.'

'I know,' said Isa. 'Your dad's sewage works used to be an iron foundry. Iron workers drink a lot. Bass was their tipple.'

'And piss a lot. God, by the time I get back upstairs I'll need to come back down again. The 'Sed' is not a pub for women with weak bladders.'

The loo was cold and clean like a mortuary. Joan checked they were alone by kicking open each closet the way FBI agents do in B movies.

'Sorry about mam and dad being here,' she said, as soon as she knew they were alone and free to talk. 'It's Dad. He's very possessive. He thinks I need looking after. He forgets I'm twenty-two. After the incident with Tobias Lacy, they knew I was upset about something. I couldn't hide my feelings. Did I really kill someone, Aunt Isa?'

'I'm afraid you did, Joan. I'm afraid you did. You are not a murderer. It was an accident. If anyone is to blame it is 'TA'.'

'I know. I know. I keep telling myself that.'

'How much have you told your mam and dad?'

'They know nothing. I've not broken the Official Secrets Act, Aunt Isa. I'd never do that.'

'Then, why are they here?'

'They know I'm upset about something. Dad keeps asking me if I'm pregnant. I've been doing a lot of crying, you see. But, I'm alright. I'm not having a nervous breakdown or anything like that. When they knew I was coming to meet you, well, there was no stopping them. Dad wouldn't let me have my car keys until Mum was in the back seat and he was sat beside me in the front. You know what he's like. "Drive," he said, "there's something fishy going on and I want to know what it is." I pay Dad rent. You know he owns the flat in which I live. You know what he's like with money. He thinks I might chuck in my job. If I do that I won't be able to pay him rent. He's got it into his head that you have something to do with what's going on.'

'I thought step-fathers were only ogres in fairy stories.'

'He has Mam under his thumb. He won't let her buy anything new. Everything has to be a bargain. Bought at the sales.'

'So,' said Isa, 'the only reason your dad is here is because he thinks he might be going to lose rent money?'

'Yes.'

'Neither he nor your mam have an inkling that number thirty-nine is a safe house?'

'None whatsoever.'

Isa told Joan about her stolen keys. About her tapped telephone. About the bug, Donald, the carpet fitter, had found.

'Tony Adder is blackmailing you, Joan, and intimidating me. At least he thinks he is. What is he expecting you to do regarding number thirty-nine?'

'I'm not supposed to tell you this, Aunt Isa, but I know you are on my side. I need all the help I can get. I don't have any allies in the service. I am the new girl on the team. The one sent out to buy the bacon sandwiches and make the tea. In a few days' time a Russian vodka salesman will be moving into number thirty-nine. I am to be his au pair. He is a KGB agent, Aunt Isa. He is not here to sell vodka. Mr Adder says he is a double agent and may be going to defect. You don't look too surprised.'

'Joan,' said Isa, 'I have been in the spying game ever since I left Cambridge. Nothing surprises or shocks me.'

The fact that Joan had questioned her reaction made Isa sympathise with Jeremy's philosophy. In the spying game no one should know more than they needed to know. If she was to tell her niece about Jeremy, that she already knew about the vodka salesman, Joan, when confronting 'TA' would have to put on an act. The 'Adder' was an old hand at the spying game. His ability to detect a lie was second to none. Under his swagger and bluster, he'd a sensitive antenna.

'Mr Adder says I am to keep number thirty-nine nice and tidy. I am, in Mr Adder's words, Aunt Isa, "to oblige the Russian's every whim and fancy". If I don't, he will lift the cover-up on my killing Mr Lacy. I will go to jail for manslaughter.'

'Would that not be better than becoming a prostitute?'

'Mr Adder didn't say he expected me to go to bed with the Russian.'

'Not in so many words.'

'Am I naïve, Aunt Isa?'

'Yes, I'm afraid you are. Do you know when this Russian is expected to arrive?'

Would her niece confirm Jeremy's version of events? She did.

'So,' said Isa, 'when the Russian arrives you will be in number thirty-nine, to bid him welcome like a good little babushka with his slippers warming on top of a samovar?'

'No. He will be arriving late. My instructions are to victual the house with coffee and Newcastle Brown Ale. I am to report for cleaning and other duties early the next day.'

'He has a key to number thirty-nine?'

'No. I am to leave a key to the house under a stone in the garden. The stone will be marked with a red star. It is one of the stones in the rockery.'

'What else?'

'He wants me to falsify my log. Remember the service mantra? Don't keep it in your head. Keep it in your log. He wants me to write nothing down about number thirty-nine. Why does he want me to do that, Aunt Isa? Do you know anything I don't know?'

'Why do you ask?'

'I don't know. Intuition, I guess.'

Sounding like a parody of Jeremy, Isa said: 'It is best you do not know certain facts. It is for your own good.'

'Am I a pawn in some kind of game? Is that what you are saying?'

'On a chessboard, Joan, pawns outnumber all the other pieces. Pawns working together can checkmate a king.'

'Do you need to use the facilities?'

'No. For our cover, I think, before we leave we should both flush.'

On their way back up the stairs, Isa told her niece: 'Never forget I am across the road from number thirty-nine. If you ever need sanctuary do not be too proud to knock on my door.'

At the bar Isa picked up her orange juice on the rocks.

'May I join you?' she said, plonking herself down next to her brother-in-law.

'It looks to me like you already have,' said Ivan. 'Joan, get your dad another cup of coffee.'

'What about Mam?'

'You know as well as I do, your mam and I share. Black, no milk.'

'I thought you liked your coffee white, Dorothy,' said Isa.

'She does,' said Ivan, 'but I don't. One coffee, Joan. Black! And hurry up. What I have to say to your Aunt Isa won't take long.'

'Joan,' said Isa, winking, 'off you go. Leave your dad to me.'

'I want to know what's going on,' said Ivan.

'And I want to talk to you about national security,' said Isa.

'Eh?'

'While Joan is at the bar, I will let you into a little secret. You know she works for Special Branch?'

'We know that,' said Dorothy. 'She is not allowed to tell us what she does. Her work is top secret and important like Ivan's is.'

'That's right,' said Isa, 'her work is important.'

'Without my efforts,' said Ivan, 'there would be no clean drinking water.'

'What if a terrorist group was thinking of blowing up the sewage works?'

'The, IRA?' suggested Dorothy.

'Dorothy,' said Ivan, 'shut up. What your sister is telling me, is important.'

'That's all I can tell you,' said Isa.

'How come you know all this and me, her dad, doesn't?'

'She just told me in the loo. I don't mind telling you, I was shocked.'

'Is that why she is upset? I know she is upset about something,' said Dorothy.

'Yes,' said Isa, 'she knows how much the sewage works means to Ivan. Ivan, she is worried in case anything should happen to you. You see, she cares for you.'

'I've always known that,' said Ivan. 'I think I mean as much to her as the sewage works means to me.'

'What I have just told you must not go any further. Please, do not let Joan know I have confided in you. It is at times like this, Ivan, that we must bury our differences. Mum's the word, Ivan.'

'You've not touched your orange juice,' said Ivan, as Isa stood up to go. 'If you don't want it, I'll have it.'

At the bar Isa told Joan, who was waiting there for the bartender to make Ivan's coffee, that she was leaving.

'Has Dad upset you?' said Joan.

'Not at all. He probably thinks I am wonderful. You see, I have made him feel important.'

'You didn't tell him, Aunt Isa, the truth, did you? Break the Official Secrets Act?'

'Don't be silly. I'm a professional. I hinted the IRA might have plans to blow up the sewage works. You, my dear Joan, are now, officially, in an emotional state, not because you killed a fellow human being, but because you are fretting for your step-father. If the IRA blow up the sewage works, he might get hurt. Will I see you tomorrow when you stock up number thirty-nine?'

'I will pop in.'

'By the way, where is Tony Adder? Do you know?'

'I have no idea, Aunt Isa. I am very junior, you know. I take my orders from the local special branch officer. I have heard rumours that he's not very happy. Something to do with Bryan and Ted being taken off his team. They are needed for more important work.'

'Bryan and Ted, being the "plumbers"?'

'You remember them?'

'Of course. Thank you for that information, Joan. See you sometime tomorrow. Bye!'

At the door, before leaving, she blew kisses at Ivan and her sister. To show he understood the situation and the role he was expected to play, Ivan gave Isa a thumbs-up.

****

Driving home, Isa pondered Joan's departmental gossip about the 'plumbers' being taken off 'TA''s team. If it was true, why had they been taken off? Who had authorised it? Was it the start of a policy to cut 'TA' down to size? For whom were the 'plumbers' working? Were they Jeremy's men or, 'TA''s?

Chapter 17

Monday. July 27. At six in the morning, Joan placed a crate of Brown Ale, six bread buns, a pint of milk and two jars of instant coffee on the table in number thirty-nine's kitchen. When she left, she hid the key to open its front door under the stone in the rockery marked with a red star.

She thought it too early to call and see her aunt as she had promised. At that time in the morning, she was sure her aunt would still be in bed.

She knew her aunt Isa worried about her. To let her know she was alright, she popped a note through her aunt's letterbox. Before she was out of the Grove, Isa – woken by Chippy's barking – was reading:

'Dear Aunt Isa,

I did not want to wake you. Early start. I have victualed number thirty-nine. Number thirty-nine's front door key is under the stone marked with a red star. I have to go to Durham University to learn Russian. Mr Adder's idea. No stone is to be left unturned to make the Russian feel at home. When I reminded him that you speak Russian, he said: "Your aunt is not part of the team. She is supernumerary. The sooner we dispense with her old-style voyeurism, the better." I did not think this to be professional but did not say so as he has me under his thumb.

Love, Joan.'

The more Isa thought about it, the more she warmed to Jeremy's instruction of removing the key. It was about time she played a trick or two of her own on 'TA'? 'Stealing my keys, indeed!'

'Letting me know my phone is tapped!'

'How dare he!'

'How dare he!'

'TA' was about to become the U-boat captain who, surfacing to sink an unarmed merchantman, sees too late his prey was hiding guns under tarpaulins.

****

Half an hour later, Isa took Chippy for his morning walk. As if by accident, but of course on purpose, she threw his ball up number thirty-nine's drive.

Unaware that his enthusiasm for chasing thrown balls was being used by the 'boss' to help her entrap a double agent and that, in effect, he was an MI5 employee, ears back – slipstreaming increased his speed – Chippy raced, pell-mell, after it.

Ostensibly to stop her dog damaging plants in the garden, but really to remove the key Joan had planted under the stone marked with a red star, Isa also charged up number thirty-nine's garden path. If anyone asked her what she was doing she would reply: 'I am retrieving my dog.' A good spy always had an answer.

A passer-by might have thought the red star was a growth of lichen that just happened to look like a star.

The key was on a silver ring. It was skewered into the soil by a plastic plant label. On the label, Isa read, not the name of a plant in Latin, but, in Russian: 'The key to our future! Love, Tony'.

'You stealing flowers?'

Harry! In her enthusiasm to get her hands on the key she'd forgotten Harry went Nordic walking before going to work.

'You have to be fit, to sell insurance,' he said, doing high kicks and knee bends between his Nordic poles.

It was every agent's nightmare that a local busybody might, by chance, witness a piece of MI5 skulduggery. Thank goodness Harry was more ego, than nosey parker. His question had been rhetorical. Harry's favourite subject was himself.

In the Lebanon, he might have had to be 'removed'. He was a witness. He'd seen her, in number thirty-nine's drive. An agent never knew when something trivial might be the cause of her downfall. Take the case of the agent who'd died because of a dog's fart. When the agent had averted her head to avoid the smell, an enemy agent had dropped a poison pill into her drink.

'Can't stop,' said Harry. 'Not long now. The street party, I mean. What about you putting up bunting on number thirty-nine? Can't be the only house in the Grove to seem to be not celebrating. It's not compulsory, but we all have to do our bit. I'm doing a new line in dog insurance. Are you interested? Talk about it later. Must be off. Unlike some folk, I'm not retired. I have a schedule.'

Then, he was off, unaware that in a different place and at a different time the British Secret Service, to stop him bearing witness, might have had him assassinated.

****

At home, the smell of her new lounge carpet made Isa want to sneeze. For a while she played with the key to number thirty-nine's front door the way Arabs play with worry beads. Joan had said the Russian would be arriving late. 'Late' was open to multiple interpretations. She could not sit and watch the house all day. She made up her mind to be only seriously on the look-out for the Russian any time late afternoon. In the meantime, she'd take Chippy for another walk. Walking helped her think. Chippy needed to do his ablutions. Where were her poo bags?

With the exception of number thirty-nine, all the houses in the street were flying some kind of red, white and blue bunting. Residents were becoming competitive.

'Fred! Next door has made Union Jack flags out of pillowcases. I'm going to make one out of a sheet.'

A man up a ladder was hanging out triangular Union Jacks. He was called George. Like, Mari's husband he was sea-going. His wife, Elizabeth, was not happy with the way he was hanging the bunting.

'More to the left, George! Wrong way!'

'Port or starboard?'

'George, you are not at sea now. This is Chillingham Grove, not the Dogger Bank.

****

Late in the afternoon, all the while keeping a watchful eye on number thirty-nine, Isa draped red, white and blue bunting over the shrubs and bushes in her own front garden. Her effort at once transforming summer-greenery, not as snow does, into silent white shapes, but into fireworks.

Harry, driving past, on his way home from work, stopped to compliment her.

'Well done! That's the spirit. Red, white and blue. Rule Britannia. Talking of spirit, I could do with a pick-me-up. I've had a hell of a day, Isa. Pet insurance is not all it's cracked up to be. When pets die their owners blame me. I'm not a bloody vet. I'm an insurance man. I offer double indemnity, not immortality. It's not my fault they haven't read clause six. Limited liability and the excess they have to pay. Get yourself across to number thirty-nine and put some red, white and blue on its bushes. You know what's keeping me going?'

'Harry, how should I know? I'm just an unmarried, retired civil servant with no prospects other than being an agony aunt to good people like yourself.'

THE LADY WITH THE WOLF

'Get on with you! You're a deep one, you are, Isa. Sticky toffee pudding. That's what's keeping me going. Jean's making it especially for me. Thinking about it all day. Helped me keep my cool when that wife whose python died was poking me in the chest. People love their pets the way I love whisky. It won't last, you know. Charles and Diana–' tapping the side of his nose– 'insurance man's intuition. Damn, there's Jean. There's my snifter down the drain. She says I drink too much.'

'Do you?'

'No more than Winston Churchill. He had a war to win. I have insurance to sell. My Nordic walking puts back in what the booze takes out. Be a good neighbour. Decorate number thirty-nine. It mustn't look like the girl who never got asked to dance.'

Isa knew what it was like to be left out. She empathised with number thirty-nine. The house was starting to look like a mouldy tangerine in a bowl of fresh fruit.

To show the house it was 'loved', she wrapped red, white and blue bunting round the pole cherry in its garden. The safe house had been part of her life for many years. She was fussing over it the way doting wives adjust their husbands' ties.

When the Russian had not arrived by midnight, she went to bed. If he arrived in the early hours of Tuesday morning, then Jeremy's plan had failed. It would look odd if she took Chippy for a walk at three in the morning and asked the Russian, if he was looking for the key to his front door. 'Silly me! I think my dog might have dug it up.'

Chapter 18

Next morning, peeking through her bedroom curtains, Isa saw a red Volvo estate in number thirty-nine's drive. Diplomatic number plates. For how long had it been there? Had it just arrived? Where was its driver? Time? Just after six.

She dressed in a hurry. No make-up. No hat. She knew she wasn't looking her best. Needs must. What the hell. Opening her front door with Chippy on his lead, she saw Harry, talking to a bear of a man.

'Isa!' shouted Harry, semaphoring her with his Nordic walking poles, 'come and meet Leo. I've told him you speak Russian.'

To be introduced to the Russian by an innocent third party was a bonus. She could not have arranged it better if she had tried.

'This is Leo,' said Harry, 'he's a vodka salesman. He's renting number thirty-nine. He has a problem. He is locked out.'

'I was to find the key to my dacha under a stone marked with a red star,' said Leo, in perfect English. 'I do not need to speak to an English woman who speaks Russian. I need to find the key to open the front door of the house I have paid a lot of roubles to rent. I have found the stone marked with a red star, but not the key. I was told the key would be under a stone marked with a red star.'

'I was telling Leo,' said Harry, 'that your dog was sniffing around in number thirty-nine's garden yesterday. Hello, Chippy. Nice dog! Nice dog! He didn't dig anything up, did he? Nice dog! I don't know why, Isa, but I never quite trust Chippy. Hi! What you doing?'

'Ha! Ha!' boomed the Russian, sounding like the end of Tchaikovsky's 1812 Overture. 'The wolf thinks your pole is a lamppost. Ha! Ha! He is an Alsatian. He pisses on the pole the way the Germans pissed on Mother Russia in the Great War. You have to watch the Germans. If you do not watch them, they will piss all over you.'

'Would you like a cup of tea?' said Isa.

'I want the key to the front door of the house I am paying many roubles to rent. I am thinking, you will be my witness for when I break down the door. You will know I am not a burglar. I have paid rent.'

'I sell insurance,' said Harry. 'Could be tricky about who pays to repair the door.'

'I might be able to help,' said Isa.

'I do not want a cup of tea.'

In fluent Russian, Isa rattled off her prepared story of how Chippy had gone into number thirty-nine's garden to look for his ball and how he had come out with a key on a fob in his mouth.

Harry hadn't a clue what she was rabbiting on about but, by god, it sounded spot on to him.

'Wait there,' she said, in English. 'I will get it for you. A good job I didn't throw it away. It may not be the key you are looking for, but I suppose we must try it. Mustn't we?'

'Found it!' said Isa, returning a few minutes later with the key. 'Found it! Where's Harry?'

'The fitness freak with the ski poles?' said Leo. 'He is off. Keeping the fit.'

'This is the key my dog found–' handing it over– '"Love, Tony", does that mean anything to you? Would that be the right key? See if it fits the lock. Off you go.'

He wasn't used to taking orders. She was not his mother. 'Off you go', indeed! Did she know to whom she was talking? On his way up number thirty-nine's drive he turned round twice to look at her. Each time, she indicated with a shooing gesture that he should get a move-on and try the key. Damn it! He was a 'Hero of the Soviet Union'. Premier Brezhnev himself had told him: 'Your chest, comrade, has more medals than the Lubyanka has cells.' Brezhnev had bad breath. It had been an honour to smell its sourness. It was the bad breath of a great man. 'Off you go!' indeed and 'Shoo!' The woman with the wolf is treating me the way a babushka treats a child.

'Dasvidaniya!' shouted Leo when he found the key opened number thirty-nine's door.

What stopped him disappearing inside, tout suite, was the sight of the woman to whom the woman with the dog was talking. Why was the new woman dressed as if she was living in the reign of Ivan the Terrible? Why was she carrying a shepherd's crook? He'd read up about Jesmond. It was not rural. Plenty of dogs and cats, but no sheep. Why was she wearing a poke bonnet?

'Privet,' shouted Beatrice who was the woman to whom Isa was talking.

Shaking his head, Leo closed his front door. Did everyone in Chillingham Grove speak Russian? Was he in a Russian-speaking ghetto? And, Tony called this a safe house! Instead of creeping in unnoticed like a spy should, by tomorrow, everyone in the street would know he was Russian. But hopefully that he was not a spy. The English were gossips. He'd done his homework on streets like Chillingham Grove.

'Who is he?' Beatrice asked Isa.

'A Russian vodka salesman. He's renting number thirty-nine.'

'I never thought you teaching me Russian would come in useful. How exciting. Does he know about the street party?'

'He must know something is going on. Unless he's blind, he must have noticed the bunting.'

'We should invite him; to the street party, I mean. I think it would be bad mannered if we didn't. I'm going to tell him. I am on the SPC.'

'So am I,' said Isa.

'I know you are, Isa, darling, but, hand on heart I think I am better at getting things done. You are retired. The way you let that gypsy fellow run rings round you yesterday, I was watching, you know, was embarrassing. What you need is a man.'

'I had one. He was called Yuri.'

'You romanticise Yuri. Memory makes you forget his imperfections. Did he lift the toilet seat when he went for a pee? That sort of thing. Do you think I should knock and tell him now?'

'If you do, Beatrice, please do not attempt to speak Russian. Do not mistake your smattering of that language for fluency. It is too easy to sound familiar when you should be formal. It would be beyond the pale if Leo … that's his name by the way … got the idea into his head that you were making eyes at him. In case you've forgotten, you are dressed as Little Bo-peep. If I may say so, you are showing a lot of bosom.'

'Am I?'

'Yes.'

'It's my fancy dress for the street party.'

'Too much bosom.'

'Ken hasn't even noticed. The Russian's a big man. I like big men. I'm going to invite him to the street party.'

'Like the spinster in the song,' Isa said, 'I'll wait for you at the garden gate.'

What would Beatrice make of the Russian? Would she see a vodka salesman or a ruthless KGB operative? Or, being Beatrice, would she see a sex god? And what would Leo make of Beatrice?

Preparatory to ringing the doorbell, Beatrice adjusted her dress to show off her bosom.

Leo opened the door with a towel wrapped around his vital organs. When the towel flapped, like a slit in a skirt, it showed a lot of leg.

After what appeared to have been an amicable conversation, a grinning Beatrice, carrying her shepherd's crook over her shoulder as if it was a cudgel, told Isa at the garden gate: 'I saw his penis.'

'He exposed himself?'

'He needed a bigger towel. He was not pleased at being disturbed. "I am showering," he told me. I apologised for disturbing him. I told him about the street party. About why I was dressed as Little Bo-peep. I told him that from nine tomorrow morning the street would be closed to traffic. "You know," I told him, "in case you want to use your car."'

'What did he say?'

'Didn't seem bothered. He knew why we were having a street party. He knew all about the royal wedding. He told me how in the great revolution the communists had got rid of Russia's royals. He called them "spoilt brats". It was when he was telling me this that he got a bit carried away. To make his point he started waving his arms. While he was exposing the iniquities of tsarist rule, he exposed himself. I saw everything. "I apologise, Little Bird" he said. Isa, he called me a "Little Bird". I told him that it was a good job I was a married woman. I begged him to come to the fancy dress. He said he would. When I was leaving, I couldn't help blurting out, "Dostivaniya".'

'What did he say?'

'He corrected my pronunciation. He told me I sounded as if I came from Vladivostok.'

'He wasn't impressed?'

'Not as impressed as I was when his towel flapped open.'

'I'd better be going. Chippy has an appointment with a lamppost round the corner.'

'Is he regular?'

'He's a dog. Regularity is a male thing.'
'Even when he's depressed, Ken is regular.'

****

From the spying and espionage point of view, Isa was of the opinion that things had gone rather well. The Russian would think Chillingham Grove was full of well-meaning, Russian-speaking idiots. Beatrice's intervention had muddied the waters. He wouldn't know what to think. He might even believe her story that Chippy had dug up the key.

She gave herself a pat on the back. Should she ring Jeremy and let him know everything had gone according to plan? Where was he? Was he still in the north-east?

Her peripheral role in whatever was going on made her feel helpless. The subterfuge made her head spin. To keep her feet on the ground, she needed to talk to someone outside the loop.

On a whim – hatless and without make-up – she decided to walk to Malcolm's. A good forty-minute walk. But why not? It was a beautiful sunny morning. Chippy needed the exercise. Now that the Russian was here, she'd need Malcolm's help. He was, after all, a co-opted member of MI5. He had to be made use of. And, like herself, he was at the bottom of the food chain.

Chapter 19

Since her last visit, Malcolm's front door had been painted blue. Powder blue. Had he been making use of the paint he'd found in the skip? WET PAINT was chalked on the door's step.

She rang his doorbell. While she waited to be let in, like a naughty child who cannot resist doing what she has been told not to do, she tapped a finger on the paint. The warning was valid. The paint was tacky.

'Hoy!' Malcolm shouted from an upstairs window. 'Oh, it's you, is it? It's lucky yuh didn't get this poured ower yuh–' showing her a chamber pot. 'Divent touch the paint.'

'Can I come in?'

'Why, aye! Give's time to cum doon the stairs. Oh, dear me! The polis after yuh? Ha! Ha!'

Since her last visit, not only had Malcolm's front door been painted blue but so had everything inside the flat, that could be painted, had been painted blue. Blue kitchen cupboards. Blue kitchen chairs. Blue doors. Blue window frames. Blue floorboards where there was no carpet.

'You've been busy,' she said.

'Oh, aye! Am never idle. Cosy, eh? Good find that pot of blue paint. It takes friggin ages to dry. If yuh gan to the bog divent sit doon. 'ave just painted the netty seat. It should be dry by next year.

Ha! Ha! Remember them handprints wuh used to dee at school? If yuh use my netty you'll be able to dee arse prints. Nee extra charge as that cheeky bloody barman telt me when a found a spider in me pint.'

'Will the paint not dry?'

'Oot of date, isn't it. Beggars can't be choosers. Cup of tea?'

'Yes, please, and a bowl of water for Chippy.'

'Oh, dear me! Am not a friggin café, yuh nar.'

As usual they drank tea out of mugs Isa would have thrown out.

'What duh yuh want? When yuh come to see me, yuh always want something.'

'To remind you to cut number thirty-nine's grass.'

'Not due to cut it until next week–' lighting a cigarette.

She told him about the Russian.

'He's called Leo. I want you to spy on him. When you are cutting number thirty-nine's grass, keep your eyes and ears open. And if he speaks to you, for goodness' sake be polite. Tell him the truth, that you used to be a collier but have been made redundant and are now a jobbing gardener. He is a communist. He will sympathise with you because you a member of the proletariat.'

'The only thing I'm a member of, Isa, is me CIU club.'

'I want you and your lawn mower cutting number thirty-nine's grass today. You will be well paid.'

'Now you're tarken.'

'The Russian will have free samples.'

'Free vodka, eh? A divent like vodka. Mind, if it's for nowt, I might get to like it.'

'I'm sure you'll do your best.'

'A will! A will! Free samples, eh? Does he sell tabs as well?'

'You'll have to ask him.'

'A divent speak Russian.'

'He speaks English.'

'Aye! Aye! A nar that, just hav'n a joke wasn't a? A like a joke. In the club last week a put a steradent tablet in Jack's pint. Oh, dear me! Yuh shud a seen his face. A thowt he was ganna smack me, but he didn't. Jack's not daft. He said: "What yuh gone on done that for?" It's a sex pill, a told him. "Cheeky bugger," he said, "a divent need one of them, afro – daisies." "Aphrodisiacs," a telt him. "Oh, aye," he said, "how cum yuh nar a big word like that? Hoy!" he told the rest of wor mates, "Malc's on the sex pills. Where'd yuh get them?"

'I told him, the "Pound Shop". He said he'd never seen them in the "Pound Shop". "You have to ask Mavis," I told him, "and they cost more than a pound." "Under the counter?" said Jack. A didn't say owt, just tapped the side of me nose. Wardle, he's one of me drinking pals, has false teeth. He'd been looking at the tablet fizzing in Jack's beer and he said: "Jack, divent worry, it's not a sex pill, it's one of them tablets that cleans your false teeth. You're a lucky bloke, you are. When you're drinking your beer you'll be cleaning your teeth aal at the same time." When it comes to catchin' on, Jack's a Ferrari. Straight away, he said: "Like when wor lass is polishin' the silver and tell'n me aal at the same time to put a bob in the gas meter." Wardle said: "Hang on, Jack when did yee have silver to polish? We'd yuh think yuh are, royalty?"

'It's this royal wedding, yuh see, Isa. Jack's missus loves the royal family like I love peanut butter. To make her feel part of the big day, she'd bought two silver spoons.

'"One has a picture of Prince Charles on its handle," said Jack.

'"And the other one has a picture of Lady Diana on its handle," said Wardle.

'"How'd yee nar that?" said Jack.

'"Me mother was a gypsy," said Wardle.

'"A nivva knew that," said Jack.

'"A nivva knew yuh had two silver spoons," said Wardle.

'"We aal have secrets," said Jack.

'"Look," said Wardle, "drink ya pint. If yuh divent need it for ya sex life, yuh dee need it to clean ya teeth."

'Good, eh? At the club they call me the racketeer.'

'Malcolm,' said Isa.

'Oh, dear me! What now?'

'A piece of advice.'

'Divent nag.'

'I'm trying to stop you getting killed.'

'Oh, aye!'

'When you are mowing number thirty-nine's pasture, keep your eyes and ears open.'

'Hoy! That's deeing three jobs at the same time.'

'If Jack's wife can do two jobs at the same time, why can't you go one better and do three? It would go down well at the club when you are playing the raconteur.'

'Do yuh think so?'

'I most certainly do. You and the Russian should get on like a fire in the Kremlin.'

'A divent want to get me fingers burnt. Ha! Ha!'

'Russians love fairy stories. They believe that one day communism will replace capitalism. Tell him about the Steradent tablet. It will no doubt remind him of all the poison pills he's dropped into the drinks of traitors to Mother Russia.'

'Are yuh finished? Oh, dear me! Me lugs are aching. You've given us the bends. That's what divers get when they come up too fast.'

'Malcolm?'

'Oh, dear me! What now?'

'Why did you put a Steradent tablet in Jack's drink?'

'A get things in me heed, divent a? It had to be done. It's like when yuh need to go for a shite. If yuh divent gan you'll fill ya pants. Yuh divent have a choice. Yuh have to gan.'

'You are a creature of impulse.'

'Am a?'

158

'Yes. When you are cutting number thirty-nine's grass, remember, this is not a game. I have worked with people like Leo. He will have murdered more people than you have drank pints of beer. And before you light another cigarette, fill Chippy's bowl with water. He is thirsty and it is a long walk home.'

'Oh, aye!'

****

Arriving back in Chillingham Grove, after the long walk with Chippy from Malcolm's, Isa noted at once that Leo's red Volvo was no longer in number thirty-nine's drive.

Had Leo garaged it? Or had he gone out? He did not seem the sort who'd bother to garage a car. If he'd gone out, where had he gone?

She was peckish. Chippy was starving. She needed the loo.

For the umpteenth time she reminded herself she could not watch number thirty-nine, twenty-four-seven. She was a one-woman band, not a symphony orchestra. It was sod's law that while she was on the loo or making a sandwich, she'd miss something.

She watched from her front room. For company, she had Chippy. For stimulus: a mug of coffee. To help her see and remember what she saw: binoculars, a notebook and a biro. She looked at the house as a sailor on watch looks at a calm sea. Why, when everything looked so peaceful, should she be on watch at all?

****

At eleven-thirty–two am she made the following entry in a notebook: 11.32 am. Van. Reg. DUS 27. Spick and Span Professional and domestic cleaning services. No job too dirty. Reversed. Number 39's drive. Rhododendron bush stopped me seeing who got out. Female? Carrying a vacuum cleaner? Think this person went into house.

159

Who let her in? Did possible female carrying a possible vacuum cleaner have a key?

Fifteen minutes later the 'Spick and Span' van reversed up Isa's drive.

'Hi! Aunt Isa,' said Joan, climbing out, before popping her head back into the van to bring out a vacuum cleaner. 'It's me.'

'I can see that,' said Isa, letting her niece in. 'Why are you dressed as a char?'

'I've come to clean your house, haven't I? The vacuum cleaner is part of my disguise. Would you like me to hoover your carpets?'

'No. I want you to tell me about number thirty-nine. Did you have a key?'

'No. Leo let me in.'

'But his car's not in the drive. I thought he was out.'

'I think there's a car in the garage. When I left, he insisted I leave by the back door. He said because I was a cleaner I should leave by the serf's entrance. For a communist he's awfully class conscious.'

'Does he know that you are not really a cleaner? That you work for Special Branch?'

'I don't think Mr Adder has told him. He thinks I come with the house. It's what he is paying rent for. By the way, I'll be quite safe. He's homosexual.'

'What makes you think that?'

'His collection of photographs. Nude men with dyed blond hair. He keeps them in a file marked "Vladivostok Vodka".

'How'd you see that?'

'While he was in the loo I went snooping. He kept shouting at me through the loo door that he was constipated.'

'Russians can be very uninhibited. Think of Khruschev banging his shoe at the UN.'

'He told me that back in Moscow he has a little sister, just like me. Maybe when he was telling me he was constipated, he thought he was talking to his little sister. Big brothers can be ever so confiding to little sisters. When he came out of the loo he told me, "That was better out then in, yes? An English expression I learn from a publican I know in Pontefract. Their liquorice cakes are great help for the vowels." Then he told me he wanted a "shit". I thought he'd just had one. "It is for the party in the street. I am going as a noble Roman. Caesar! Cicero! I need a shit, maybe two, shits for my toga. You go to a shop and buy me them. I give you money and a big tip."'

'His vowel sounds and his bowels are not, I fear, in tip-top condition. Will he not be suspicious that you have called here?'

'I told him you were a customer; that as soon as I'd vacuumed for you, I'd go and buy the sheets. To make him think you really are a client I think I'd better stay for a while.'

To let nosey neighbours know she was, indeed, a char and that she was doing what she'd been paid to do and was not a secret agent up to no good, Joan made a point of going outside into her aunt's front garden and fluffing dusters. For good measure she also emptied a bucket of soapy water over a rose bush. She also polished the knocker on her aunt's front door and swept imaginary dirt off its step.

Every so often, Isa scanned number thirty-nine through binoculars. She was surprised the Russian had garaged his car. Maybe he'd a fetish about keeping cars in garages. The Russian winter? Or security? A car locked in a garage was that little bit more difficult to bug. Fetishes were funny things.

In the Lebanon she'd known an assassin obsessed with keeping his nails looking as if they belonged to a concert pianist. He'd looked after them the way he'd oiled his sniper's rifle.

After a suitable time had passed, Joan left. Isa did not wave her niece goodbye. That would have been out of character. Like Winston Churchill letting Clem Attlee go first through a door.

****

To vary her surveillance, Isa went outside to keep a watchful eye on number thirty-nine from her front garden. Weeding and dead heading would be her cover.

Surfacing from pulling up a weed lurking under the leaves of a magnolia, she found herself face-to-face with Beatrice.

'What a fright!'

Beatrice had been crying.

'Ken doesn't like my Bo-peep costume. He says it makes me look like a tart. Sob! Sob! You don't have a spare diazepam, do you?'

'I'm afraid not.'

'May I come in for a chat?'

'Of course.'

'You're not busy?'

'Just killing time before tomorrow's big event. The street looks gay, doesn't it?'

'I suppose so. It doesn't cheer me up. Isa, when I'm talking to you would you mind looking at me and not across the road?'

'Sorry.'

'Are you sure I'm not disturbing you?'

'Of course not.'

'I need to talk to you about my problem. You are worldly. You have travelled. You know a lot about men. The people in the street look up to you. If the street had to elect a mayor, they'd elect you. I know they would.'

'That would not please Angus or Harry. But, never mind them. What's your problem?'

'I'll tell you inside. I'll die, just die if I don't have a coffee.'

Casting a wistful look towards number thirty-nine, Isa, once again lamenting her lack of back-up, ushered Beatrice inside.

In the kitchen Beatrice confessed: 'I'm a nymphomaniac. There, I've said it. I feel better already. I'm not a Catholic but I can see how confessing one's sins is a help. You see, I can't get enough of it. In fact I'm not getting any of it.'

'What?'

'Sex! I keep feeling randy. Just looking at the red hot pokers in your front garden turns me on. I'm wicked, aren't I?' Taking a dog biscuit out of a saucer on the kitchen table, she added: 'Nice! Salty but moreish. Where'd you get them?'

'Morrisons.'

Beatrice stayed an interminable hour. An hour when goodness knows who might have come and gone at number thirty-nine.

'We'll have a great time at the street party,' she told Beatrice at her garden gate. 'I'm sure Ken will come round to liking your Bo-Peep costume. It might help if you didn't show quite so much bosom.'

The red Volvo was back. Damn! What had she missed?

****

Later that day she watched Joan deliver Leo's sheets to number thirty-nine; the sheets he needed for his toga. In a notebook she logged Joan's time of arrival.

When she saw 'TA' through the binoculars she was using she nearly dropped them. If only she'd been looking at him through a sniper scope. A minute later, he and Joan were opening her garden gate.

She opened her front door to them before they'd knocked.

'You were expecting us,' said 'TA', trespassing into her kitchen as if he had a search warrant.

Behind his back Joan mimed to her aunt that she'd not a clue as to what was going on.

'TA' was dressed for debauchery. If there is such a thing as a catamite Sloane Ranger, he was it. He was wearing a t-shirt which proclaimed he loved Renoir. His shorts were too tight and too short. His legs were luminous with a post-waxing oil. Flip-flops. No socks. His toenails were painted, alternately, red, white and blue.

163

His aftershave went up Isa's nose like a fizzy drink. She thought of the wolf, in Little Red Riding Hood: 'What big teeth you have, Grandma!'

He sat down. He crossed his legs. They were so oily the uncrossed leg kept giving the crossed leg a trip down a slide.

Isa and Joan stared at him like naughty schoolgirls waiting to be told why they'd been called into the headmaster's study.

'Sit,' he said, 'I will not be towered over.'

They sat. Chippy ambled in. A bouncer smelling trouble.

'Your bodyguard will not be needed. My men told me what happened at the telephone box. Set your dog on me and I will kill it. How did you know where to find the key?'

'I didn't. My dog found it. He was looking for his ball.'

'I don't believe you. You were the same in the Lebanon. Always poking your nose in. The clever pleb who could do algebra and pick up a language in less time than it would take the Artful Dodger to pick a pocket. People like you, make people like me, look stupid–' threatening her with a teaspoon– 'and we are not. Keeping a moated castle in the same family for six hundred years takes brains.'

'Put the teaspoon down, Tony. Strike me and Chippy will attack you. You are scantily dressed. Your flesh is vulnerable.'

'You may think you have a better brain than me, but you lack an attribute without which no spy can survive.'

'Inherited wealth? The old boys' network? The ability to use a teaspoon as an offence weapon? Put it down, Tony, before Chippy bites you.'

'The attribute you lack, my dear Ms Weddle, is the ability to enjoy lying and cheating. Cheating someone and getting away with it helps me sleep at night. You lack cunning. You are not ambitious. You are not greedy. You are too comfortable with your lot. I mean, let us get real. Living this far north. In this godforsaken city when, simply by turning a blind eye to this and that, you could be living the good life somewhere warm and sunny with a toy boy thrown in, if that's what turns you on.'

'Like the south of France,' said Isa, 'where Renoir and Cezanne painted their rubbishy pictures?'

'TA' looked at Chippy. If that bloody dog of hers hadn't been looking at him as if he were a lamb chop, he'd have punched her in the face. That's what he wanted to do. Punch her in the face. Ms Weddle was a pleb. How dare she criticise Renoir and Cezanne. Calling them 'rubbish' was sacrilege.

Ms Weddle was a loose cannon. She knew every trick in the book. Had her comment about his beloved Impressionists been an innocent remark? Had the t-shirt he was wearing suggested it to her? Was it an en passant remark that anyone might have made? Or was she goading him? Letting him know she knew about his passion for the Impressionists? If the latter, how did she know?

If this damn woman was hinting that she knew about his infatuation, who had told her? She'd been out of the loop for years. At university he'd studied geography. He'd shown no interest in the arts because he'd had none. His love affair with those who had the skill to make oil on canvas shimmer like real water had been a Damascene conversion. When he'd worked with her in the Lebanon, he'd had no interest in modern art. If she did know, how did she know?

Too late, Isa realised, she'd made a slip. Jeremy had told her about 'TA's' love affair with the Impressionists. If he'd not told her, she'd not have known. 'TA' had provoked her. She had responded in an unprofessional way.

As a diversion she tapped Chippy's leg. On cue, the dog growled and snarled.

'I'm telling you, keep that wolf under control or I will kill it.'

'It's alright, Chippy,' said Isa, stroking the dog's ears. 'The man you would like to bite is not an enemy. He is an old friend. Ha! Ha!'

'Very droll, I'm sure,' said 'TA', standing up to go. 'I have come to remind you and your niece of your positions. As far as number thirty-nine is concerned, you have nothing to tell London. Do you understand? If you so much as hint to London that I am at number thirty-nine, I will expose Joan for what she is. A murderer. A bungling assassin, responsible for murdering a high-ranking MI5 officer. A friendly-fire cock-up of epic proportions. One for the Guinness Book of Records. You two are under my thumb. If you don't do as I say, you know the consequences.'

His performance left Isa feeling underwhelmed. People who make threats are scared. 'TA' was a blunderbuss full of feathers.

'I will let myself out.'

'I am impressed,' said Isa. 'Wow! You are capable of opening a door all by yourself. I thought posh boys like you had servants to do that. You are coming down in the world, Tony. Next you will be having to wipe your own arse.'

When he'd gone, Isa and Joan looked at each other as if a film they'd been watching had come to an end and they needed time to gather their thoughts before passing comment.

'Well?' said Isa.

'I don't want to go to jail, Aunt Isa. I have to do as he says.'

'He's scared I tell London.'

'If you do, my career in MI5 is finished. The press will hound me. Dad will lose his job at the sewage farm.'

'Has it ever occurred to you how difficult it will be for 'TA' to keep the death of a fellow officer secret?'

'I've not thought about that.'

'Well, you should.'

'Aunt Isa, what are we going to do?'

'Have a cup of tea and a chocolate biscuit.'

'It was an accident, Aunt Isa. I was set-up. I know I was. You know it too.'

'For goodness' sake, do not start to cry. When women cry, men think us silly weak creatures and despise us. Get out of the habit. If I can stop smoking, you can stop blubbing.'

'Yes, Aunt Isa.'

'Besides, you are upsetting Chippy. While I make the tea, stroke his ears. He likes that and it will calm you down. If Beatrice my neighbour had a dog she wouldn't need diazepam.'

Over mugs of tea and more than one chocolate digestive biscuit, Isa told her niece a few home truths about been a secret agent.

She told her about some of the things she'd done in the Middle East. Learning from the horse's mouth that in her younger days her aunt had been an MI6 assassin made Joan go quiet.

'I am confiding in you, Joan, these secrets of my early life, to drum it into you that I know, from experience, the idiosyncrasies of the British secret service. What you might call its funny little ways. When it suits us, we Brits are as ruthless as the Russians. If 'TA' has the support of those higher up the chain of command, the disposal of the mortal remains of Tobias Lacy will be a formality. His cremation ... he will be cremated ... a body can be dug up ... exhumations and post-mortems play the devil with the best laid plans ... no, he will be cremated and with, of course, all the correct paperwork. It's amazing how having the right piece of paper makes everything seem above board.'

'I have heard rumours, Aunt Isa,' said Joan, 'MI5 has its own undertaker.'

'MI6 had, in the Lebanon. Believe me, Joan, what you have heard in the locker room is not rumour. It is fact. Take that from me. I know about these things. The cause of Tobias's death will depend upon the imagination of 'TA'. I have been out of the loop for many years, but I am inclined to think Tobias will have been given what we in the trade used to call a "Porton Down" death. While on a visit to Britain's top secret laboratory dedicated to researching nasty toxins, one Tobias Lacy caught anthrax. That sort of thing. To prevent the spread of the virus, the coffin will be screwed down. The cremation will be private. A member of MI5 will be present. He will have watched Tobias rise up out of his burning coffin as if he were alive.'

'Aunt Isa, please!'

'To make his family feel good they will have been told he died in action. What concerns me is the lack of an obituary. Tobias was very well connected. His family are titled. They have their own coat of arms. They own a lot of land. One of his ancestors was a mistress to Charles the second. I'd have expected a few lines in the Daily Telegraph. Nothing. It is possible the family are acting up. They may be smelling a rat. The aristocracy know a lot about smelling vermin. To play ball they may be demanding compensation. What you and I would call hush money. More tea?'

Later, at Isa's garden gate, the two women hugged. Emotion had made them forget, Joan was a char and Isa, her customer.

'How will it all end, Aunt Isa?'

'My dear Joan, I have no idea. As Prime Minister Macmillan once said: "Events, dear boy! Events!" Things happen, Joan. Let us hope they happen in our favour. Oh dear! We shouldn't be seen talking like this. You are my char. We are forgetting our roles. Shall I raise my voice and accuse you of not having dusted the piano?'

'I can feel eyes looking at me from behind net curtains.'

'You have forgotten your vacuum cleaner.'

'Damn!'

'Without your vacuum cleaner you are Hamlet without a skull. Your vacuum cleaner makes you look the part. Go and get it. I do hope Chippy hasn't attacked it. He dislikes vacuum cleaners.'

Joan struggled to get the vacuum cleaner into the back of the van. A spy trained to observe such fumblings might well have concluded that Joan was not a char.

Isa shook her head. The courses Britain's secret service agents were sent on these days were not as thorough as they had been when she had fought for queen and country. If she'd not learnt her lines when, years ago she'd been disguised as a Zoroastrian fortune teller in Tel-Aviv, the sheik for whom she'd been forecasting (he wanted to know if his camel would win the annual derby) would have cut off her ears. Being a secret agent and forgetting your lines wasn't the same as an actor forgetting his lines. A secret agent did not have a prompter waiting in the wings to save his bacon.

Waving Joan off, Isa looked up and down the street. Dominic and Irene were out tying red, white and blue shields to lampposts. Dominic was up a ladder, shouting at his wife that if she didn't steady the ladder he would fall.

'You two are doing a great job,' she told them. 'The street is looking wonderful.'

'Irene!' shouted Dominic, as Irene, fancying a chat with Isa more than she fancied keeping the ladder steady upon the top rung of which her husband was wobbling, ambled over to Isa's side of the street.

'Dominic's in a mood, 'Irene explained to Isa. 'Now he's a carnivore his moods are worse than when he was a vegan. He does the opposite of everything I say. Yesterday I told him I fancied a weekend in Skegness. He said he fancied Llandudno.'

'If you wanted to have a weekend in Skegness you should have told him you wanted to go to Llandudno.'

'Should I? I've started smoking again. Have I told you? I have ringworm. Don't tell anybody.'

'Why? It's not a sexually transmitted disease; is it? How's your dandruff?'

'I don't have dandruff.'

'Irene! I need you to come and hold the ladder.'

'I'm coming! Does the Russian who is renting number thirty-nine know the street will be closed to traffic tomorrow?'

'Who told you he was Russian?'

'He's a vodka salesman, isn't he?'

'So I've been told.'

'Irene!'

'I know this is none of my business, but do you have anything to do with number thirty-nine?'

'Irene!'

'Why do you ask?'

'All the comings and goings between it and your house.'

'Oh, you mean my niece Joan. She is working for Spick and Span.'

'I saw the van.'

'Spick and Span have the contract to keep number thirty-nine, well … spick and span.'

'Irene! For the last time …'

'The Russian has someone staying with him, doesn't he? A man wearing tight shorts and a flowery shirt. Do you think that was fancy dress he was wearing?'

'For the street party?'

'Irene!!'

'You know what I'm thinking? I'm thinking it was fancy dress. He was having a try on ready for tomorrow. The royal wedding is making all of us let our hair down. Beatrice is coming as Little Bo-Peep, isn't she? I'm coming as a nun. Dominic says I shouldn't. When he wants to be he can be very touchy about his Catholicism. He never misses going to church. I just wish he'd clean out the bath after he's used it. Mind you, I'd draw the line if he got circumcised.'

'Why on earth would he do that?'

'A Jewish school is advertising for a headteacher. I wonder how I caught ring worm. I wish I hadn't started smoking again. You know I'm pregnant?'

Across the road, a postman, dressed as John Bull, was wagging a finger at Dominic in such a way as to suggest he was giving Dominic an ear-bashing.

'Oh dear,' said Irene, 'it's that bloody postman again. His son is in Dominic's class. Every time he delivers us letters, he knocks to complain that Byron, that's his son, can't read and that it's all Dominic's fault.'

'I suppose anyone who calls their son Byron expects him to come top of the class in reading and writing,' said Isa.

'Irene! Help me with these will you?'

'Do you think homework might help?' the postman was asking Dominic, as the latter, trailing behind him the postman as a convict trails behind him the ball and chain to which the law has shackled him and, to boot, carrying a pair of step ladders on his shoulder, in the manner of a Victorian lamp lighter, came over to join his wife.

'It might. Irene, go and bring the shields I've left over there. I can't carry everything.'

Ignoring her husband, Irene told the postman: 'I love your costume. Is it for the royal wedding?'

'I'm flying the flag, aren't I?' said the postman, sticking out his chest to show off his Union Jack waistcoat. 'You're the wife with the wolf, aren't you?' handing Isa a pile of mail. 'They are all yours, wolf woman. Ha! Ha! I like a joke.'

'Chippy is a German Alsatian, not a wolf,' said Isa.

'Where is it now?'

'At this moment my dog is watching you from behind a potentilla.'

'Eh?'

'The big bush with yellow flowers.'

'I'll tell you this, Mrs, every time I gan up your path me gob gans dry. When he sees me he doesn't see a postie, he sees a chop. Show me a dog what doesn't have it in for posties and I'll show you a councillor what isn't on the fiddle. Oy! Oy! Here's trouble.'

'Mr Postie or, should I say, John Bull?' said Mr Pratt, master butcher, leaning out of his car's window the way people do when they are asking a stranger for directions. 'Any letters for me? Number ninety-nine. Detached property. Top end of the street.'

'One more nine, sir, and you'd be an emergency service, wouldn't you? You'd be expecting me to deliver your letters as if you'd rung in and said you'd broken a leg. I'm not an ambulance driver, sir. I'm a postie.'

'And a most eloquent one. Do you have any letters for me?'

'I don't know.'

'Why don't you look?'

'I don't deliver letters, sir, to first come, first served. I don't deliver letters the way they hand out loaves of bread from the back of a lorry to those black folk I saw on the telly last night what were starving. I'm a servant of her majesty the queen, not a charity shop.'

'It's a letter from Her Majesty that I'm expecting,' said Mr Pratt. 'You see–' looking, superior and smug– 'I'm expecting a gong.'

'A knighthood?' said Isa.

'Not yet but, it's a step in the right direction. It's on the cards I'm going to get an OBE.'

'What for?' said Irene.

'Services to retail butchery. What swung the balance was my Charles and Di venison burger. They are selling like hot cakes. I'm letting street parties have them at cost price, plus a little bit for you-know-who. You sure you can't look in your bag? What about a free burger?'

'I'm a postie, sir. Not a councillor. I don't take bribes.'

'I hope you are not suggesting that I do.'

'All I'm thinking, sir, is, if you can get an OBE for selling sausages, why can't I have one for delivering letters; in the snow and when the snowplough can't get through.'

When the withering look Pratt gave the postman failed to make the postman wobble like a jelly on a plate balanced on the dashboard of a lorry driving over cobbles, Pratt, expressing his frustration through acceleration, put his foot down and drove off at speed.

'Ha! Ha!' said the postman. 'I do have a letter for him. It's not from Buckingham Palace, it's from the Inland Revenue. If he's not fiddling his tax, I'll never eat another ginger snap for as long as I live. I loves ginger snaps.'

'Do you dunk?'

'Is a postman's mail bag red?'

'Quite!' said Isa. 'Here, Chippy!' placing in the dog's mouth the letters the postman had handed to her earlier. 'Chippy likes to carry my mail into the kitchen.'

Chippy, tail wagging, head held high, pleased to be pleasing the 'boss', took the letters into the house.

'Never thought I'd be made redundant by a wolf. A wolf delivering letters. Whatever next? He should get an OBE for that.'

'Can animals get medals?' said Irene.

'Lots of sly foxes and cheeky monkeys get medals,' said Isa.

'Do they really?'

'Yes. They are called politicians.'

'Isa, you and your teasing. And here was I believing your every word.'

'Pratt!' said the postman. 'He's well named, isn't he? They say folk get like their pets–' looking at Isa. 'I wonder if they can get like their surnames? I'm alright. Mine's Noble.'

On which happy note he sauntered off down the street, whistling Rule Britannia.

'If a butcher can get an OBE for selling sausages, I think it's a disgrace that I'm not given one for all the extra-curricular activities I do at school,' said Dominic. 'I run a stamp collecting club and a table tennis club. All the children in my class can spell philatelist. I was thinking of starting an RSPB club. I don't think I will, now.'

****

In high dudgeon and feeling undervalued, Dominic and Irene walked off down the street in search of another lamppost on which to tie a red, white and blue shield.

What would they have thought if they'd known that she, Ms Isa Weddle, was the recipient of a gong quite high up in the pecking order of gongs?

At first Isa did not recognise the blue car coming down the street at the speed of a hearse taking a dead body to be buried or burned. She did, though, recognise the blue trailer it was pulling – a Heath-Robinson contraption made out of scrap wood, with bicycle wheels.

Surely, he hadn't? But, he had. Malcolm had painted his car blue; had hand painted his car blue by the looks of the way in which, in some places, the paint had run. The lawn mower in the trailer was also blue.

Outside number thirty-nine, where he'd parked, the street looked blue; as if his blue car, blue trailer and blue lawn mower were making the statement that if rain can fall from clouds, why, on a summer's day, can a clear sky not precipitate blue?

Before sauntering over to chat with his cousin, Malcolm lit a cigarette. As he came up to her – showing off, as usual, by blowing smoke rings out of his nose – Isa saw that her cousin's forehead was smudged with streaks of blue paint.

'The smoke rings go with your war-paint,' she told him.

'Eh?'

'You have blue paint on your forehead.'

'Have I?'

'Yes.'

'Bloody skip-paint, that is,' he said. 'Bloody won't frigg'n dry; will it?'

He looked at his hands. The tips of his fingers were blue.

'Am like, Mickey Midas, aren't I? Everything a touch a turn to blue. Ha! Ha! Like me new car?'

'It's your old one painted blue.'

'Howay man! Divent spoil me fun. Blue's me favourite colour. Did a ever tell you that?'

'Yes.'

'Hello, Chippy. Nice doggy! Where's its cage?'

'Chippy does not need a cage. If he needs anything, he needs love.'

'You saying he needs a woman?'

'He has been castrated.'

'Ouch!'

'He is pleased to see you. You don't understand dogs.'

'Do a not?'

'No. You do not. He is wagging his tail.'

'At least he's got that to wag. Heh! Heh!'

'He knows you are naughty and give him treats. If he could talk, he'd call you the "Biscuit Man".'

'Get away–' looking at Chippy before changing the subject to money. 'Am a still on danger money? Like, getting double time for working on Sunday?'

'Yes. It is unfortunate you do not know how to use a Glock.'

'You call'n me im-po-tent?'

'Malcolm, I said, "Glock"!'

'Ah heard what yuh said. I was hav'n a joke, wasn't a? Oh dear me, Isa, things is bad, very bad, when yuh can't take a joke.'

'Malcolm, cut out the wise cracks. How many times must I tell you? This is not a game. You will be earning your danger money.'

'Will a?'

'Yes.'

'Oh, dear me! Am too young to die. Heh! Heh!'

'Are you wearing clean underwear?'

'Hoy! That's personal, that is.'

'I'm asking in case the Russian shoots you and you have to go to hospital.'

'You taking the piss?'

'Yes.'

'You're a funny one, you are, Isa. Yuh had me ganin there like Mary did last neet. Heh! Heh!'

'When you are cutting number thirty-nine's grass, I want you to be the three wise monkeys.'

'Oh, dear me! It was a lot easier working doon the pit.'

'Keep your eyes and ears open and your mouth shut. You may see and hear nothing of importance. On the other hand, you might. Hide your belligerence to authority under a bush.'

'What have a to hide under a bush?'

'Your "belligerence".'

'Oh, dear me, Isa. I wish yuh wouldn't use long words. They dee me heed in. What have a to hide under a bush?'

'Your "belligerence".'

'Will a need a shovel?'

'Off you go. Your very first spying mission. Pretend you are James Bond.'

'He gets the women, doesn't he?'

'Always.'

'In that case, I'm off. Divent tell Mary.'

****

Isa watched Malcolm push his lawn mower up number thirty-nine's drive. He stopped only once to blow smoke rings into the air as if he were a Red Indian sending her a smoke-message. While he was cutting its grass, she could take time off from watching the house. If anything untoward happened, he would be sure to tell her.

****

What with all that had been going on she'd forgotten all about the letters the John Bull-postman had given her and which in turn she'd given to Chippy They were on the kitchen table where, as he'd been trained to do, Chippy had dropped them.

Adverts on three of the envelopes told her who they were from. One was for car insurance. One was for corn plasters. One was from a firm selling double glazing.

The Lebanese stamp and Lucy Miller's handwriting – instantly recognisable to Isa – told her who had sent her the air-mail letter.

Why had Lucy replied so quickly? Their habit was to write to each other, maybe, twice a year. It was normal, for months, not weeks, to pass between their letters. It made Isa suspicious when someone changed the habit of a lifetime. Had Lucy done something silly, like falling in love? Was she going to get married? Heaven forbid! Could it be an invitation to a wedding breakfast?

'Hi! Isa,' Isa read, *'I'm so busy at the moment. Outbreak of typhoid. And in such big trouble! I will come straight to the point. I don't have much time.*

You are wrong about that sodomite, Tobias. He is NOT dead. Believe me, he is very much alive.

I banged into him coming out of a brothel – not me, HIM. He wouldn't have stopped if I hadn't made him. He must have been cursing. He did not want to talk. He told me it would be best if I was to forget I'd ever seen him.

Now! The scary bit. The next day my boss told me I'd been accused of selling drugs on the black market. If I agreed to fly to Bolivia tomorrow, it would all be hushed up. He was sure it was all a "terrible mistake". I was told that if I was sensible I would know which way the wind was blowing.

Tomorrow, I fly to Bolivia in an RAF Hercules. If you don't hear from me ever again, do not assume the worst. Cross your fingers and think, Bolivia has a rotten postal service. Lots of love, Lucy.'

Isa read the letter three times. It was Lucy's handwriting? It was not a forgery. But how could Tobias not be dead? She had seen him, with her own eyes, stretched out, in her front room, bleeding to death?

To have survived a 'hit' he must have been wearing body armour. With what type of bullet had 'TA' loaded the rifle?

She remembered seeing a ring on Tobias's little finger. Had there been a spike on its underside? Some kind of sharp projection he'd used to burst open a sachet of blood.

When she thought about it, the 'plumbers' had arrived on the scene awfully fast; they were like firemen arriving at the scene of a fire before the fire had started. They must have known what was about to happen. Had they been on standby to ring her bell before the shot had been fired? And 'TA', screaming exhortations at her through the broken window; he too had been quick to arrive on the scene.

The more she went over the time-line relating to these events, the more she came to the conclusion that 'TA' and the 'plumbers' had known in advance that Joan was going to shoot Tobias. She and Joan were victims of a sting operation.

'TA' had not wanted her to go back into her front room where Tobias was supposedly lying, mortally wounded. What had he said? 'No need for you to see more than you have already seen.' As if he'd wished to spare her feelings. Bullshit! 'TA' had never spared anyone's feelings in his life. If she had gone back into the room, she'd have seen Tobias sitting up, alive and well and more than likely swigging brandy from a hip flask.

And, what had Joan told her? Something about 'TA' getting very uptight and anxious when she'd suggested a head shot. He had insisted it must be a chest shot. 'No fancy shooting if you don't mind.'

If Joan had gone for a head shot, then Tobias really would now be dead.

To help her think, she dusted a Toby jug. A pirate. A grim looking fellow with a black patch over one eye and a parrot for a handle. A priority was to let Joan know she was not a murderer.

She worried that Tobias might have told 'TA' he'd been spotted by Lucy. What was Tobias doing in Beirut? Was he there on holiday? Was he retired? Was he there on official business? The fact that Lucy was being flown out by the RAF, suggested he was still working for MI6. He still had 'pull' to make false claims against Lucy stick. How discreet had Lucy been when she'd posted the letter?

When 'TA' had taken charge of number thirty-nine, had he been told she was a 'watchful eye'? If he hadn't, was that a deliberate oversight or, was it because she'd been forgotten? It was a few years since she'd reported any suspicious comings and goings.

She recalled a clerk in the British Embassy in Cairo. Apart from sharpening pencils and doing the Times crossword, he did no work. He used a monocle to examine the points of the pencils he'd sharpened. His nickname was the 'Fire Engine'. 'You'll see,' a senior member of staff had told Isa, 'what he does when there's a fire. I went to school with his brother. He comes from a very good family.'

She knew how MI5 and MI6 worked. Warts and all. Jeremy had said 'TA' had been given carte blanche to run number thirty-nine. It was his fiefdom. He could do what he liked with it. 'TA' would be just loving the irony of meeting his KGB control in one of MI5's very own safe houses. A house way up north, in a dull suburban street full of middle class bores who didn't know a Renoir from a dirty postcard. And best of all, a long way from London.

How had he found out about her involvement? Gossip? By chance? So many possibilities. Number one: He and Tobias gossiping in their London club. A glass of something alcoholic in front of them. 'TA' had told his long-time pal about his new job. 'I'm looking after a safe house. It's up north.' Tobias says: 'Remember that cow, Isa Weddle? She was from up north. Roman Wall country. I heard a rumour she's still on our books. Still taking the Queen's shilling.

Works from home or so I was told.'

'TA' had tracked down her file. How shocked he must have been when he realised she, of all people, was being paid to keep a watchful eye on number thirty-nine. When he was popping in and out, she was certain to recognise him. She'd be on to him like a leopard jumping on the back of an impala. How could he stop her giving him away? Stop her telling London all about his comings and goings? Number thirty-nine was a safe house. With her watching it, he knew it would not be a safe house for him.

He knew she would not take a bribe. Everyone had an Achilles's heel. What was hers? Had more research revealed she'd a niece working for Special Branch?

Isa recalled 'TA''s and Tobias's penchant for cruel and dangerous practical jokes. She made a note to ask her niece how she'd been seconded to work with 'TA'. She'd bet it had not been by accident.

'TA' and Tobias had hatched a plan to fool Joan into thinking she'd killed a senior member of the British Secret Service.

'She'll take the bait.'

'We'll have her, hook, line and sinker.'

'Ms Weddle needs putting in her place. Needs to be taught a lesson.'

What they'd done had been dangerous to the power ten. It suggested desperation. Were they another Burgess and Maclean? If they were, how the top brass must be squirming at once again being let down by their own kind. How much easier they'd have found it to believe that Ms Isa Weddle had betrayed the land of her birth.

'What do you expect? Typical product of a bog-class comprehensive. As Aesop said in one of his fables: Never trust a pleb. I think it was Aesop. It might have been Herodotus or Aristophanes. An education in the classics gives one so many sources from which to pick a suitable epigram. I have the same trouble deciding which waistcoat to wear for Ascot. The silver spoon the plebs keep going on about is not always that easy to suck. Ha! Ha!'

It was years since she'd reported to London. At first they'd sent her telegrams to tell her that number thirty-nine was to be occupied at such and such a date. No names. Then, the telegrams had stopped. When new people arrived, she assumed London knew all about them. In the meantime, she kept getting paid. She claimed expenses for Malcolm cutting its grass. No questions asked.

Fanning herself with the 'bombshell' letter, she walked into her front room. Staring across at number thirty-nine she saw Malcom's blue lawn mower, unattended, in number thirty-nine's front garden. No sign of Malcolm. Where was he? A man, carrying a bunch of flowers, was walking up her drive. The doorbell rang.

'Hello,' she said to Derek, the doorman who'd looked after Chippy, when she'd met Jeremy at the County Hotel. 'How many jobs do you have?'

'Ah! You recognised me. As does your wolf who scares the living daylights out of me. Nice dog! Nice dog! Do you like my disguise? I'm supposed to be working for Inter-Flora–' pointing to the logo on the blue dust coat he was wearing.

'Without your top hat you don't look as tall.'

'I have a message from the colonel.'

'You mean Jeremy?'

'You may call him that, Ms Weddle. I may not. Sir wishes to meet you, ASAP on board HMS Newcastle. That good ship is on a courtesy visit to the city after which she is named. You will find her moored close to the Tyne Bridge. Between the hours of three and six she is open to the public. When you gets there you are not to join the queue. There will be a queue. Visiting warships is very popular on Tyneside. Geordies like to see what they're getting for their taxes. The officer of the watch will be on the look-out for a lady …'

'With a wolf?'

'No, ma'am. For a lady wearing a Queen Elizabeth rose pinned to whatever she might be wearing. That's one of the pink roses in the bouquet which, to make the part I'm acting look the full Monty,

I am hereby delivering and must ask you to sign for just in case any nosey neighbours are peeking at us from behind their net curtains. Sign here,' he said, producing a pencil from behind an ear and a notebook from a pocket.

'Thank you,' said Isa.

'One more thing, ma'am. The colonel told me I was to tell, you. I am delivering flowers to Joan. I believe she is your niece. The colonel wishes her to be present at the pow-wow on HMS Newcastle.'

'Joan!' exclaimed Isa. 'She is going to meet Jeremy?'

'That's right, ma'am. She's getting the same bouquet as you has.'

'Will she have to wear a Queen Elizabeth rose in her buttonhole?'

'You catch on quick, ma'am. Yes. The standardisation of identification signals reduces the chance of confusion. Now, if you'll excuse me, I must be off. Afore I go, I'll tell you this. It was easier when me and the colonel was in the SAS than me having to dress up as an Inter-flora delivery man. The street looks nice. You are having a street party, I believe. It's alright for some. As one old soldier to another, ma'am, you are, if I may make so bold to say so, ma'am, quite a lady. The colonel has told me a little of the work you did in the Lebanon.'

Walking back to his van he whistled, 'Here comes the bride'. The forthcoming royal wedding was on everyone's subconscious the way a spinster who likes men never stops thinking that one day she will marry.

Before Isa had time to mull over what he'd told her and put on her hat and coat and decide how best to get to the quayside – taxi? Bus? Walk? Drive? – Malcolm rang her doorbell.

'I'm bursting,' he told her.

'The toilet's up the stairs; and lift the seat.'

'A divent want a Jimmy Riddle, man. I'm bursting to tell yuh aboot Leo. He's a canny bloke. He gave me these–' holding up a twenty packet of Players cigarettes– 'and guess what else? Two bottles of Stalingrad vodka. He calls it "Mig fuel". He told me, "It will make you poop the loop." "Poop the loop?" I said. "You mean, it will make me piss and fart?" He liked that. Isa, am think'n am good at handlin foreigners. He said he could tell I was a peasant. He wanted to give me a bear hug. "Hoy!" a told him, "That's enough of that".'

'Malcolm,' said Isa, 'he was bribing you. He was buying you.'

'Duh yuh not think a nar that? I'll tell yuh something. A like been bribed.'

'Were you in the house?'

'Oh, aye. He made us a cup of Rosie Lee. He put a poker in it. Yuh nar! A drop of vodka. We sat there drinking like old mates. He's a big bloke, isn't he? We had lots of "pokers". He said he didn't like tea but he was drinking it 'cos he was in England. "When in Vladivostock," he said. "I beg your pardon," I said. "A Russian saying," he said, "it is like when you English say, when in Rome." "Oh aye," a said. He wanted to know aal aboot you, Isa.'

'Did he, indeed?'

'Oh, aye!'

'What did you tell him?'

'A told him your mother was Russian and that yuh loved dogs.'

'Why on earth did you tell him my mother was Russian?'

'It just popped into me heed, didn't it? I'll tell yuh this, Isa, it made the bugger think. He knew I'd worked doon the pit. He spotted the coal dust under me skin. He's sharp. Doesn't miss much. When he asked me if I was a pitman, a said, "Why aye!" Charlie, the doorman at the club is always ganin on aboot how he used to work doon the pit. When he takes wor subs, him, and the secretary wear their miner's helmets. They put the lights oot and we all have to pay by torchlight. Heh! Heh! That's so as he can short change yuh oot of a pund note. Heh! Heh! Clever, that.'

'Malcolm, stick to the point. About the Russian?'

'Oh, aye! Him. He puts them sweet things in his tea instead of sugar.'

'Saccharine?'

'Is that what it's called? He was ganna put some in mine but a told him: "Hang on, bonny lad!" He said, "Sorry" but a knew he didn't mean it. 'ave been aroond the clubs long enough to nar when someone's trying to spike me drink. Oh, dear me! A divent feel well.'

'Malcolm, what's wrong?'

'I'm seeing double.'

'Oh, my god! What did the Russian put in your tea? You didn't drink the tea, did you?'

'Of course, a didn't. Am not that daft.'

'Then, why are you seeing double?'

'Am not.'

'But you just said you were.'

'Having yuh on, wasn't a? I'll tell yuh this, Isa, a wasn't having any Russian putt'n a poison pill in my tea.'

'Malcolm, they'd be saccharin.'

'You didn't see what I seen. The plastic case he kept his tablets in had a front door and a back door. You told me to be on my guard and a was. When he put the tablets into his tea, he used its front door. When he was ganna put tablets into my tea, he was ganna use its back door. Am a mak'n sense?'

'You are not making this up, I hope?'

'Am tell'n yuh the truth. Cross me heart and hope to die. Oh, dear me! A divent feel well. Heh! Heh! Yuh should a seen his face when a dropped a Rennie in his tea. Yuh nar? Tit-for-tat. A always keep a packet of Rennies in me pocket for me heartburn. A thowt he was ganna kill us. Yuh nar, if looks could kill and aal that. That's when a challenged him. "Drink my tea and I'll drink yours." But, he wouldn't. I'd called the bugger's bluff. That's when a took the handkerchief … yuh, nar … the initiative. A went at him like he was a low seam.'

'You didn't hit him, did you?'

'Course a didn't smack him! Am not daft! Anyway, he's bigger than me. I blew him up with one of these–' holding up a stick of dynamite. 'I'll show yuh.'

In between finding his cigarette lighter, getting it to work and using it to light the long fuse on the stick of dynamite, Malcolm explained to Isa that he'd taken to heart her warning that the Russian would be dangerous and that he'd gone into number thirty-nine well prepared.

'With Rennies?' said Isa.

'Aye! Cleva that. I'll bet there's not many secret agents used a Rennie as a poison pill. Cleva that.'

'I am assuming,' said Isa, eyeing the spluttering fuse, 'that while the fuse is real, the rest is dud?'

'Aye, that's reet. A bit of black powder, that's all. It'll make a bang like a fat wife farting, that's all. Duh yuh want to hear the fart?'

'Not really.'

'There yuh are,' he said, licking his fingers and extinguishing the fuse with his saliva, 'safe as a hoose with all its doors locked.'

'Where did you get it?'

'From the pit. I did work there for years, yuh nar. We used it to give the bosses we didn't like the shits.'

'That was cruel.'

'Aye! And so is the rain when it dashes daffodils.'

'I beg your pardon?'

'When a was young a wanted to be a poet. Heh! Heh! Howay man, Isa, take a joke. When I threw this at the Russian, yuh shud have seen the bugger run. He ran oot the room shouting, "Tony! Tony!" Hi! He's got a squeaky voice for a big bloke; hasn't he? We's Tony?'

'There is another man in the house.'

'Oh, dear me! There was two of them, was there? I've had a narrow escape.'

'Believe me, you have. Leo has probably blown up more people with dynamite than you have blown up tonnes of coal.'

'Oh, aye?'

'Tony is Tony Adder. I call him 'TA'. He is a British secret agent. He works for MI5. He is selling British secrets to the Russian for money.'

'Yuh mean he's a blackleg?'

'He is a traitor.'

'Same thing.'

'Because of your eavesdropping, you are up to your eyeballs in the spying game.'

'Ouch!' said Malcolm, crossing his legs.

'I said "eyeballs",' said Isa. 'Do you sleep with innuendo?'

'A might have done. A don't always nar their names.'

'Are you listening?'

'In for a penny, in for a tanner. A miss the old money. Gives a kiss'.

'You have had too much vodka. You are not in a fit state to be in charge of a lawn mower, let alone drive a car.'

'Oh, aye!'

'You are a loose cannon.'

'Am I?'

'To keep you out of trouble you'd best come with me.'

'Where to?'

'To a meeting with my niece Joan and a posh boy called Jeremy. He is top-drawer.'

'Is that where they keep the sharpest knives?'

'Sadly, no. The top drawer is full of penknives who think they are rapiers. Can you stand?'

'Course a can friggin stand! We're ganin now?'

'Yes.'

'Where's it at? A mean, is it far?'

'It is aboard a British warship moored under the Tyne Bridge.'

'Isa, you're not the pressgang, are yuh? A mean, when a gan on this ship a, won't wake up in Shanghai, will a? What aboot me lawn mower? And, me car and trailer?'

'Stop fussing! They will be quite safe. This is Chillingham Grove. Excuse me while I put a rose in my hat.'

'Can a not have one?'

'You are not wearing a hat.'

'A was ganna put it behind me ear like a tab.'

'Malcom. Shut up!

'Oh, aye!'

****

Isa was excited about meeting Joan. How do you tell someone they are not a murderer? It would be like telling Joan she'd won the football pools.

The day was warm and sunny. The news that her niece was not a murderer made Isa want to do a handstand. As she was no longer young and not up to acrobatics, she decided to show her joie de vivre by driving to HMS Newcastle with the Mercedes' hood down. Driving al fresco made her feel young.

'Aye!' said Malcolm, as he watched the Mercedes' hood fold into the car's boot. 'It's the poor what gets the blame and the rich what gets the pleasure. Hoy! Why have I got to sit in the back seat?'

'Chippy always sits in the front seat.'

'A divent like play'n second fiddle to a dog. Hoy! What's that on me lawn mower?'

Stopping the car to look, Isa saw a cardboard placard, swinging from its handles. On the cardboard, in big, bold, black letters: DOSTAN MENYA!

'What's it say?' said Malcolm.

'"Come and get me",' said Isa.

She hoped 'TA' and Leo were watching. Driving with the hood down, made her feel she was telling them to 'Fuck off'!

****

Malcolm had never sat in a Mercedes with its roof down before. It made him feel like royalty. It made him feel like the Pope. At traffic lights he blessed pedestrians with the sign of the cross. If only they would pass one of his girlfriends. If Mary saw him she'd think he'd come into money. Enjoying the 'good life' made him forget about wanting a ciggy. Living the dream made a bloke forget aal aboot nicotine.

****

Newcastle is a compact city. In fifteen minutes Isa was there, under the Tyne Bridge, parking close to the stern of HMS Newcastle.

Behind a life-belt, on a stand decorated with the ship's crest, a queue of visitors was waiting to board.

From bow to stern the ship was flying flags.

'Doesn't she look pretty,' said Isa.

'Howay man! It's a friggen ship, not a fairground ride,' said Malcolm. 'It's a kill'n machine. It's meant to scare yuh. Not give yuh a kiss.'

The gangway closest to its bow was covered with a white plastic awning like a posh gazebo at a country club. Coming down the utility gangway at its stern, a sailor was waving at them.

'We've been spotted,' said Isa.

'Ms Weddle, ma'am?' said the sailor, rolling towards her, as if the quayside's concrete was the heaving deck of a ship and to keep his balance he'd to sway from side to side.

'That is I,' said Isa.

'Petty Officer Jefferies, ma'am. The colonel sends his compliments. I am to escort you on board.'

'That's very kind. You were quick to spot my pink rose.'

'Not a bit of it, ma'am. It was the wolf I spotted. The colonel told me not to bother looking for a rose but to look for a wolf. Believe it or not, ma'am, it's not every day a chap sees a wolf driving a Mercedes.'

'Hoy!' said Malcolm. 'How do I get oot of here?'

Isa pressed the button which allowed the driver's seat to fold forward. Malcolm, under the influence of too many 'pokers', staggered out.

'Sir,' said Petty Officer Jefferies, coming to attention.

'Yuh alreet, bonny lad?'

'Local man, are you, sir?'

'Why aye.'

'So am I.'

'Where duh yuh drink?'

'The "CP" and the "Low Lights Tavern".'

'A nar where yuh mean. You and me is ganna get on just fine.'

'Follow me.'

'Oh, dear me! That's what the Pied Piper said to the rats.'

'But,' said Isa, 'we are not rats. We are the good guys. Chippy. Stay!'

They went down ladders and up ladders. They squeezed through doors stencilled with warnings that when at sea they must be kept closed. PO Jefferies kept telling Malcolm to duck.

'I don't want you meeting the colonel looking like a bruised apple, sir.'

Their journey through the labyrinth ended when PO Jefferies showed them into a cabin just about big enough to take two table tennis tables.

In her time Isa had been in many such rooms. It was where admirals talked about using nuclear weapons.

Jeremy, resplendent in the uniform of a Royal Marine colonel, all smiles, bid them welcome. When he stood so did Joan who was sat next to him. In front of him on the faux Chippendale table were plates of triangular sandwiches, a bottle of Moet in an ice bucket, champagne flutes, thermos flasks, cups and saucers, and serviettes. The crockery (bone china) and serviettes bore the crest of HMS Newcastle.

'Ms Weddle, Isa,' said Jeremy, extending a hand, 'welcome to the pow-wow. Who is your friend?'

'My cousin, Malcolm. He cuts number thirty-nine's gardens. He has upset 'TA' and Leo.'

'He is in jeopardy?'

'Yes.'

'You can vouch for him?'

'Yes.'

'On whose life?'

'Chippy's.'

'If you are prepared to swear on the life of your wolf that this fellow is bona fide and to be trusted with our secrets, I believe you. Ms Weddle, Malcolm, please take a seat. Tea and coffee in the flasks. Or, shall we start with the Moet? Smoked salmon in the Bermuda triangles. Caught the fellow myself. Put up a helluva fight. I apologise for the cucumber. It is not home grown. I believe it is from a supermarket called Morrisons. Buy, three, get one free, so my ADC told me. Who wants three cucumbers?'

The NO SMOKING sign, between two black and white photographs, of previous HMS Newcastles, made Malcolm wonder what the world was coming to. Who would want to join the navy if you couldn't smoke? And, as for this bloke, Jeremy. Well, yuh bugger! Last time he'd found anything so out of his comfort zone, was when he'd found a fossil in a lump of anthracite.

The champagne looked to be a bit of alreet, though. He'd once had champagne at the club. Christmas Day, 1973. A barmaid who fancied him had given him a freebie. 'Prosecco', she'd said, 'it's the same as champagne.'

'Moo-et?' said Jeremy, handing Malcolm a flute of fizz.

'Moo!' said Malcolm, taking the flute with a mischievous grin. 'Yee impersonating a cow?'

He knew how to handle posh buggers. Yuh let them know from the start that yuh weren't the back end of the pantomime horse.

'Yuh alreet, bonny lad?'

'A local man?' said Jeremy.

'Why aye! How'd yuh nar?'

'I have no idea. Put it down to intuition.'

'Isa says you're a spy. Pleased to meet yuh. Glad we are both on the same side. I'm a spy as well, yuh nar. Me cousin Isa deputised me. Yuh nar, like yuh see in the cowboy films. We're like a posse, aren't wuh? Heh! Heh! Oh, dear me! This fizzy stuff is giv'n me hay fever. It's bringing tears oot me eyes and snot oot me nose.'

To shut Malcolm up, Jeremy took out his glass eye, breathed on it, cleaned it with a napkin and without a by-your-leave, popped it back into its socket. As a blabber-stopper, it never failed.

'Oh, dear me!' said Malcolm. 'How'd yuh dee that?'

His head was spinning. How many 'pokers' had he had with Leo? He couldn't remember.

'Are yee the ship's conjuror?'

'Malcolm,' said Isa, 'shut it!'

'Eh?'

'Shut it!'

'Oh, aye!'

'Help yourself, dear boy!' said Jeremy, gesturing towards the Moet.

'If yuh divent mind,' said Malcolm, 'a think a will.'

'Jeremy,' said Isa, 'I think it's time we put our cards on the table.'

'You go first.'

'Because I am a woman?'

'Strategy, Ms Weddle. Strategy. No room for good manners in the spying game.'

Looking Jeremy straight in his good eye, she said: 'I know he's not dead.'

'Do you indeed?'

'Who is not dead?' said Joan.

'I have not had a chance to tell you. Joan, Tobias Lacy is alive and well. You are not a murderer.'

'He has to be. Aunt Isa, I didn't miss. I know I didn't. I'm a marksman.'

'He was wearing a bulletproof vest.'

'Really?'

'Yes.'

It took Joan a few seconds to even begin to think that she might not be a murderer. Ever so slowly the stiff-upper-lip dam she'd built to keep her emotional reaction to what she'd done under control began to show signs of cracking.

She was the victim of a sting operation. She was like the patient who'd been told she'd a malignant brain tumour but was now being told she'd been misdiagnosed.

She put her head in her hands. Her shoulders began to heave. She did her best to stifle her sobs. She did not want to let the side down.

Despite her best efforts, her sobs of relief were as audible in the small room as church bells are on a frosty Sunday morning when their rolling peels sound as if they are breaking ice on the village pond.

Isa and Jeremy ignored her disintegration. In the grand scheme of things she was not important. And Malcolm was drunk.

'What's the matter with her?' he said. 'Canny stuff, this, moo-cow. Heh! Heh!'

'You knew all the time he wasn't dead, didn't you, Jeremy?' said Isa.

'Yes, I did. Who told you?'

'Who told you?'

'The "plumbers".'

'They are working for you?'

'Yes.'

'But 'TA' thinks they are working for him?'

'Yes. They are wizards with the technical stuff. Clever. Not public school.'

'You trusted two plebs!'

'As I trusted you, Ms Weddle.'

'And when you are finished with us you will throw us to the wolves.'

Jeremy sighed.

'You find my point of view exasperating?'

'I'm afraid, I do, rather. One of these days that chip on your shoulder will give you a permanent list.'

'We's Brahms and Lizt?' said Malcolm. 'A think am pissed. Yee alreet, bonny lad? Hoy! What aboot me lawn mower?'

'Joan,' said Isa, 'would you be so kind as to pour Malcolm a café noire. I need to talk strategy with Jeremy.'

'Oh, dear me! Brahms and Lizt,' said Malcolm, then, in his best RP voice, '"I need to talk strategy." Yuh alreet, bonny lad?'

'Malcolm,' said, Joan, stifling a sob on the point of turning into a giggle, 'if you don't shut it, I'll shoot you.'

'Aye, yuh would, as well. Is that for real?' pointing at the: NO SMOKING sign. 'Ave never seen a sign like that before. What aboot me lawn mower? It's on the never-never. Tick! Tick-tock. Tick-tock. A think am a clock. Heh! Heh! Tick-tock. Tick-tock.'

As adult wild animals – even the crocodile and hippopotamus – tolerate the waywardness of their offspring while getting on with the business of staying alive, Isa and Jeremy ignored Malcolm and discussed the rendition of Tony Adder.

Jeremy told Isa, the 'plumbers' had planted bugs in number thirty-nine: ''TA' knows nothing about them. I now have conclusive

193

proof: Tony Adder is a traitor.'

'What will happen to him?' said Isa.

'The highest authority has told me his treachery must not become front page news.'

'The PM?'

'That is for me to know, Ms Weddle, and for you to speculate. I have carte blanche to use the usual facilities. Pray, do not raise your eyebrows. Please to remember, Tony Adder was responsible for the blowing up of Yuri.'

'And for you losing an eye.'

'Just so. Quite. You are in agreement with my plan for tomorrow?'

'The little of it you have told me, yes.'

'I think we understand each other.'

'Are you saying, we see eye to eye?'

'That, Ms Weddle, is an inappropriate colloquialism to use when chatting to me.'

'Sorry.'

'By-the-by, how'd you come to know that Tobias was not dead?'

****

For the drive home, Joan and Malcolm sat in the back seat of the Mercedes. As usual, Chippy (droit de seigneur) sat in the front seat. The car's roof was down. The dog sniffed the air flowing over his wet nose as a connoisseur sniffs a brandy whose grapes had sucked in sunshine before Napoleon had been defeated at Waterloo.

'I'm not a murderer,' said Joan, arching back her head to look at the sky. 'I'm not a murderer.'

'Hoy!' exclaimed Malcolm. 'That bloke, Jeremy, with the eye trick. Canny bloke, him. Yuh nar what he slipped me?' Holding up a bottle of navy rum sporting the crest of HMS Newcastle. 'He might be a posh bugger but he's alreet. Where's me fags? A was think'n of joining the navy until a saw that no smoking sign. Oh, dear, me!

Give's a turn; that did.'

Placing a cigarette between the receptive O of his mouth, Malcolm clicked his lighter. Each time its wick flared, the car's wind speed snuffed it out.

'Friggen wind! And look at me hair. It's aal ower the place.'

Malcolm's top hair consisted of strands of side hair drawn across his scalp the way curtains which do not meet in the middle are drawn across a window. Only Malcolm believed they hid the fact that on top he was as bald as an egg.

'Friggen wind! Oh, dear me! We've got a wolf sitting in the front seat and now, a can't light me tab.'

'This reminds me of the "Planet of the Apes",' said Joan.

'I beg your pardon?' said Malcolm, putting on his posh voice.

'I mean,' said Joan, 'the animals have taken over. Chippy in the front seat. As if he owned the car and Aunt Isa was his chauffeur. And, do you know what? I don't care. I'm not a murderer.'

'Aye!' said Malcolm, looking at Joan and then at Chippy. 'The "Planet of the Apes", eh? That's good, that. I like that.'

****

Isa dropped off Malcolm first. His car and lawn mower would have to stay at number thirty-nine. He was in no fit state to drive.

'Are you alright?' she asked him.

'Why aye, am alreet! Why shouldn't a be?'

'Don't drop your rum.'

'Nee fear of that. 'am vexed, mind. A left the two bottles of vodka Leo gave me, in his hoose; didn't a?'

'You will get them back.'

'Will a? Tomorrow neet?'

'Yes.'

'Av nivva done an abduction before.'

'Would it help if you thought of it as a seduction?'

'Aye! Heh! Heh! It would. A nar a lot aboot seduction. Mary Battles seduced me behind a dustbin in the back lane when a was fifteen. What will Jeremy ... Oh, dear me! A can't say that withoot laugh'n. A divent think there's anyone called Jeremy at the club. What will the posh guy dee to this 'TA' bloke?'

'He will be taken to a safe house and debriefed.'

'"Debriefed"! What if he's wearing boxer shorts? Heh! Heh! Get it? Good, eh?'

'Give me your key.'

'Why?'

'Because the keyhole you are trying to find is not at the bottom of the door.'

'Oh, aye! Hoy! What aboot me lawn mower? And, me van and trailer? There's a few thousand quids worth of equipment there. If I lose them I'll need compensation. A bloke at work got a thousand quid when he lost a finger. He tried to get more by telling the board he was a concert pianist, but they wouldn't believe him. Nee body trusts anybody these days. It's a good job blood is thicker than watta. Div a get a kiss?'

'Certainly not!'

'Heh! Heh! Oh, dear me! This is not my day. Pip-toodle!'

'What on earth made you say that?'

'It's what a heard the posh bloke say. I am not as drunk as yuh think a am, Isa. Hoy! What if a went to the Evening Chronicle? Yuh, nar? Sell them my story. Tell them aal aboot the spies at number thirty-nine?'

'First of all, they wouldn't believe you, and second, MI5 would arrange for you to have a fatal accident. Do you understand what I am saying? For the umpteenth time, Malcolm, this is not a game!'

'Divent worry, Isa. A nar what you're gannin on aboot. Malcolm's not daft. Good neet.'

****

'We need to talk,' Isa told her niece, as she drove off, 'somewhere quiet.'

Jesmond Dene, a public park of many acres, is a green and leafy place. It has waterfalls, stepping stones and a fairy glen. Off his lead, Chippy sniffed and squirted. Only a five-minute drive from the centre of Newcastle, its acres of greenery made Isa and Joan feel as if they were out in the country.

'Why did Mr Adder do it?' said Joan.

'For money,' said Isa.

'Mr Adder is not a nice man, is he?'

'Not a nice man, indeed!' If he was to pop out from behind that bush and I had a gun, I'd take him out. Nothing fancy. A chest shot. Maximum target area. I am feeling vengeful. Damn the consequences.'

'That's not like you, Aunt Isa, to want to take the law into your own hands.'

'Could you not kill him?'

'I might be tempted, but I wouldn't. When I thought I'd killed Mr Lacy I couldn't sleep. It is a terrible thing to take a human life. It was a risky stunt Mr Adder and Mr Lacy pulled. If I'd tried to be clever and gone for a head shot, Mr Lacy really would be dead and I would be a murderer.'

'I have killed,' said Isa.

'Does it bother you? You have mentioned it before. I mean, do you have nightmares?'

'No. If I hadn't killed them they'd have killed me. I was lucky. Each time I shot a bad guy I have kept the shoes I was wearing. I call them my "lucky shoes".'

'How many "lucky shoes" do you have, Aunt Isa?'

'Too many. Not a wardrobe full but, too many.'

'Oh!' said Joan. 'I'm a rookie, aren't I?'

'Yes.'

'Aunt, Isa, what will happen to Mr Adder?'

'Don't ask. I think you know. Keep your suspicions to yourself. A suspicion is not the same as a fact. As long as you only suspect, there is hope that you might be wrong. Dear me, we can't let it become common knowledge that HMG condones bumping folk off. Can we? That would never do. Mum's the word, Joan. Tomorrow?'

'I carry on as if I do not know I am not a murderer. I play the role of a skivvy to Mr Adder and Leo. If Mr Adder wants a tin of baked beans from Morrisons, I go get him one. No questions asked. I am under his thumb. If I don't play ball, he spills the beans on me.'

****

Back home, after having first dropped off her niece, Isa – before she'd even had time to take off her coat – received a deputation from the SPC. Dominic, Irene, Beatrice and Angus were at her front as agitated as if they'd lost their budgerigar and wanted to know if she'd seen it.

'We don't want coffee,' said Dominic.

'That's not what you said before,' said Irene. 'You said, "Isa's bound to offer us coffee".'

'Irene! Shut up!'

'Dominic, don't talk to me like that! Don't forget I'm pregnant. What have I done now?'

'I was hoping for a whisky,' said Angus. 'A shy bairn gets nowt. Isa is known for her generosity. You ask her, Beatrice. It was a tradition in the glen that if a Campbell asked a Macdonald a favour, you knew it would rain for a fortnight.'

'Angus, what are you going on about?' said Beatrice. 'Are you mad?'

'Was I blather'n on?'

'Yes.'

'Don't blame me. Blame the wedding. I keep toasting the happy couple. Three times I've raised a glass to them tonight. Morag says

I'm drinking too much. I tell her, blame Charles and Di. Morag loves the royals more than she loves watching salmon jump the weir at Pitlochry.'

'What is it you want to ask me?' said Isa. 'Chippy, stop licking Angus's hand.'

'It's the whisky I spilled on it,' explained Angus. 'Aye! The wolf has good taste. That was ten-year-old malt.'

'I think Dominic should ask,' said Irene, 'after all he is our chair.'

'To cut to the quick,' said Domenic, 'your gardener's car and trailer are in the space the street plan has allocated for the conjuror and karaoke.'

'You must tell your gardener to move his car and trailer,' said Beatrice. 'If it's not moved our street party will be ruined. People will blame me. I know they will. Everyone knows I'm on the SPC.'

'What I want to know,' said Angus, 'is ... what's going on? I mean he's never left his car in the street before. He's some kind of relation of yours, I believe?'

'He's my cousin,' said Isa. 'The sad truth is that while he was cutting number thirty-nine's grass he was led astray by the gentleman who is currently renting number thirty-nine. Vodka!'

'He is Russian,' said Beatrice. 'I've met him. I took the liberty of inviting him to the street party. I said hello and goodbye to him in Russian. He was ever so impressed. I think he rather fancied me.'

'He's a vodka salesman,' said Isa. 'I'm afraid he plied my cousin with too many free samples. I'm ashamed to say Malcolm was in no fit state to drive home.'

'If he doesn't move it,' said Irene, 'our street party will be ruined. You can't expect Dominic to draw up an alternative plan at this late stage. There isn't time. And what's that bit of cardboard say on the lawn mower? For sale?'

'Is the Russian selling second hand lawn mowers?' said Angus.

'Next thing it will be beds,' said Beatrice.

'Or wardrobes,' said Angus, 'next thing you know the Grove will look like the forecourt of a second-hand furniture shop. House prices will plummet.'

'The note on the lawn mower, says: "Come and get me",' said Isa.

'Why does it say that?' said Beatrice.

'Leo, the Russian renting number thirty-nine, is as keen for Malcolm to come and collect his lawn mower as you are for him to come and remove his car. I will pass your instructions on to him. I assure you he is a most obliging fellow.'

'That's not the impression I got,' said Beatrice. 'Do not forget, Isa, I have met him. I don't mean to be critical of one of your relations, but it seems to me he is the sort of fellow who is too fond of women. When he looked at me I got the strong impression he was taking off my dress.'

'Ladies, please,' said Angus, 'I was brought up by Presbyterians. About your cousin's car, Isa?'

'I will get in touch with him and tell him he must remove it before the street is closed to traffic. Promise.'

'There we are, wonderful what diplomacy can do. No need to burn Isa at the stake. I'm looking forward to tomorrow night.'

'So am I,' said Isa. 'I have a feeling it will be a party I will remember for the rest of my life.'

Chapter 20

Malcolm did not have a home telephone. To get in touch with him to tell him to remove his car and trailer, Isa drove to his house. She took Chippy with her.

She knocked and rang his doorbell. No answer. The blue paint he'd found in the skip and with which he'd painted his front door was still tacky. Would it ever dry? She'd smudges of it on her fingertips. It was like a virus. The Blue Paint virus. Go anywhere near it and it got you.

To get the paint off her fingertips she did a finger-tip print on a red brick. Making the print made her feel like a cave woman doing a hand-print in a cave with a fire at its entrance to keep out wolves.

If he was out, she knew where to find him. Malcolm's second home was a CIU club. Parking outside its urine-splashed walls, she put up the Mercedes' hood. Not because the crime rate in the area was high, but because of seagulls. Their droppings went through upholstery like sulphuric acid. The car was safe with Chippy guarding it. To give him air, she let a window down.

Cairo, Damascus, London – private clubs were the same the world over; to get in you had to get past the gorilla on the door.

'I've forgotten my membership card,' she told the CIU door man sitting on a plastic chair, behind a table in a kind of booth. He was an old man, dressed to kill in a black shirt with pearl buttons. His white bow tie had come straight out of the washing machine. He looked at her through a cloud of cigarette smoke.

In front of him he'd a saucer. Ah! The begging bowl. You scratch my back and I'll scratch yours. Into it Isa dropped two pound coins. When he did not look impressed she dropped in two more.

'Alreet, pet, in yuh gan. You're not a prostitute, are yuh?'

'Certainly not! Do I look like one?'

'Nar! Nar! Sorry. They come in aal shapes and sizes, yuh nar. They're like leeks. Do you grow leeks? Nar! Nar! Silly question. Am on the committee. Sub-committee chair of "Pathetic Mushrooms". Ethics and morals.'

'I am looking for Malcolm.'

'Oh, him! There's only one Malcolm. Does he have castanet hair? When it's windy it bangs up and doon … yuh, nar … open and shut like a netty door when yuh are trying to read the paper and yuh nar the neighbour's watching yuh from behind her net curtains? Have yuh not got good lugs? A mean, can yuh not hear him? Shut the door and shut oot the traffic and listen.'

In the ensuing quiet Isa heard singing.

'That's him. He's the boy! Loves Frankie Vaughan. Most blokes like dee'n Elvis, but Malcolm's a Frankie Vaughan fan. It was the same when he was doon the pit. He always had to be different. He once came to work wearing a bow tie. I mean, fancy ganin doon the pit wearing a bow tie. Tut! Tut!' shaking his head and exhaling a cloud of cigarette smoke. 'A think he was mak'n a point. He's what wuh call a character. Just listen to him! Yuh sure you're not on the game? Did a tell yuh, am on the committee? It's my job to keep the club free of drugs and make sure folk aren't hiding in cupboards deeing things with broom handles what they shouldn't be deeing.'

'May I go in?'

'Why aye! You've paid the ferryman.'

****

202

The air in the concert hall was foggy with cigarette smoke and evaporating sweat; a toxic mixture locals called Gothic Butter. Caught on stage, between the beams of two spotlights, Malcolm wearing a top hat and with an NHS walking stick over his shoulder to represent a gentleman's walking cane, was putting his heart and soul into singing Frankie Vaughan's sixties hit 'Give me the moonlight'. Impersonating his hero singing that song, was Malcolm's party piece; what chefs call their signature dish.

Being on stage made him feel important and wanted. It made him feel loved. And Malcolm was a great believer in love.

On stage, tipping his topper at the women, any woman who caught his eye, he wasn't an out of work pitman, struggling to make ends meet, he was a star of stage and screen.

Taking his bow, he received sporadic applause and two wolf whistles. A woman who might have been a man in drag threw a pair of y-fronts at him.

Semaphoring him through the Gothic Butter, she caught his eye.

'Are yuh alreet, cus?' he said, coming over to join her. 'Did yuh see us on the stage? A was good, wasn't a? Ave got a lot of fans, yuh nar. What yuh deeing in here? Yuh look as out of place as a daffodil does in the park in August. Duh yuh want me autograph?'

'I want the keys to your car.'

'What for?'

She explained.

'Oh, dear me! A secret agent's work is never done, is it? Give us time to tell Mary am ganin haem. She'll not be pleased.'

The kiss Malcolm exchanged with Mary was long and passionate, as if he was going off to war and she might never see him again.

'See yuh, Tommy!'

In the car park Isa said, 'Malcolm, I'm puzzled. Why did that woman you were kissing call you "Tommy"?'

'Yuh niva tell woman what fancies yuh, your real name. If yee dee they'll be after holy-money; yuh nar ... alimony. Anyway, she's from "Alnwick Castle"–' 'lighting a cigarette– 'they're rough. Back seat?'

'In you get.'

'And tell Chippy to stop licking me, will yuh?'

'It's because he likes you.'

'Aye, well … a divent like him. He's like a foreman we had at the pit. When he was nice to yuh, yuh couldn't trust him. Yuh always knew he was after something. Nice doggy!'

At his house, giving her his car keys, he gave her sage advice concerning the idiosyncrasies of the car's gears: 'When you put it into third, keep your hand on the gear stick, otherwise, it'll pop oot.'

Nodding, to show she understood, Isa said: 'Was that woman a plant?'

'What duh you mean? Like a geranium?'

'No. The woman who threw y-fronts at you, was she for real or had you planted her in the audience?'

'Nar! Nar! She was for real. If she was a plant she'd be a bedding plant. Heh! Heh! She fancies me. Can I not drive me car home?'

'No. You have had too much to drink.'

She left him, drunk and weary, watching a 'load of shite' on television, about the royal wedding.

Back home she parked the Mercedes in her drive. With Chippy at her side, she walked across the road to Malcolm's car, where he'd parked it with its trailer outside number thirty-nine. It started first time. That was a miracle. If he complained about dog hairs, tough!

In less than fifteen minutes she was back at his flat and had parked his old banger and trailer outside his blue front door. Posting the car's keys through his letterbox, she could not resist touch-testing the front door's blue paint. Still tacky. Alongside the finger-tip print she'd done earlier, she left a second print.

She and Chippy walked home.

****

Before turning in for the night she looked across at number thirty-nine. No sign of life. What were 'TA' and Leo doing? Was Leo writing down in longhand what 'TA' was telling him? Did Leo have a tape recorder? 'TA' had worked for MI6 for a long time. The story he had to tell would be a long one. More 'War and Peace' than a sonnet.

In number thirty-nine's front garden, moonlight made Malcolm's lawn mower look like a Henry Moore sculpture. It would have to stay there. There was only so much a supernumerary paid to keep a watchful eye on a safe house could do.

Wednesday 29th July 1981.

The day of the royal wedding dawned bright and sunny. A beautiful day on which to get married. Was it the right weather, though, for an assassination? When a dastardly deed was to take place, should there not be thunder and lightning?

According to anecdote, whenever the Nazis had held one of their rallies, the sun had always shone. Germans had called it 'Hitler Weather'. Every house frau knew her washing would dry when the Nazis were marching.

Carpe diem. She opened doors and windows. A through breeze brought into the house the subtle scents of an English summer's day. Bees were pestering a lavender bush the way no doubt Charles and Di would be pestering each other later that evening. The perfumed air relaxed her the way Yuri used to make her feel relaxed when he'd massaged her neck. Yuri! Dear Yuri! Was this the day he was going to be avenged?

Chippy wandered out into the front garden and flopped down onto the cooling grass. It was a hot day for a dog. When humans were hot, they could take off their clothes. He couldn't. All he could do was pant.

****

Isa was trying on her cowgirl costume when Chippy barked. Going out to see why he was raising the alarm, she found Harry leaning over her garden gate as excited as a horse poking its head out of its stable door when it thinks it's going to get an apple.

Harry! Dear Harry! Out for his morning bout of Nordic walking. He was wearing white running shorts, a yellow singlet advertising the name of the insurance company for which he worked and … a tricorn hat; the hat looking as out of place on him as a pair of shoes for sale would look in the window of a fish shop.

'You were as good as your word,' he said, doffing the tricorn and standing back from the gate, to give himself room to make a sweeping bow, as if he was an English gent, circa 1790.

'You mean, I kept my word about removing Malcolm's car?'

'Angus told me about the deputation. That your fancy dress for tonight?'

'I'm coming as a cowgirl.'

'I'm coming as a town crier. Hence the hat. Like it? Dominic has loaned me a hand bell from his school. Funny bloke, Dominic. I met him in Pratt's buying rib-eye steaks. I thought he was vegan.'

'He used to be.'

'Changed his mind, has he? Seen which way the wind's blowing.'

'Irene told me, he knows someone in education with influence who is a carnivore.'

'I know where he's coming from. If you want to get on, you have to fit in. My boss is a Methodist. I tell him I don't drink. I don't think he believes me. That lawn mower in number thirty-nine's front garden doesn't do the Grove any favours, does it? How long is it going to stay there? Do you think the hat suits me? I do. How does this sound? Oh, yeah! Oh, yeah! Bring out your dead!'

'Harry, we are celebrating a royal wedding not the plague.'

'If I come as a town crier folk will expect me to do a bit of hollering. Jean is coming as Little Bo-Peep.'

'Does Jean not know that Beatrice is coming as Little Bo-Peep?'

'Is she? Is she really?'

'A rival Bo-peep could send Beatrice over the top.'

'If she had to sell insurance for a living, Beatrice would have something to go over the top about.' Looking at his watch. 'I'd best be off. I'm under strict instructions to be back in time to watch the wedding. I'm only doing five miles this morning. I told Jean, no royal wedding is going to come between me and keeping fit. If I'm not fit I can't sell insurance. If I don't sell any policies I won't have money to pay the gas bill. The domino effect. Ipso facto. I must keep fit.' Looking at his watch again. 'If I'm slower than usual I'll blame the tricorn. Wind resistance. Bye!'

****

For the umpteenth time Isa pondered what might be going on inside number thirty-nine. She imagined 'TA' talking to Leo in sessions of one hour. If the Russian had done his homework, he'd have a list of prepared questions. Over vodka – perhaps in bed together (she did wonder about their relationship) – he'd be pumping 'TA' for information about the workings of the British Secret Service. Nothing would be sacred. Who was who in the British embassy in Moscow? The names of sleeper agents. What he knew about the CIA. Gossip and facts would be spilling out of 'TA' the way coins cascade out of a slot machine when someone hits the jackpot.

If only Jeremy had taken her more into his confidence. Did he have a plan? He had the confidence of Genghis Kahn. On board HMS Newcastle he'd spoken in the broadest of brush strokes. 'TA' was going to be rendered. Ok. But how? He probably thought telling 'TA' 'You are nicked, bonny lad' would be a whizz. In case it wasn't, at the street party tonight, she'd be carrying the Glock Desmond had sent her. She'd carry it in one of the holsters she'd be wearing as part of her cowgirl costume. To make it look like a toy gun, she'd wrap white electrician's tape round its butt.

She'd borrowed the holster from the twin boys who lived next door. They were no longer into playing cowboys and Indians. That was kids' stuff. They were into 'Star Trek'. As a thank you she'd let them look through her telescope. The sight of Saturn's rings had shut them up for all of five minutes.

They were out now, watching her through the beech hedge separating their gardens.

'Bang!'

'You are dead!'

'I can see you, so I'm not dead. I knew you were there all the time. It is not British to shoot an unarmed cowgirl. Look! My holsters are empty. I am unarmed.'

Isa was ambivalent about children. They should be seen but not heard. If her view was old fashioned, well, so be it. After all, apart from being an assassin she was also a spinster.

'Bang!'

'Gotchya!'

Water squirted out of the beech hedge.

'Ambush!' shouted Isa, doing her best not to sound like a spoil sport.

'Alfie! Isaac!' shouted their mother. 'Do come in and watch the wedding. I hope you are not shooting water at snails. I know they eat mummy and daddy's plants but, like all living things they have their uses and we must treasure them.'

Alfie and Isaac went in, Isa suspected, not to watch the wedding – which they probably couldn't give a toss about – but because they were guerrilla fighters. As soon as he has killed, a guerrilla fighter disappears.

What would they have thought if they'd known they'd doused a secret agent? Such a pity she could not tell them she was a marksman. That she had killed for her country. That her old biddy act was a piece of stage scenery.

Wouldn't it be amusing if the conjuror hired to entertain them, in the afternoon, sawed one of them in half.

****

The street was now officially closed to traffic. In the middle of the road, Dominic and co-opted members of the SPC were unhinging legs hidden under tables. Higher up the no-go area, entrepreneurial residents were making a children's playground. A swing, a slide, a see-saw and a blow-up paddling pool were appearing in real time, in the middle of the road, at the speed a delayed action film shows, in seconds, the years it takes for a twig to grow into a tree. Had they permission from Dominic? As far as Isa knew it had never been part of the SPC's plan to have a children's playground. She hoped Dominic would be flexible. It was never a good idea to stifle free enterprise. Free enterprise had made possible the British Empire.

As is the way with amateurs who have done something for the first time and are feeling pleased with themselves, those responsible for the ad hoc playground, now stood back – arms folded – hands on hips – to admire and fine-tune their handiwork. Perhaps the swing should be a few more centimetres away from the kerb.

'Excuse me!' shouted Irene, leaning over Isa's front gate. 'I've put a tea pot (meaning a cardboard cut-out of one) on your wall. You are down as a tea-station. It's on Dominic's master plan in one of the coloured inks he uses. Anyone who wants a cup of tea at this end of the street will come to you. Here is a supply of paper cups. Some folk will bring their own cups. Some might not. Just in case. Do you think number thirty-nine will know what the tea pot means? He's Russian, isn't he? Will he be joining in? I mean, if he's a Russian he'll be a communist, won't he? They don't believe in kings and queens; do they? They murdered their king. He wasn't called a king. He was called a tsar. Did you know that? Yes, you did. I can tell by your face that you did. Have I put my foot in it? Dominic is always telling me I have cow shit on my shoes … you know; from putting my foot in it.'

'Oh, yeah! Oh, yeah!' shouted Harry, striding up and down the street, dressed as a town crier and ringing a hand bell.

'Oh, yeah! Oh, yeah! To the good people of Chillingham Grove let it be known that Her Majesty the Queen has left Buckingham Palace. If you don't want to miss Charlie boy saying, "I will" get yourselves inside in front of the telly, now!'

'A street party needs someone like Harry,' said Isa.

'Dominic's coming as a highlander,' said Irene. 'He's going to wear his kilt. You'll see his knees. He has lovely knees.'

'I can't wait,' said Isa.

'He's going to play his bagpipes.'

'Oh, yeah! Oh, yeah!'

'Isa, do you think Harry's town crier's cravat is a pair of men's Y-fronts?'

'Yes. Think of it as making the private, public.'

'What do you mean?'

'Never mind. I'm going in to watch the wedding,' said Isa. 'I'm beginning to feel emotional just thinking about it. The Wedding March makes me cry.'

'Dominic,' said Irene, going over to her husband who was doing something with a spanner under a trestle table, 'Harry's made his town crier's cravat out of Y-fronts. I didn't know we were going to have a town crier.'

'Nor did, I. Nor a children's playground. Things are getting out of hand.'

'It would serve Harry right if he got arrested for indecent exposure like my Uncle Tom did when he'd had too much to drink and couldn't find a Gents.'

****

During the wedding ceremony the street emptied, apart that is from a toddler who found crawling through lengths of corrugated plastic tubing more moreish than watching a royal wedding. His parents, no doubt absorbed in watching the big event, had forgotten all about him; like the couple who, in the excitement of going on holiday, left their dog at home and after driving for an hour had to turn back.

Isa's TV was in her front room. While she watched it, she could also keep a watchful eye on number thirty-nine. Because she was a woman, she found multi-tasking easy.

Though the day was warm none of number thirty-nine's windows were open. It looked to be an empty house. A deserted house. The bunting Isa had wrapped around the pole cherry in its front garden had failed to do what it had been meant to do, namely: make the house look as if it was joining in the street party. Malcolm's blue lawn mower, instead of hinting at occupation, suggested number thirty-nine's front garden was a scrap yard.

Were 'TA' and the Russian watching the royal wedding? Its pomp and circumstance made her brood about what she had lost when terrorists had killed Yuri. If he had lived, would they have married? After all these years his loss still hurt. The fanfare announcing the arrival of the Queen and Prince Philip gave her goose bumps. When the congregation stood, she stood. As if she was there and not three hundred miles away. Who else but Queen Elizabeth the second could make a serving member of MI5 stand to attention in front of a television screen?

'God Save the Queen' made her want to cry and that was before the Wedding March began to play merry hell with her nervous system.

It was 'reality' in the form of Joan walking up number thirty-nine's front path that made her sentimentality do an emergency stop.

Why was Joan walking? Where was her 'Spick and Span' van? Of course, the street was closed to traffic. Living in a street temporarily turned into a pedestrian precinct – like driving on the continent –

was going to take a lot of getting used to.

Was her niece the only adult in the UK not glued to a television set? As far as Isa knew, Joan was not a republican. She was carrying a hold-all. What was in it? Tea? Coffee? A weapon from MI5's arsenal?

Through binoculars she saw 'TA' take the holdall, then, at least from his body language (it was like watching a silent movie) give Joan what the posh boys called a bloody good dressing down.

Joan walked up Isa's drive with her head bowed. Chippy, on guard in the front garden, greeted her with the single bark he kept for people he knew.

Dropping the binoculars, Isa ran to meet her niece.

'What happened?'

'If you don't mind, Aunt Isa, I'll stand on the doorstep. He'll be watching. I want him to know I have delivered his message. Don't look so worried. I didn't buckle.'

'Thank god for that.'

'He reminded me to do as I was told. If I did not, I knew the consequences.'

'You didn't even hint that you knew Tobias … Mr Lacy was alive?'

'Of course not. Aunt Isa, each day I'm getting more professional. When he threatened me, I pretended to let him know I knew which side my bread was buttered on. I acted humble when, really, I wanted to scream at him. I wanted to tell him, "Go fuck yourself, Mr Adder, I know Mr Lacy isn't dead". I don't like being a doormat. Now that I know I am not a murderer, I am like a guy who has been told he is no longer on death row. I feel invincible.'

'You don't think he suspected?'

'Stop worrying, Aunt Isa. I'm a good actress. He was in a helluva mood. Malcolm has really upset him. He is adamant you find a new gardener. If Malcolm plays anymore tricks with dummy dynamite he says he will have him assassinated. That's what he said.'

'Did he indeed! What did you deliver?'

'A laurel wreath. It's for Leo's fancy dress; you know, to go with the toga.'

'The mind boggles.'

'Also, plus fours, a black beret and pantomime dame boobs. Mr Adder is coming as "Cezanne the Dame Golfer". He rang up HQ and told me to get them and the laurel wreath.'

'And you didn't let him down?'

'I wouldn't dare, would I? He's blackmailing me. I have to do as I'm told. Ha! Ha!'

'Well done, Joan. You've not let the side down. I'm thinking there's a lot of iron in the Weddle blood. I'm surprised 'TA' is coming to the fancy dress. I'd have expected him to keep a low profile. On the other hand, he's such an egotist he'd hate to be left out. No fear of him being the girl who never got asked to dance.'

'I think it's Leo's idea. Leo might be a communist, but I get the impression he likes us Brits. I think he wants to get to know the neighbours.'

'In which case he should put 'TA' in a pantry and lock the door. A street party to celebrate a royal wedding is not the place to introduce a cross-dresser into Chillingham Grove's polite society, Joan. 'TA's' fancy dress will raise eyebrows but not open doors. I wonder how much Jeremy knows about such goings on.'

'Aunt Isa, who is Jeremy?'

'A good question.'

'Do you trust him?'

'Yes and no. My gender and upbringing bar me from the upper class male world in which he operates. I know he is ruthless. Stand in his way and he will crush you.'

'By the way, I know where 'TA''s parked his car. It's on Front Street. I was told where to find it.'

'By whom? '

'By Jeremy. He rang me at home. How he got my number, I don't know. He told me where it was and that I was to immobilise it. I have let its tyres down. Mr Adder won't be driving anywhere without first using a foot pump. When I was letting the air out of them, they hissed like, adders.'

'Joan, for goodness' sake put a brake on your imagination. You are in danger of allowing your fancy to influence your judgement. It is clear to me, Jeremy is using you to tighten the noose MI5 is placing round 'TA''s neck. You and I, Joan, are cogs in a plan we know too little about.'

'If you say so, Aunt Isa.'

'I do.'

'I'd better go. He will be watching. He will have seen I have delivered his ultimatum. By the way, I'm coming to the fancy dress as a Keystone cop.'

'You are coming to the fancy dress?'

'Yes. Jeremy told me to think of my role as a fire engine. I might not be needed but if there was a fire I would be.'

****

At two-thirty, Isa gave Chippy, who was on guard duty in the front garden, a marrow bone. She fondled his ears. He wagged his tail. Soon, according to Dominic's itinerary, the party would be starting.

The start of the pedestrianized area of the street was marked with a row of red geraniums in terracotta plant pots. The SPC had discussed whether or not to use plastic plant pots. Morag had insisted on terracotta. Plastic plant pots, she'd said, made her shudder the way she'd seen a man last week in her golf club's dining room wearing an open necked shirt. No tie! Whatever next? Beans on toast on the menu? Cut-loaf sandwiches? French baguettes?

Isa thought a row of red geraniums as a demarcation line, so much more civilised than a row of brutish soldiers standing behind an electrified fence, armed with Kalashnikovs.

'Isa!' shouted Dominic, as busy as a bee in a garden full of flowers. 'Have you any chairs you can spare? We are three short.'

'I have some in the garden shed. You are not frightened of spiders, are you?'

'I'm more frightened of my mother-in-law. If she doesn't have a seat, she'll accuse me of murder.'

'Will there be an official opening?'

'As chair of the SPC I was going to make an announcement, but Harry has persuaded me to let him do it. He's a town crier, you know. He's in love with a tricorn hat.'

****

Without the fear of being run over by a car, children were skipping and climbing through plastic hoops in the middle of the road. Someone brought out a length of clothesline and began a girls-versus-boys tug-of-war game. An impromptu egg and spoon race ended in screams when eggs fell off spoons and splattered.

'Should they not have been hard boiled?' said Irene.

A toddler fell into the paddling pool.

'What do you expect?' said his mum. 'He's Aquarius.'

The owner of an out-of-control Jack Russell was told in no uncertain terms that the sandpit and paddling pool were not canine loos.

Tables were being set up and laid with white tablecloths. A nurse with experience of looking after the elderly shook her head: 'Take my word for it,' she said, 'the golden oldies will make more mess with their jelly and ice cream than the children. I know how hard it is to get jelly stains out of white linen. If those tablecloths are hired, we'll not get our deposit back.'

Pratt, the master butcher, elbowing his way through the growing throng of residents and their extended families with a tray of pies on his head was hollering: 'Make way for the pies! Let the pies through.

Can't have a street party without Pratt's pork pies.'

It was like watching the tide come in, in so much as the tables, as if they were a beach, were being covered, ever so slowly, not with sea water but with plates of food covered with cling film. One resident brought her contribution in a children's pushchair. Everyone wished they'd thought of that.

There were one-bite sausage rolls; plates of sandwiches cut into triangles; slices of toast buttered with anchovy paste. Various salads. An olive oil dispenser brought by an avant-garde family who, that year had holidayed in Naples, raised eyebrows. Everyone knew you put olive oil in your ear to soften wax, but what had olive oil to do with food?

To show off his pies, Pratt moved a Victoria sponge cake behind a jug of water. Big mistake! The cake's baker was what in local parlance was called a Byker Granny. She was the sort of woman with whom shopkeepers never argued. She was also a Methodist (staunch) and a member of the WI. For weeks after the royal wedding, Pratt wondered why his takings were down.

A row broke out between Dominic and Beatrice.

'We need to take chairs from the tables to make an auditorium for the conjuror when he comes,' said Dominic.

'This is ridiculous,' said Beatrice.

'I want the chairs in rows of six,' said Dominic. 'I've put chalk marks on the ground where I want them. Follow the chalk and you can't go wrong.'

'I've heard secret agents in films say, "Follow that cab!" but never, "Follow the chalk!",' said a co-opted resident. 'This is like a "Carry on" film.'

'It must have been easier building the pyramids,' said a chap who worked in a bank and was not used to physical labour.

'I thought running a post office was hard work, but this is slave labour,' said a resident who was a postmaster.

'We should be given free Angus Tokens for doing this,' said a man who'd recently moved into the street from Whitby.

'Dominic!' shouted Harry, appearing on the scene, dressed as a town crier. 'I have decided to announce the arrival of the conjuror as if he was a weather forecast. Oh, Yeah! Oh, Yeah! All is well on a clear and frosty night. What time's the fellow due?'

'It's on the flyer I gave you.'

'I've lost it.'

'I went to a lot of trouble printing those flyers. You seem taller than usual.'

'Lifts on my shoes. A town crier should be tall; like policeman and firemen used to be tall. It's part of my costume. What time's this conjuror chap coming?'

'Three o'clock.'

'Can't wait. I'm thinking, a town crier's costume is not a bed of roses. I'm as hot in this bloody get-up as a wrestler's you know what's, in a jock strap.'

****

Dominic was fretting but not yet sweating. Where was the conjuror? The fellow had come highly recommended by a friend of a friend. He hadn't liked hiring someone through Chinese whispers, but beggars couldn't be choosers. Every SPC in the area was after hiring a children's entertainer. It was a sellers' market.

Two forty-nine. Where was the bloody fellow? If he didn't turn up, Dominic knew his name would be mud. He was chair of the SPC. The buck stopped with him. His watch was right because he'd synchronised it, that very morning, with a BBC time signal. If he'd had his way he'd have had all members of the SPC synchronise their watches with his. Irene had said that was a silly idea. Who did he think he was? He was organising a street party, not the D-day landings.

At two-fifty-nine he heard clapping; the sort of desultory clapping small groups of spectators give runners at the half-way point in a marathon, when the runners are passing them, in dribs and drabs, like water dripping from a tap.

The clapping was for two clowns struggling to man-handle a sedan chair over the red geraniums – in terracotta pots – marking the start of the no-go area for vehicles.

After having negotiated those obstacles – a feat they achieved, it must be said, without knocking over one terracotta pot – they set off down Chillingham Grove at the double as if whoever was inside the sedan chair had looked at his watch and told them to get a move on, otherwise they'd be late for the party.

'He's here!' said Dominic.

'Oh, Yeah! Oh, Yeah!' shouted Harry, ringing his hand bell. 'On a warm and sunny day in July let the festivities begin. Pray make way, for the magician. Make way for the magician before he makes you disappear.'

As events turned out, it was Harry who disappeared. Wobbly on his pins because of the lifts on his shoes, not to mention an overenthusiastic ringing of his hand ball, he slipped on the remains of an egg dropped by a runner in the egg and spoon race, and twisted an ankle.

Using hand signals similar to those used by ground crew to guide an aeroplane to its terminal, Dominic indicated to the clowns that they were to lift the sedan chair onto a step-high stage made out of boxes.

At once parents began pushing their children into the seats at the front of the stage.

'Little ones at the front, if you please,' shouted Dominic, 'big ones at the back. We want everyone to see. Will the girl at the front please take off her sun hat … if you don't the girl sitting behind you won't be able to see.'

'Patience,' said the girl's mother, 'leave your hat on. If you take it off, you'll get sunstroke.'

'She can sit in the back row with her hat on but not in the front row, with it on,' said Dominic.

Telling Chippy to stay and guard her garden, Isa joined the residents gathered in clusters round the make-shift stage.

The two clowns, one at each end of the sedan chair, letting go of the chair's carrying poles, now drew Colt 45 revolvers from holsters, slung very low, on their hips.

Isa knew about guns. She was certain the revolvers weren't replicas. They were heavy, like real Colts. She knew they were heavy by the way the clowns were holding them. A Colt 45 was not a lady's gun.

To get everyone's attention, the clowns fired the Colts into the air. Bang! Bang! Bang! Bang! Everyone, including Isa, jumped.

A lot of smoke. Black powder? A reduced charge? The guns were real, alright. Why were two clowns carrying real guns?

'Fools! Idiots! Imbeciles!' boomed a voice magnified by a loudspeaker. 'Turn me round! My door is on the other side.'

After pretending they did not know what to do and bumping into each other and falling down, the clowns lifted and turned the chair.

Out of it stepped a dark-skinned man dressed as a sultan. Coloured lights on his turban flashed on and off. The cut of his three-quarter length golden coat looked as if it had been tailor made in Savile Row. His golden trousers were wide and baggy, like jodhpurs. His golden slippers had turned up toes.

'Good afternoon, boys and girls, mams, dads and nannies. I am Charlie the Caliph from Chipping Norton. Good afternoon,' he said, bowing. 'Let me introduce my two helpers. Their names are "One Smile" and "Two Smiles".'

His voice boomed. Somewhere on his person – perhaps in the golden torque around his neck – there was a hidden microphone connected to an amplifier.

At the mention of their names, the two clowns bowed to their audience with an over-the-top obeisance. At the same time as they were ingratiating themselves, two wooden hands, twice the size of normal hands, began, with hydraulic smoothness, to extend themselves out of each end of the sedan chair.

At a nod from 'Charlie', 'One Smile' and 'Two Smiles' began pumping these wooden hands up and down as if they were shaking hands with a long-lost friend.

After three ups-and-downs of the wooden hands, a bubble the size of a football floated out of the sedan chair's roof.

'Mam,' said a tiny-tot, pointing at the bubble as it floated upwards, 'there's a bird in the bubble.'

When the bubble burst, a dove, after falling a little – as a rocket does when it is launched from under the belly of its mother ship – flapped its wings and took to the air under its own power.

After a few circuits it landed on Charlie's outstretched hand whereupon, throwing over it a bandana the colour of a Buddhist monk's saffron robe and pointing a wand at it (produced from goodness knows where) he made it disappear.

After getting over the surprise at what they could not believe they'd seen, adults and children clapped and clapped. Dominic breathed a sigh of relief. The conjuror was as good as the Chinese whispers had said. Money well spent. His reputation was safe.

More bubbles emerged from the chair's roof. In each bubble, a dove. When the bubble burst the dove flew circuits before landing on Charlie's outstretched hand, from which perch, Charlie the Caliph from Chipping Norton made it vanish.

He made coins cascade out of children's noses. He made playing cards disappear into thin air. He pulled a rabbit out of a top hat. He let the children in the front row stroke it. It really was a rabbit. To make the rabbit disappear he fed it 'magic lettuce'. When he put it back into the top hat he changed it, by magic, into a Labrador puppy.

At the end of his act, bowing and well aware he had the audience in the palm of his hand and could do with them what he liked, he held up his hands for silence.

'Dear audience,' he began, 'as a thank you for your warm applause I am giving a bottle of champagne to whoever lives in the house whose number is drawn out of this top hat,' holding up a top hat by its brim, with two hands, as if it was a jug too full of water and he didn't wish to spill any. 'A spot prize to celebrate the marriage of Charles and Di. In the hat are pieces of paper. On each piece of paper is a number. I give you my word that the number of every house in Chillingham Grove is in there. Who will be the lucky winner? "Two Smiles", take the hat round and let this wonderful audience see for themselves that I am a man of my word. Ladies and gentlemen, please feel free to inspect the contents of the hat. By the by, no trying to find your house number and put it on the top of the pile. I know the people of Chillingham Grove. When they play Bingo they don't shout, House! They shout, Bungalow!'

While 'Two Smiles' took the hat round for its contents to be inspected, Charlie and 'One Smile' amused the children by making animals out of balloons.

They blew up the balloons from the mouth of an intaglio cherub on a shield above the sedan chair's door.

The balloons they were blowing up were long and thin. Ideal for making Dachshunds and the long necks of swans.

A little girl who said she wanted a wolf-dog like the one the lady had who lived in that house over there caused Charlie to scratch his head.

'Wolf-dogs are tricky to do,' said Charlie.

After the audience had inspected the numbers in the hat, 'Two Smiles' handed it back to Charlie.

As he did so, Isa was surprised to see 'One Smile' making his way towards her.

'The hat and its contents have been inspected,' boomed Charlie. 'To make sure the number plucked from the hat is plucked, without favour or prejudice, I need an independent dipper. "One Smile", touch the person closest to you.'

Like a policeman making an arrest, 'One Smile' dropped a hand on Isa's shoulder. Gun oil. It might have been his grease paint make-up but she didn't think so. It was the smell of the basement armoury in the British Embassy in Beirut.

'Bring the gallant lady over, "One Smile".'

Standing next to Charlie, Isa knew, beyond any shadow of doubt, that the conjuror, dressed in all the golden finery of an Oriental ne'er-do-well, was indeed none other than Jeremy, and that the two clowns were none other than the 'plumbers'.

Close up, there was no mistaking Jeremy's glass eye.

'What is your name, madam?' said Charlie/Jeremy.

'Isa.'

'Isa. Would that be short for Isabel?'

Isa nodded. What else could she do but play along?

'Is a bell necessary on a bike? Never mind. I was hoping you might have been called "Dipper". Isa ... Isabel, one dip. One piece of paper. One lucky house number.'

'Shall I close my eyes?'

'Should she close her eyes?' Charlie asked the audience.

'Yes,' shouted Harry, sitting on a garden wall with his poorly foot up on the saddle of a child's tricycle. 'We don't want any cheating. And if she picks her own number she'll have to pick again. Fair do's!'

Isa closed her eyes and pulled a number out of the top hat.

'And the number of the lucky house is?' said Charlie/Jeremy.

'Number thirty-nine,' muttered Isa.

'Speak up, Isa.'

'Number thirty-nine,' she shouted.

'Is number thirty-nine in the audience?'

'It's the rented house,' said Irene, 'he has just moved in.'

'Who will be postman?'

There was a gift tag around the neck of the bottle of Moet.

'I'd deliver it, if I wasn't a wounded soldier,' shouted Harry.

'I don't trust you,' said Beatrice, 'I believe you'd drink it.'

'No need to kick a man when he's down. I'll have you know I have a sprained ankle. I should be compensated.'

'I'll deliver it,' said Beatrice, taking the bottle off Charlie/Jeremy.

'Thank you, madam. A lady with a social conscience. Ladies and gentlemen, a round of applause for Isa.'

People clapped. Somewhere a balloon burst. Harry rang his hand bell.

'Thank you for your help,' said Charlie/Jeremy, handing Isa a bunch of real flowers. She'd no idea where they'd come from. They had a wonderful perfume. Inside the bouquet there was an envelope.

'Bye!' Charlie/Jeremy told the crowd as he paused at the sedan chair's door the way the president of the United States pauses at the door of Air Force One.

Closing the sedan chair's door, he drew its curtains. As far as Jeremy was concerned it was mission accomplished. Accompanied by much clapping 'One Smile' and 'Two Smiles' carried him off down the street at the double as if they were sedan chair porters on piece-work.

****

To spread the word it was time for the elderly and children to sit down and eat. Harry, in a wheelchair he'd managed to get his hands on, was being pushed round the street by Isaac and Alfie.

'Oh, Yeah! Oh, yeah! Time to eat! Tea stations, go and fill your kettles! Oh, Yeah! Oh, Yeah! You two! Gee up! Faster! Faster! Warp speed five!'

Isaac and Alfie knew what that meant. They'd seen the rings of Saturn through Ms Weddle's telescope.

'Faster! Faster!' said Harry. 'Warp speed ten!'

They were young and full of snap, crackle and pop. Adults were always telling them 'No!' The Pole Man – their private name for Harry (his Nordic walking) – was on their side. He was an ally. An adult who was on their side. Whoopee!

'Faster! Faster! Get me to the church on time.'

They took their new pal round lampposts on one wheel. They bumped him on and off the kerb. They did three-point turns. They pushed him up and down the street as fast as they could go.

'Faster! Faster!'

They lost control in the children's play area. To avoid a tricycle, they tipped the wheelchair onto one wheel and, unable to keep control and not looking where they were going, tipped Harry – waving his arms as a novice roller skater does when he knows he is going to take a tumble – into a foot of water in the children's paddling pool.

A resident with a Super-8 cine camera and the sang-froid of the true professional at once zoomed in on the incident.

'Harry,' said the true professional, 'could you spurt water out of your mouth? You know, pretend you are a gargoyle. In the movies when some idiot falls into water he always comes up for air squirting water out of his mouth.'

'Piss off!' said Harry.

****

The elderly ignored the incident. It was feeding time. They didn't want farce, they wanted ham sandwiches; they wanted Victoria sponge cake; they wanted a sit down and a cup of tea. Finding a seat and somewhere to park your walking frame was like reversing a car into a tight parking space. If you wanted to make sure you got a seat next to your pals, be prepared to use your elbows; play by the Queensbury rules and you might not get a sausage roll.

Angry glances were launched at the fat couple who lived at number eighty-nine. Was it true they'd brought doggy-bags? If it was, they'd have to be told. The war finished in 1945. This was not a VE Day party. There was not a food shortage. This was a party to celebrate a royal wedding.

An old man, a widower, left standing all alone, looking for a seat, was rescued by Mari.

The children, sitting at their long table, were kept under control by a posse of fussing mothers. Isaac's water pistol was confiscated.

Isa watched Beatrice and Leo talking outside number thirty-nine's front door. Beatrice was delivering the champagne. Leo seemed pleased. Dear me! Whatever next? Leo was kissing Beatrice on both cheeks. Now he was giving her a hug.

Spotting Isa, Leo gave her a wave. The sort of wave neighbours, who have known each other for years, exchange. She waved back. What had MI5 in store for him? He had diplomatic immunity. When all this had blown over, would he be told to leave the country?

When Leo had disappeared back into number thirty-nine, Beatrice walked across the road to talk to Isa.

'It's alright for some,' she said, eyeing Isa's bouquet.

'You've had a bear hug.'

'I'd rather have had the flowers. When he hugged me I felt like a tube of toothpaste. I'm here to deliver a message. He wants to know when Malcolm is coming back for his lawn mower. The gift tag on the Moet put a smile on his face. You'd think he'd won the football pools. I think there's something funny going on at number thirty-nine. I like him. Do you think you could persuade him to come to your Russian class? I mean if you start them up again in the winter.'

'Let's wait and see how he fits in, shall we? If he's a communist he will hate capitalists.'

'He doesn't dress like a communist. That sports jacket he was wearing wasn't off the peg. I know quality when I see it. I told him, "I didn't recognise you with your clothes on." "Ah!" he said, "English humour." He is doing his best, bless him, to fit in. I'm having a lot of bother with my Bo-Peep costume. I'd better go and see if Ken is out of bed?'

'Will Ken be coming to the fancy dress?'

'He has a migraine.'

'How awful.'

'He always has a migraine when he doesn't want to do something. It's an excuse. He hates parties … always has. I love them. I don't know why I married him.'

'Marriage is a funny business.'

'But not funny, Ha! Ha! Not like that magician. I wonder why he picked you … you know, to draw the number out of the hat? I'm running around delivering his prize and you get the bouquet. Life is so unfair.'

'You did volunteer.'

'I suppose where men are concerned, I'm a sucker for punishment.'

'I think you have an inferiority complex.'

'Do you really?'

'Yes. You need to come out. You need to be yourself.'

'Do I?'

'Come to the fancy dress as a Bassarid.'

'Isa, I know you are cleverer than me and went to a posh university, but, while I know what a "bastard" is … what is a "Bassarid"?'

'A "Bassarid", Beatrice, is a female who helped the pagan god Dionysus with his orgies. They dressed in goat skins and did naughty things with men while under the influence of …'

'Evil spirits?'

'No, Beatrice … wine.'

'I think,' said Beatrice, 'I am more Bo-Peep than one of them other things. On the other hand …'

Holding up her bouquet, Isa said: 'I'd better put these in water. Put the kettle on as well. In case you have forgotten I'm a tea station.'

'I'm a server. I don't know why I volunteered.'

****

Isa opened the envelope Charlie/Jeremy had sent her, sitting down, which was just as well because what she read might have made her fall down.

'My dear Ms Weddle, How are you? Did you like my disguise? I am writing to bring you up to date and to let you into a secret.

My plan for dealing with, you know who, is well under way. Even as I write I am dotting the "i's" and crossing the "t's".

The secret? Leo, the Russian to whom Tony is selling our secrets, is also a traitor. He is betraying Mother Russia. He loves Savile Row suits and English fish and chips.

When the action starts, if, by any chance Leo should get in the way, please don't shoot him. Remember, he is on our side. He is batting for us.

I am assuming, this evening, you will be carrying the weapon Desmond sent you. Yes, I know about the Glock! You may need it.

Leo is stressed. He drinks too much. He fears his minders at the Russian embassy in London are on to him. They wish him to return to Russia for a rest. We all know what that means.

*We have a duty of care to defectors. After Tony has been
safely abducted, Leo will be granted asylum. He will be given
a new identity. MI5 will make him disappear.*

*The bottle of Moet I wangled into number thirty-nine was
my way of letting Leo know that the plan I'd discussed
with him months ago – would you believe it in of all places
a mortuary – was rolling along as planned. He was not to
worry. The players were in the pavilion putting on their
whites and oiling their bats. A cricketing metaphor. You
have been around posh boys long enough to know we all love
cricket.*

*As I am in the confessing mode I will come clean about
why I wanted you to find the keys to number thirty-nine
under the stone marked with a red star. It was by way of
introducing you to Leo. He was told you were MI5. If things
had gone wrong his instructions were to ring your doorbell
and ask for sanctuary. You were to be a safe house for the
occupant of a safe house which was no longer safe.*

Jeremy

*PS I will be coming to the fancy dress party tonight dressed
as a Victorian undertaker.*

*PPS Give this epistle to Chippy. It is written on rice paper.
In lieu of the absence of coal fires on which to burn evidence
I have found the jaws of a dog to be an equally reliable
method of destruction. Should your house be burgled by
Russian agents we don't want them reading this, do we?*

Isa gave Chippy the note wrapped round a dog biscuit. She watched him destroy it the way spies in movies watch fire burn a code book.

****

For the next couple of hours she served tea to anyone who fancied a cuppa. She liked being a Tea Station. She was meeting people who'd lived in the street for years but to whom she'd never spoken.

On a folding table at her garden gate she'd an aluminium teapot. It had two handles. When it was full you needed two hands to lift it.

One resident – Isa knew his face but not his name – while watching her pour, called it a 'belts and braces' teapot.

'You know,' he explained, 'if your braces go, ping! Your belt stops your trousers falling down … see what I'm getting at? Your teapot has two handles.'

'Don't mind him,' said the man's wife, 'he has a funny sense of humour.'

'Milk and sugar?'

'The conjuror was amazing!'

'Someone told me they saw the sedan chair in the back of an army lorry.'

'Strange.'

****

As a 'server' dedicated to keeping the elderly supplied with tea, Beatrice was kept busy dashing to and fro between Isa's 'Tea Station' and the table reserved for the street's senior citizens.

'More refills,' Beatrice told Isa. 'And just look at my knees …' lifting up the Charles and Di plastic apron she was wearing over a summer dress, to show them.

'They're dirty. What have you been doing?'

'Crawling on my hands and knees looking for a hearing aid. They are so damn fussy. One of them has a hip flask. You'll never guess what they keep talking about.'

'The state pension? Mrs Thatcher?'

'Sex and doodlebugs. And, you'll never believe this, they've had a farting competition.'

'Beatrice!' a voice boomed across the street. 'Where's my tea?'

'That's Mary,' said Beatrice, raising her eyebrows. 'She lives at number seventy-six. Her husband's hard of hearing. She's used to shouting. I'd better go before I have a mutiny on my hands.'

****

'Refill that, will you, pet?' said a man handing Isa a china cup on a saucer.

She'd seen him around. He lived in the street. She did not know his name. Like a lot of little men, he was loud. Very full of himself. If he'd been a dog he'd have been a Jack Russell. The sort who'd bark at a Great Dane.

'The cup or the saucer?'

'I ask you, pet, do I look like the sort of man who'd drink tea out of a saucer?'

'You are my first cup and saucer customer,' explained Isa, 'up till now I've only had mugs.'

'Well, I'm not a mug. And I don't like drinking tea out of one. I'm cup and saucer. I have a sense of tradition. No one what lives in Chillingham Grove should drink tea out of a mug. If they do they are letting the side down. It's like playing cricket in a ginger jumper. The Grove is not a council estate. What's the lemon for? To keep the flies off the sugar?'

'A slice of lemon in one's cuppa is favoured by some as a substitute for milk.'

'You taking the, you-know-what? That's foreign, that is. You under the influence of the Russian renting number thirty-nine? A commie in the street. I'm not happy about that. The Grove is true blue. Might be one or two closet socialists but they know which side their bread is buttered on. If the socialists had their way we'd be singing the "Red Flag" instead of "God Save the Queen". And, I'm not having that. Three sugars, please. No lemon. Wait until I tell the missus. She won't believe me. She says I've got no imagination. So she won't believe me when I tell her you wanted to put a slice of lemon in my tea instead of a splash of milk. Lemon in your tea, never heard of anything so ridiculous in all of my life.'

****

At around six o'clock Dominic and his team began turning the street into a beer garden. After much humping and some bad language and much standing back to talk about the best way forward, they'd made a corral out of trestle tables. In its 'safe' middle, as if they were placing holy relics in a shrine, they put the two barrels of beer purchased by Harry at cost price with a little something added on for the drayman; whoever he might be.

To make it clear to any resident who might be tempted to treat himself to a pre-party slurp, Dominic covered the barrels with Charles and Di tea towels.

On the stage, occupied in the afternoon by Charles the Caliph of Chipping Norton's sedan chair, the conjuror – who everyone kept talking about – wasn't he amazing – there now stood boxes of sound equipment as big as cabin trunks.

A young man with long hair called Rob was tap-testing a microphone, on a tripod.

'It's not working,' he told Dominic.

This infuriated, Dominic. He'd tap-tested it earlier and it had worked. Why was it not working now?

The woman into whose house it was plugged ran out to apologise.

'I think I might have unplugged it when I was drying my hair. I don't normally dry my hair downstairs but I wanted to watch the royal wedding.'

****

Looking at his watch and seeing it was the time Dominic's flyer had said the party should start, a Superman, holding out his cape behind him as if it was windswept and he was flying, flew twice around the beer corral.

His bravado caused a domino effect. Within seconds of him landing back at his own garden gate – where his wife, who was dressed as Nell Gwyn, gave him a kiss and a glass of wine – a Dennis the Menace and a Friar Tuck, who hitherto had been hovering at their garden gates waiting for someone to take the plunge, were out in the street giggling and laughing at their costumes.

From the top of the street a Laurel and Hardy danced towards the bar singing 'In the Blue Ridge Mountains of Virginia'.

A Batman and Robin brought out deckchairs for themselves along with glasses and a bottle of wine.

Neighbours who'd known each other for years, failed to recognise each other.

'Mary, it's me!'

'Is it really?'

'Yes.'

'I'd never have recognised you.'

'I'm Jane Austen. I've always wanted to wear a poke bonnet.'

Leaving Chippy to guard her open front door, Isa, dressed as a cowgirl – two guns in hip-holsters hanging from her belt – one a toy gun, the other the Glock Desmond had sent her – joined the revellers. Number thirty-nine looked an empty house. No lights. No open windows.

To let everyone know it was party time Dominic, wearing a kilt and a Tam O'Shanter, fired a rocket from a milk bottle.

Bang! Bang! Bang! Cloud bursts of red, white and blue chrysanthemums lit up the darkening sky. The PA system blared into life, playing a well-known popular song.

Angus, wearing a kilt and a bowler (so he looked like a barman), whipped the tea towels off the barrels of beer.

'Angus Tokens!' he shouted. 'Angus Tokens!'

Down the street Pratt the master butcher wafted a tea towel over the smoke coming off his barbecue.

Too late to declare the party open – as had been his heart's desire – Harry hobbled out of his front door on a crutch, shouting: 'Avast, me hearties! Avast!' Attached to one of his ears by an elastic band was a rubber ring from a Kilner jar. A cardboard parrot cut out of a Weetabix box wobbled on his shoulder.

'Harry! You look absolutely wonderful,' Isa told the incorrigible extrovert, 'but why have you come as Long John Silver? I thought you were going to be the party's town crier.'

'Town crier's costume is soaking wet, isn't it? And my ankle's giving me, hell. I had to come up with a character who uses a crutch. Ouch!'

'You need a paracetamol.'

'I need a whisky. Ouch!'

'Excuse me!' said a large woman. 'I'm Little Red Riding Hood. I'm looking for a big, bad wolf.' Then, looking at Harry: 'You're the town crier who fell in the paddling pool … aren't you? I do so admire a man who is not afraid to make a fool of himself. I'm sure you did it on purpose to amuse the children. My son thought it hilarious. What's your parrot called? Don't tell me … let me guess. "Splash!" Ha! Ha!'

'Excuse me,' said Isa, 'I'm off to mingle.'

While she made polite conversation with neighbours – the topic invariably being about the fancy dress they were wearing –

Isa thought of herself as a player in a play within a play. The two guns in her holsters summed it all up. The toy gun was the play to celebrate the wedding of Charles and Di. The, Glock – the real gun – was the other play.

Looking round for an actor in the real life and death drama she spotted Derek, the doorman from the County Hotel; he who delivered flowers; Jeremy's odd-job man. What the hell was he doing here? He looked lost and lonely but terribly dignified in the finery of a doorman employed by a five-star hotel: pink swallow tail coat, green waistcoat, black trousers and a black top hat, pinned to the side of which was a blue rosette of the sort you normally see, pinned to the harness of a winning horse at a gymkhana.

'Good evening, Ms Weddle,' he said, saluting with a white gloved hand, 'you recognised me?' Then, looking round to make sure he'd not be overheard: 'What I'll earn tonight will pay for my TV licence. MI5 pays well. Spying doesn't come cheap. You can't buy spies the way you buys gobstoppers. Three for the price of two. You'll know that. Everything has to be paid for, doesn't it? How's that little doggy of yours? Still eating a sheep a day, is he? Ha! Ha! He likes liver, I know that.'

'Where's Jeremy?' said Isa. 'If you are here that means he's not far away.'

'I am reconnaissance, Ms Weddle. The tip of the spear what will soon be all bloody. The colonel, madam, is nearby, hovering, like an, hawk waiting to pounce.'

'Dressed as an undertaker?'

'That is correct, Ms Weddle.'

'Have you seen Batman?' said a woman (tipsy), dressed as Robin.

'Madam,' said Derek, lifting his topper, 'turn left at the Charlie Chaplin over there, chatting up a nun and, if I'm not mistaken, you will find a Batman talking to a Snow White.'

'Th - ank you,' said Robin (tipsy).

When she walked off in the direction, opposite to the one he had suggested, Derek, replacing his top hat with a sigh, gave a wry smile; as a real doorman he'd seen it all before.

'We were talking about the colonel,' said Isa, 'What's his plan? What if Mr Adder makes a run for it?'

'He won't get far. See that Santa Claus, over there? Special Branch. Name of Henry. The street is closed to traffic. Your niece has sabotaged Mr Adder's get-away vehicle.'

'You know of Joan's involvement in all of this?'

'Only what the colonel tells me, Miss. And another thing, Miss, and begging your pardon before I say it, I see you are carrying a Glock. The electrician's tape round its butt doesn't fool me.'

'Are you not armed?'

'I have my doorman's truncheon. Old Lignum has never let me down. Let us hope no one gets a bloody nose except him what deserves it and no firearms are needed. Your niece, I understand, is coming as a keystone cop. No doubt she'll have a truncheon, like what I have, but while I will keep mine hidden she'll be a twirling hers, no doubt, like a drum majorette in one of them juvenile jazz bands.'

****

Under the liberating influence of alcohol, residents were letting their hair down. A ballerina had her hand up a priest's soutane. Angus, full of whisky, had long ago stopped serving at the bar: 'Och! What did it matter if folk were pulling their own pints?'

A 'tiger' pushing up his face mask and wiping perspiration of his face with the frond of hair on the end of his tail, said to a man wearing a grass skirt and carrying a spear: 'It's alright for some. I wish I'd come as a Zulu.'

'Actually, I'm a Maori. You live at number twenty-nine, don't you?'

'I do … opposite that chap with the three big Swiss mountain dogs.'

'I've been tempted to give you a knock.'

'Have you?'

'You drive down the street too fast.'

'Do I?'

'Yes, you do.'

****

The night wore on. Rob, he who had been tap-testing the microphone earlier, had made it clear to everyone from the start, that he was in charge of the PA and karaoke.

'That's Rob,' a woman told Isa, 'he wants to be a pop star. I live next door to him. He's in PR. When he's on his drums, Nelly … that's my Dachshund … won't stop barking.'

To watch what was going on in the street and number thirty-nine all at the same time, Isa retired to a deck chair in her front garden. Chippy kept her company.

The PA system was playing, what Isa believed was called, 'Heavy Metal'. Dancing to its hypnotic beat were ghouls, Goths, a nurse wearing a short black skirt, one Pinocchio and a couple wearing wet suits. No sign of life from number thirty-nine, though.

During a lull in the PA, she heard bagpipes. 'Scotland the Brave'.

Marching down the street, his cheeks puffed out as he blew air into his pipes, came Dominic, in the full regalia of a Highlander. His black busby made him look tall. Behind him, looking the way a deputation of trade unionists look when they are going to give management a piece of their minds, marched Irene and two of her teenage daughters. They were carrying swords with basket handles and wearing kilts. Their plaids were kept in place with shiny, silver pins with thistle handles.

Whether they liked it or not, the residents of Chillingham Grove were going to watch a display of Highland dancing.

The old woman, dressed as Britannia – the woman Isa had met in the post office – told Isa – over the top of Isa's garden wall: 'The queen has her very own piper. He pipes her awake every morning. It's right and proper we should have a piper. It's like icing on the cake, isn't it? If her majesty has her very own piper, why shouldn't we?'

'Your helmet is full of holes,' a passing Dennis the Menace told the old woman.

'I know it is,' she said, 'it's a colander.'

****

Around about this time a light came on in the window above number thirty-nine's front door; seconds later the door opened and out came Leo singing the Volga Boatmen. He was wearing a toga made out of bed sheets and carrying a picnic table. Behind him, as if he was the Russian's bag carrier, came 'TA', carrying two folding chairs, one in each hand, the way dads carry deckchairs from the car parked on the road to the beach.

'TA''s fancy dress was a cocktail of styles. If he'd been a real cocktail – say a Bellini or a Bachelor's Dream – he'd have tasted corked.

He was wearing golfer's plus fours, brogues with leather tongues and an artiste's beret. His enormous boobs and rouged cheeks made him look like a pantomime dame.

When they began handing out free vodka everyone thought them the best thing since the invention of the wheel.

Isa's surveillance of 'TA' and Leo was interrupted when a keystone cop and a coal miner walked up her garden path.

'Hi! Aunt Isa,' said Joan.

'Yuh alreet, pet?' said Malcolm.

'No, I am not alright,' said Isa.

'What's wrong?'

'The light on your miner's helmet is hurting my eyes.'

'Am a dazzling yuh? A dee that to women, yuh nar. Yee in a mood?'

'Joan, where the hell is Jeremy?'

'I don't know, Aunt Isa. I am a foot soldier. I obey orders. I was told to dress up … be here before ten … that I was to come armed … just in case. My carrying of a firearm is all legal and above board.'

'Bloody hell!' said Malcolm, 'you're carrying a shooter. Am thinkin a need danger money.'

'You shouldn't be here,' said Joan. 'This assignment is no place for amateurs.'

'Hoy! I'm here because me cousin Isa deputised me into the Secret Service.'

'Don't be so ridiculous, Aunt Isa does not have the power to deputise anyone into the Secret Service.'

'You're a hard woman, Joan,' said Malcolm, lighting a cigarette. 'A hard woman. A thought yuh might have humoured me, yuh nar, like giving a bairn a smile. It costs nowt.'

'Stop bickering,' said Isa. 'Joan … Malcolm, I want you to go and talk to Leo and my glavniy protivnik.'

'Ya what?'

'My main enemy. The man with the big boobs. I want to know what 'TA' and Leo are up to.'

'Hoy!' said Malcolm, 'a nar am dressed as a miner and 'ave coal dust aal ower me face, but what if he recognises me?'

'Tell him you want your lawn mower back. Tell him that when you threw the dummy dynamite at him you were having a bit of fun. Tell him if he can't take a joke there's something wrong with communism.'

'Oh, dear me, Isa … you've done it again.'

'What?'

'Twisted me arm. Heh! Heh! Hi! What if he kills me?'

'Leo will not harm you.'

'How'd yee nar that? He's a communist, isn't he? Is that because I'm a miner?' Yuh nar … one of the workers and a sing "Keep the red flag flying" at the Picnic.'

'Jeremy has given me new information about Leo. If he harms you it will be by accident, not by intent … more than that I am not at liberty to say. Malcolm, if you come to grief on this mission, I promise I'll give you a funeral that your pals at the CIU club will never forget.'

'What have yuh got in mind?'

'What about a hearse pulled by four black horses and an undertaker dressed as Frankie Vaughan singing, "Give me the moonlight"?'

'A like the sound of that. Aye, that's canny! A like it. Divent buy the committee a roond of drinks mind. They're tappers.'

****

Joan and Malcolm were crossing the road over to number thirty-nine – which was like crossing a dance floor, so full was the road with people twisting and jiving – when the PA said: 'Elvis says stop'.

'Elvis says, "Wave your hands".'

And everyone did; including Joan and Malcolm.

'Elvis says, "Act your part".'

'What do you mean?' shouted Irene.

'He means,' said a man dressed as a sailor, 'that if you are a sailor, like me, you dance a hornpipe. If you are a keystone cop like that young lady over there, you twirl your baton.'

'I never knew we were going to play, "Simon Says".'

'I don't think any of us did,' said the sailor, who Irene sort of knew. 'Anyway, it's not "Simon Says", is it? It's "Elvis says". The chap dressed as Elvis on the microphone is called Rob. He's in PR. Letting him anywhere near a microphone is like telling a rabbit to look after a lettuce.'

'That was pathetic,' boomed Rob through the microphone. 'Let's try again. Elvis says, "Let's jump up and down".' And everyone did, including Joan and Malcolm. 'Elvis says, "Act your part".'

On cue, Charlie Chaplins sauntered around doing Charlie Chaplin penguin walks. Laurel and Hardys bowed and fluttered their fingers. From her front garden Isa drew her toy gun and shouted 'Bang! Bang!' when she fired it into the air. Supermen pretended to fly. Dominic blew air into his bagpipes. Irene did a Highland fling dance. Joan twirled her nightstick like a keystone cop.

'What duh I dee?' said Malcolm.

'You're a coalminer,' said Joan, 'pretend to wield a pick axe.'

So it was that Joan and Malcolm – a keystone cop and a coalminer – baton-twirled and pick axed their way through the melee of amateur mime artists, like a ship tacking, all the way across the road to number thirty-nine where 'TA' was shouting: 'Where's Cinderella? I want Cinderella to wash my underpants.'

Acting his part, Leo was shouting: 'Hail Caesar!'

'The peasant has come to pay homage,' said 'TA', quick to recognise that the keystone cop was Joan. 'What do you want?'

'My aunt, you know, Ms Weddle ... she sent me.'

'What for? You do not take orders from her. You are on my staff. She doesn't tell you what to do ... I do. Why did she send you? I do hope you are not forgetting our bargain?'

'I really don't know why she sent me, sir. Maybe it was to let you know we are keeping to our bargain ... you know ... so that you protect me from the consequences of what I did.'

'Now you are here you might as well make yourself useful. Leo, you fancy a burger?'

'Hail Caesar!' said Leo.

'That's a "yes",' said, 'TA'. 'Off you toddle, Cinders ... two burgers ... tabasco sauce on mine.'

'Capitalist tomato ketchup on mine,' said Leo. 'Hail Caesar!'

'Yes, sir!' said Joan.

'TA', watching Joan walk off, wondered why she'd such a spring in her step. Why was she twirling her keystone cop's baton as if she'd not a care in the world? The working classes amazed him. He'd treated her like a doormat and, instead of being cowed, she had a spring in her step. Why was she so full of herself? Her jauntiness worried him.

'Hoy!' said Malcolm, drawing attention to himself by squeezing 'TA''s falsies as if they were bulb horns. 'That's nee way to treat a secret agent.'

'Do you mind,' said 'TA', 'Buzz off!'

In between shouting 'Hail Caesar', Leo had been studying Malcolm.

The man dressed as a pitman – orange overalls, knee pads, steel capped boots and a light on his miner's helmet which the impertinent fellow was using the way he'd often used a bright light to intimidate a suspect – reminded him of someone. The fellow's face was black with coal dust. The whites of his eyes glowed.

'A want me lawn mower?' said Malcolm.

'Ah! Mr Dynamite!' said Leo. 'I thought I recognised you.'

'The gardener?' said 'TA', 'Ms Weddle's cousin?'

'That's me,' said Malcolm, 'alreet if a gan in the garden and get me lawn mower?'

'No, it is not alright,' said 'TA'.

'Hoy! That's me livelihood you're talking aboot.'

'My daddy,' said 'TA', leering, 'employs three gardeners. He has over a thousand acres.'

'If his son doesn't let me have me lawn mower, he'll have two acres ... reet between his legs,' said Malcolm.

The pantomime dame was beginning to annoy Malcolm. In the pit, when a prop creaked too much – almost as if it was tarken to yuh ... as if it was tell'n yuh it wasn't happy, yuh did something aboot it

241

… that is, yuh did if yuh wanted to stay alive. Yuh either put in more props or yuh got oot, fast. If yuh did nowt aboot it, yuh were deed.

Leo was taking a close interest in the altercation between Tony and Malcolm.

The English class system fascinated him. It was in his interest to study it. If things went according to plan, he would soon be part of it. Like all systems it would be full of loopholes and fault lines. Find them and you could exploit them. If only he did not so much love Savile Row suits and supermarkets full of food. The West was a whore. He wanted to enjoy all the good things she offered.

If Tony and Dynamite Man came to blows, how might that affect his defection? What if some upright citizen phoned the police and an honest British bobby marched them and him, off to jail?

'Piss off, Mr Underground worker,' said 'TA'. 'Think yourself lucky I don't have my riding crop with me. If I had, I'd thrash the living daylights out of you. Next time, I will come prepared.'

'Yuh shud have been in the Boy Scouts, like me,' said Malcolm, 'a always come prepared. A neva leave the hoose without one of these,' tapping 'TA''s nose with a condom.

While 'TA' ogled, Malcolm produced from a pocket in his orange boiler suit a crocodile clip; a 'Big Daddy', used doon the pit to jump start generators.

'Fucking pleb!' exclaimed 'TA', raising a hand to stop himself being blinded by the light on Malcolm's helmet.

Gaffing 'TA''s raised hand with the crocodile clip, Malcolm said: 'Divent call me a "fuck'n pleb". Reet?'

It is a well-known CIU aphorism that hell hath no fury like a posh boy gaffed by a pleb.

Removing the crocodile clip, 'TA' smashed an empty vodka bottle on number thirty-nine's garden wall and, holding it by its neck, would have smashed it into Malcolm's face but for the sudden appearance on the scene of a tall man, dressed in black and wearing a top hat with three black ribbons fluttering from its back.

With the walking stick he was carrying, the apparition whacked the broken bottle out of 'TA''s hand. Then, he was gone. And so was Malcolm. They'd disappeared in a cloud of mist. Where had the mist come from?

Rob, he who worked in PR but yearned to be a pop star, was at the microphone singing one of his own compositions. A doleful ballad about lost love. To bring theatricality to his performance, he'd plugged in a mist machine.

The mist it was pumping out was turning the street's lights into gauzy moons and those dancing in the street into apparitions.

'The mist reminds me of Siberia,' said Leo. 'Hail Caesar! I feel very much at home.'

'TA' did not feel at home. He disliked the north. It was a barbaric place. It had never changed since the time of William the Conqueror. The locals spoke a lingo he could barely understand. His fingers were bloody and sore. He sucked the bruise on his hand where the man in black had whacked him. Who was he?

Did that upstart Geordie not know he'd committed GBH on a senior MI5 officer? If he could get his hands on him – the impudent sod – he'd snap the crocodile clip on him, where it would really hurt.

'Coming prepared, indeed! By the time I've finished with you, my man, you won't need a condom because you won't have a cock.'

Leo was a barbarian. He was coarse and rough. His hands were large like a workman's. He might know the difference between a MIG and an F16 but not the difference between a Pissarro and a pissoir. Give him a pastry fork and he'd use it to remove dirt from under his nails. The things one had to do to own something one loved. Why were Impressionist paintings so bloody expensive?

The mist machine was puffing out mist as if it were a male dragon trying to impress a female dragon. And, as for that crooner … bloody awful song.

He kept seeing the face of the man in black. The fellow had winked at him. Why? He knew that face. He knew of whom it reminded him. Desmond Lavery. But, Desmond was in Bolivia. Wasn't he? He'd been Ms Weddle's London contact. He'd requested to go back on active service. The usual moan of an active man weary of doing a desk job.

If only he could remember if the man dressed in black had a glass eye. What he did remember was the 'wink' and the 'knowing look'. It was as if the fellow was saying: 'Look at me! Do you not recognize me? Don't you know who I am?'

Ms Weddle had been in Beirut. Desmond had been in Beirut. They'd been in Beirut at the same time. He was responsible for Ms Weddle losing the love of her life. He was responsible for Desmond losing an eye. Desmond had been Ms Weddle's London contact. It was too much of a coincidence they were both at a street party in a suburb of Newcastle. Ms Weddle needed to be confronted. Where was Joan? He could smell the barbecue but because of the mist could not see it. Was she still queuing or had she, too, vaporised like that fellow in black? Ms Weddle needed to be reminded that if she'd blabbed, her precious niece Joan would be up for murder.

It worried him that Leo had also disappeared. Where had the Russian gone?

****

The transmitter MI5 had placed in one of 'TA''s falsies enabled Jeremy – aka Desmond – aka Charlie the Caliph of Chipping Norton – aka the peripatetic gypsy who sharpened knives – to hear – through the earpiece he was wearing – every word and curse 'TA' muttered.

The boffin who'd installed the device had told him: 'It will keep you abreast of events, sir.'

As soon as he knew 'TA' was off to confront Ms Weddle, Jeremy (as we will continue to call him, at least for the time been) told Leo: 'Pack your bags. Mr Adder is no longer your concern. I will take care of him. ASAP you will be driven to a safe house. Her Majesty's government will keep its word. You will be well looked after.'

At Jeremy's side, Joan and Malcolm were tucking into the burgers 'TA' had ordered for himself and Leo.

'Good, these,' said Malcolm. 'Did a dee alreet, Jeremy? Did I irritate him, like yuh said I had to?'

'You have a talent, Malcolm, for getting under people's skin.'

'Yuh mean am like coal dust?'

'If you say so. You will not be surprised to learn, I am not as familiar with the idiosyncrasies of the coal mining industry as your good self.'

'Nar, am not.'

'Sir,' said Joan, 'should we not be going across the road to help my aunt? I mean, if Mr Adder turns nasty because you've let him know you are here, and you've made him suspicious that he might have been rumbled … he might kill her.'

'Or,' said Jeremy, taking out his glass eye and breathing on it, preparatory to licking it clean with his tongue, 'your aunt might kill him.'

'A wish yuh wouldn't dee that,' said Malcolm. 'It puts me off me burger. Me granny used to dee that with her false teeth … yuh nar … licking them clean. A used to think that was bad … but to dee it to a glass eye … Oh, dear me! A think that's arful. Am sensitive, yuh nar.'

****

The vapour the mist-making machine was pumping out was turning trees, bushes, lampposts and street dancers into weird shapes. One dancer was dancing with a headless partner.

Crossing the street to Ms Weddle's house, 'TA' reminded himself that if his worst fears were realised, his first line of defence was to protest his innocence. He'd lots of aces to play. He belonged to the upper echelons of British society. He knew who liked little boys.

Sucking his gaffed finger, he tasted blood. He knew people in the service who, for a bit of cash up front, would smack that Geordie coalminer so hard he'd spend the rest of his life in a wheelchair.

The dancers he was weaving through, annoyed him. People wanted to dance with him. A woman who fondled his falsies told him: 'I'm glad they're not mine.'

He didn't feel at home among plebs. He didn't trust drunken Geordies. They might take out his falsies and use them as footballs.

Ms Weddle and Desmond had been in Beirut at the same time. Had they worked together? Had they known each other? There was an age discrepancy. When he lost his eye, Desmond would have been twenty. A junior officer in the SAS. Ms Weddle? A middle-aged high flyer in the embassy. He knew they had both been in the restaurant when terrorists had blown it up. All a long time ago. How well had he covered his tracks? Was it possible that after all these years they were working together? Were they after revenge? Were they freelancing or did they have at their disposal all the resources of the British Secret Service?

'He's behind you!' someone shouted, in his face.

He wanted to shout 'Piss off!', but didn't. He was a pantomime dame. If he stepped out of character these drunken northern louts – he thought the women worse than the men – might do unspeakable things to him.

'Who is, darling?' he said, in a squeaky, high pitched female voice.

'The undertaker!'

Mist had turned the revellers into grey silhouettes. He'd no idea who had called out. Why was an undertaker behind him? Why not a Charlie Chaplin? In fact, why not anyone, other than an undertaker. How many undertakers were there at the party? It took a black sense of humour to come to a fancy dress party as an undertaker.

'You are supposed to say, "Oh no he isn't!",' said a female Mephistopheles.

'Oh no, he isn't!' croaked 'TA'.

'Sound as if you mean it,' said a Bishop, poking his falsies with a trident. 'Are they balloons?'

A chorus of phantom revellers chanting, 'He's behind you!' and 'Oh no, he isn't' escorted 'TA' all the way to Ms Weddle's garden gate.

Their hounding ceased when the wannabe crooner on the PA system – somewhere in the mist – stopped singing and barked out the order, 'Play your part!'

Only when he was close to Ms Weddle's front door, peering through the mist, did he make out her shape and that of her dog.

'What do you want?' said Isa, stepping out of ribbons of mist as if she was walking through a cobweb.

'I want you to keep that dog under control. If you don't, I will kill it.'

'Down, Chippy! Down!'

'Give the brute a bone.'

'Would you care to donate your tibia?'

'I am warning you … keep it under control. If you don't, I will kill it.'

'What with? Your bare hands?'

'No, with this,' pointing a handgun at her.

'Down, Chippy! Down!'

'Inside!' threatening her with the handgun. 'The wolf stays outside. Do I make myself clear?'

'Stay, Chippy! Stay!'

They sat in the kitchen.

'Coffee?' said Isa.

'What is Desmond doing in Chillingham Grove? He's supposed to be in Bolivia. Tell me and I promise not to kill your dog.'

'You think Chippy is my Achilles's heel, do you? Once a blackmailer always a blackmailer.'

'You know I don't make idle threats … refuse to play ball with me and your dog is dead. You love that dog … killing it would be like me breaking your heart. It's an easier way to make you talk than breaking your arms. Desmond!' Banging the table and making a spoon jump. 'Why is he here?'

'Desmond who?' said Isa.

'You know damn fine well who I mean. You talked to him often enough when he was your control. It took a lot of arm twisting for me to get my hands on your file. I've read the notes he made about you. He was very thorough. Played by the rules. You didn't like him much, did you?'

'He was a pompous ass. The same as you. You all come from the same stable. He thought Britannia still ruled the waves … India was still a jewel in the imperial crown. I was surprised when he told me he was going to Bolivia. Give him a year and he'll be pleading to come home. His derring-do in the tropical rainforests of South America will become the stuff of legends. If he's a good storyteller, he'll not have to buy a drink for the rest of his life. 'A whisky for a tale, Desmond, old boy!' His club will more than likely have already made him an honorary member. Do Pall Mall clubs have honorary members? I wouldn't know, would I? I'm a pleb and a woman.'

Isa's description of Desmond was so far off the mark it prompted 'TA' to ask: 'Have you ever met him? I mean, Desmond, in the flesh.'

'No. Of course not. You know the rules of the game. When it suited him he rang to tell me things about number thirty-nine he thought I should know. There was a gulf between us. He was "upstairs" and I was "below" stairs. Often we did not speak to each other for months. If I had no need to contact him and he had no need to contact me, why should we? We were not having a telephone love affair. Until all this brewed up and you arrived on the scene, I'd the strong impression I'd been forgotten about.'

'So,' said 'TA', for the first time wondering if Ms Weddle just might be telling the truth, 'if you did meet him you wouldn't know what he looked like?'

'Correct.'

'What if I told you your description of him could not be more wrong? The Desmond I know is no desk bound dreamer. That great naval hero of ours, Lord Nelson lost an arm and an eye in the service of his country. So far, Desmond has only lost an eye. I wonder if he will ever give England an arm … perhaps a leg as well. The Desmonds of this world always try to go one better.'

'Desmond lost an eye in the service of his country?'

'He has a glass eye. When he wishes to give himself time to think, he takes it out and cleans it.'

Jeremy had a glass eye. He took it out to clean it in the way 'TA' had described. Jeremy liked disguises. He was a chameleon. At the County Hotel he'd played the part of a hunting, shooting and fishing toff. He'd disguised himself as a gypsy. He was Charlie the Caliph of Chipping Norton … what if … what if he was also Desmond?

The very idea that Desmond and Jeremy might be the same person made her feel dizzy. Whoever he was, where was he? Where was Joan? Where was Malcolm? She needed help. Where was the fucking cavalry?

The front door was open. Chippy was in the front garden. If she called him and he came bounding in, would 'TA' shoot him? She could hear music and singing. Mummy wrappings of artificial fog were drifting into the kitchen as if a long dead cadaver was making a feeble attempt to come back to life.

'TA' had an anecdotal history of abusing women. At Cambridge his connections had allowed him to slither free of a possible murder charge. He was an extremely dangerous man with whom to be alone under any circumstances.

'You are stressed, Ms Weddle,' said 'TA'. 'The lady with the wolf is stressed. I ask myself, why? Have you something to hide?'

'I am stressed,' said Isa, 'because you are pointing a gun at me. It might go off.'

'Talking of guns ... and I want you to do this very slowly ... unbuckle your gun belt.'

'You are scared of toy guns?'

'Just do as I say. For once in your life obey an order. One of the guns is real. If any gun is going to go bang! It will be mine, not yours. I know you are a marksman. Unbuckle ... slowly.'

'Like in the cowboy films?'

'If you wish. Put it on the table.'

Not wishing to provoke him, she put the toy gun belt, with its two holsters, down on the table as carefully as if she was a waitress serving a customer a too-full cup of coffee.

'Kneel on the floor. Fold your arms.'

Kneeling on the floor brought her eyes level with the kitchen table. Lucy's letter! To Isa, its Lebanese stamp made it stand out like a tangerine, in a bowl of grapes.

The table was cluttered with, among other things, Chippy's dog lead, a Daily Telegraph and an assortment of mugs and jugs. All Isa could see was Lucy's letter and its Lebanese stamp.

She reacted the way sunbathers react when a cloud blots out the sun. She began to feel cold.

'TA' was quick to notice her change of mood. What had wiped the smile off her face? At the start of the interrogation, she'd been full of herself.

'Look at the floor. Keep your arms folded.'

For many seconds, she did not know what he was doing. Outside, the revellers were singing a Beatles hit. In the kitchen? Silence. Had he tip-toed out and left her kneeling there? So quiet. Her heart was working overtime. Her mouth was dry. Where was Jeremy? Joan? Malcolm? If 'TA' knew she knew Tobias was alive, what would he do?

The dog lead noose he dropped round her neck answered her question. He had read the letter. He was strong. Hell bent on vengeance. He began pushing her away from him with his knee in her back while at the same time pulling her head backwards with the improvised noose. She tried to prise off the lead. Pointless. Its bite was deep. Not a millimetre of slack between it and her flesh. Chippy's dog whistle – its sound inaudible to humans – was attached to the lead by a plastic spiral. After much frantic clawing at 'TA's' hands, she blew it until she thought her lungs would burst.

****

She came-to on the floor, propped up against the Aga. The heat from it was like a hot water bottle. Her neck ached. Chippy was licking her face.

Two big men dressed in surgical green smocks were lifting 'TA' onto a stretcher. He looked more dead than alive.

To bring herself back to life, she rotated her head and hunched her shoulders. Who were these men? What was happening? 'TA' looked as if he'd not a drop of blood left in his body. And maybe he hadn't. He was covered in dog bites. He'd a torn lip and a minced ear.

'She's coming round, sir,' said Joan.

Standing next to her niece was a tall figure dressed in black.

'She'll live,' said Jeremy. 'Let's get your aunt up off the floor, shall we?'

They sat her in a chair.

'I'll make you a cup of tea,' said Joan.

'You are an extraordinarily brave woman, Ms Weddle,' said Jeremy.

'Chippy and Mr Jeremy saved your life,' said Joan. 'You'd have been a gonna if sir hadn't clobbered Mr Adder.'

'I was the bait in the trap, wasn't I, Jeremy? Or, should I say, Desmond?'

At this allusion to his double identity, Jeremy with a twinkle in his biological eye and a cheeky smile – contrasting sharply with his undertaker's fancy dress – gave Isa a bow and removing his top hat with a certain theatricality, said: 'I am surprised I got away with it for so long. I apologise for my teasing,' then, replacing his topper as if it was a candle snuffer and he was snuffing out his apology, he said: 'You were such an easy target.'

'Was the chip on my shoulder that obvious?'

'Aunt Isa,' said Joan, 'another cup of tea. It will do you good. After what you have been through, I don't think you can have too many cups of tea.'

'The party is still in full swing,' said Isa, 'I can hear it.' Then, looking hard at Jeremy while at the same time rubbing the weal on her neck, 'Shall I call you Jeremy or Desmond?'

'I don't mind. I'm not partial. It is not as if you are asking me to choose between whisky and gin.'

'No doubt you were baptised with a necklace of Christian names. How many salmon rivers will you inherit?'

'I have no idea. In my circle it is considered infra dig to mention one's possible future assets. Two or three! Ha! Ha! Clearly, Ms Weddle, you are well on your way to a full recovery. A near-death experience has not mitigated your instinctive need to poke a finger at a toff.'

'For an undertaker, Jeremy, you are a cheeky chap.'

'It is the silver spoon in my mouth. No matter how hard I try I can't stop sucking it.'

'I have a plastic one.'

'I had a pony.'

'I had a scooter.'

'Ms Weddle, must you always have the last word?'

'I am letting you know I am alive.'

'Quite! Just so! Sadly our banter, like all good things, must come to an end. My men and I have work to do. At this very moment one of my team … he is dressed as a chicken … you wouldn't believe the bother I had in persuading him to dress up as a chicken … is persuading the ego who has commandeered the microphone for most of the evening, to order everyone to "Act your part". When he does, our nemesis, 'TA' ... temporarily comatose on a stretcher in your passage, will be carried out of your life, at the double. I must say, the plebs do love a knees-up.'

'You can't stop teasing, can you?'

'It's in my genes. Family history says that in the reign of Henry the eighth, one of my ancestors married a jester.'

'Are you trying to blame your flippancy on a lowly marriage? I am beginning to think you have more in common with my cousin Malcolm than I ever thought possible. Where is he by the way?'

'Who?'

'Malcolm.'

'The last time I saw him,' said Joan, 'he was kissing a woman wearing a sheepskin rug. She'd a bit of paper pinned on her back letting everyone know she was , Bassarid ... whatever one of those might be.'

'Oh, my god!' said Isa. 'Does she know who she is kissing?'

'Enough of this parochial chit-chat,' said Jeremy, 'as soon as I hear "Act your part" my men and I will be off. When we have gone, Ms Weddle, you will find, in your passage, a mannequin. Think of it as the detritus of war. My men brought it in on the stretcher. When the law-abiding folk of Chillingham Grove see Mr Adder on the stretcher they will think ... if they are capable of thinking ... most of them are as far gone as members of the Bullingdon Club on a good night out before Michaelmas ... that they are seeing the dummy they earlier saw my men parading round the street while acting their part as medics taking a casualty to hospital. Pride before a fall and all that but I do think I have thought of everything.'

'Jeremy ... Desmond,' said Isa, 'how come, when I met you at the County Hotel, I did not recognise your voice? You sounded different on the phone when you were Desmond.'

Jeremy/Desmond smiled the sort of smile a schoolboy smiles when he is about to show a mate his pet mouse.

'As you are part of the team, Ms Weddle, I will tell you.'

'Me, part of the team? Who are you kidding?'

'You are part of the team … just not part of the inner sanctum. In the reign of Henry the eighth you would be allowed face-to-face contact with Cardinal Wolsey … '

'But not the king?'

'Definitely not. We all have our place in the pecking order. The lion eats the antelope, etcetera. The reason you did not recognise my voice is quite simple. When I was Desmond, speaking to you from London, I pressed a button. A bit like a scrambler. Clever bit of kit. Electronic. It removed certain frequencies from my voice. Made me sound like Paul Robeson singing "Ol' Man River". I played a small part in its invention. It's called "DRF" … device for removing frequencies. It's all part of the spies' cloak and dagger world. Nothing is what it seems. There's a bush. Wrong! It's a chap with a lot of twigs stuck on top of his helmet. Ha! Ha! In the old days one put a handkerchief over a phone's mouthpiece to distort one's dulcet tones. Never liked doing that … germs, you know. Never know what you might catch. Bit like fishing the Amazon. Fishing the Tweed, I know what to expect. As for the Amazon, I shudder to think.'

'When will 'TA''s obituary be in the "Times"?'

'All in due time. Proper procedures will be observed.'

'But,' said Joan, 'Mr Adder isn't dead. He's been bitten by a dog and has had a knock on the head … nothing that can't be put right.'

'Quite right, too,' said Jeremy. 'May I suggest, young lady, that you pop outside and when the time is right help my men push the gurney on which Tony is now resting, to his car. Tony is a big man. They will appreciate your help.'

'To his car? I let its tyres down.'

'Then, blow them up. Off you go. Oh, I almost forgot. Mr Adder has a listening device in his left falsie. Please remove it and return it to Special Branch's technical section. Off you go.'

Isa and Jeremy did not speak until Joan had left.

'So,' said Isa, 'you were listening in to everything 'TA' and I were saying to each other.'

'Yes. You see, you were never in any danger.'

'Was I not?'

'No. I would never have let him murder you.'

'Thank you,' said Isa, rubbing her neck which was sore and swollen. 'I fear my niece is young and naïve. If I am correct, 'TA' has not much longer to live.'

'The young are so touchy and moral about murder. I have it from the top ... the very top ... 'TA''s treachery must not be allowed to go public. HMG cannot afford another Burgess and Maclean ... not to mention that top drawer villain, Philby. Tobias will of course also be made to walk the plank. He too was selling secrets to the Russians. He and 'TA' were a team. Adder and Lacy. They watched each other's backs. Tobias betrayed his country because he thought communism a better form of government than capitalism. I find that tricky to understand. I mean chaps who betray their country for an ideology are slippery to understand. A simple fellow like me, just can't grasp what they're on about. Greed, on the other hand, I find easy to understand ... not condone, but, understand. Would I betray my country to own the River Tweed and all its fishing rights? No ... so I suppose I must, in my old fashioned way, have morals ... not a portmanteau full of them but a little purse stuffed with one or two.'

'Are you not forgetting why 'TA' wanted the money? His motive was aesthetic. He wanted to sit and ogle Impressionist masterpieces all by himself.'

'Does the end justify the means? I think not. 'TA' and Tobias are traitors. I have a theory. They betrayed their country not because of money or believe in an ideology, but because they got a kick out of lying and cheating. When they got away with it, they felt empowered. Some people covet power, don't you know? It is a drug. Once you get hooked, you can't stop.'

'Would that be like revenge? We both owe 'TA' a punch on the nose. Is that why we went after him? Not for love of country?'

'You are saying we live in an Old Testament world, Ms Weddle? Very few turn the other cheek. Motives are always mixed. I am obeying orders. I lost my eye a long time ago.'

'I lost Yuri a long time ago. His loss still hurts. How will 'TA' join the angels?'

'The flames of hell, more likely ... if you believe in that sort of thing–' then, looking at his watch– 'Tobias will now be dead ... this time, really and truly dead. I have it on good authority that he was given a sedative at zero four hundred GMT this morning and pushed out of a Hercules over the Indian Ocean at forty thousand feet. His obituary in The Times will say he died in action. We might even give him a medal. I am never averse to putting icing on a cake. A dollop of fresh lemon icing on a bit of mouldy cake makes it edible.'

'You are bribing his relatives?'

'In a manner of speaking, yes.'

'And 'TA'?'

'My men have instructions to drive him to Otterburn firing range. His car, with him in it ... heavily sedated, I might add, will be target practice for Howitzers. He will be blown to smithereens. His obit will say he died as a result of friendly fire, which, in a manner of speaking, will be true.'

'Sir,' said one of the big men dressed as a medic – coming to attention in front of Jeremy, 'the ego on the microphone has announced, "Act your part".'

'I'm on my way,' said Jeremy. 'Ms Weddle, before I go ... two things. First of all I want you to ... act your part. If you don't join in the party your neighbours will want to know why. You know the spies' maxim: at all times do your best to fit in. Forgive me for telling an old hand how to suck eggs. Now, where is my tape measure? When I act my part I will measure people for their coffin. Ah! Here it is—' producing one from a pocket. 'It has been a pleasure working with you … Ms Weddle … Isa.'

As if under a spell, Isa allowed Jeremy to take her hand and kiss it.

'Before I vaporise into the night, Ms Weddle, I leave you with a conundrum. My real name is not Jeremy … nor is it Desmond. Au revoir.'

At her garden gate, to show the revellers he was a good sport, Jeremy measured a Charlie Chaplin for a bespoke coffin.

A Santa Claus (Henry?) had taken charge of the mist-making machine. Under his supervision it was pumping out mist at a tremendous rate.

'Act your part!'

'Make way, please! Casualty!'

'Well done the medics!'

Jeremy, Joan and the medics pushing 'TA' on the gurney, disappeared, at the double, into the mist.

****

As she'd been ordered to do, Isa re-joined the party. A cowgirl bandana hid the red weals on her neck.

She accepted a glass of wine from Dominic and Irene, telling them she'd enjoyed their display of Scottish dancing.

'I never knew you could play the bagpipes, Dominic.'

'And he's a wonderful organiser, as well; isn't he?' cooed Irene. 'I just wish he'd paint the bathroom. I think eating red meat has given him energy. When he was vegan, I had to cut his toenails.'

'I'm off to mingle,' said Isa.

She was asked about Chippy. Where was he? Guarding the house, she explained. Some asked if she was alright. Oh dear! Was her acting not good enough to hide the fact she'd nearly been murdered? The bandana hid the scars on her neck. What she found difficult to hide was her mental state. She kept going over her near-death experience. Thank god for the mist. In its swirling vapour, everyone looked traumatised.

Coming out of the phantasmagoria making man-made mist hanging around number thirty-nine's front gate she saw Leo, still wearing his toga. A young man wearing a boater and a purple jacket with green and white stripes was linking him. One of Jeremy's men?

In Russian, Leo explained to Isa he was off to begin a new life in a safe house somewhere in the south of England. He didn't know where and he hoped none of his enemies did either. He was looking forward to a wardrobe full of Savile Row suits.

'Dasvidaniya,' he said, kissing her, Russian style, on both cheeks. 'Dasvidaniya,' said Isa.

'I say, Leo, old boy,' said the young man. 'I rather think we should be getting a move on. I don't want to put up a black on my first mission.'

At which urging they disappeared into the mist.

Leo's Volvo was still parked in number thirty-nine's drive. Who, she wondered, would come to remove it? Someone from the Russian embassy in London when they heard Leo had defected? Would they know where it was? Was it bugged? Would an MI5 staffer drive it to London? Park it outside the Russian embassy with a note under its windscreen wiper saying, 'Thank You'?

Mingling, she bumped into Angus.

'Your gardener's been sowing seed,' he told her. 'Morag's disgusted … caught him and Beatrice doing, you know what behind the hydrangea bush in my front garden … don't know what the Grove is coming to … wouldn't have happened in my day. Wonder if this wedding between Charlie boy and Di will last? You wouldn't fancy giving your neighbour a whisky, would you?'

****

A week later Isa received a letter from Lucy. Tobias had disappeared. No one had an inkling of where he'd gone. It was all a bit of a mystery … rumours were flying. She wasn't going to South America. Her job with Medecins Sans Frontieres was safe. The charges against her had been dropped. A nice man from the British embassy had brought her a bunch of flowers and a bottle of champagne.

****

When a red flag is NOT flying, the British army's firing range in Redesdale, Northumberland is open to the public. Notices tell visitors: 'Stick to defined tracks. Be aware of unexploded ordinance.'

Three days after the royal wedding, an ophthalmologist, out on a ramble across the range, stopped to pour himself a coffee. Walking the moors helped him unwind. Folk had no idea how stressful it was looking all day into people's eyes.

While sitting back on a cushion of bracken and enjoying the scenery, something splashed into his mug. Looking up he saw two corbies engaged in aerial combat. Looking into his mug he saw a human eye.